First Light

First Light

BILL RANCIC

G. P. PUTNAM'S SONS

New York

PUTNAM

G. P. PUTNAM'S SONS
Publishers Since 1838
An imprint of Penguin Random House LLC
375 Hudson Street
New York, New York 10014

The Library of Congress has catalogued the G. P. Putnam's Sons
hardcover edition as follows:

Names: Rancic, Bill, author.
Title: First light / Bill Rancic.
Description: New York : G. P. Putnam's Sons, 2016.
Identifiers: LCCN 2016027134 | ISBN 9781101982273 (hardcover)
Subjects: LCSH: Wilderness survival—Fiction. | Married people—Fiction. |
Reminiscing—Fiction. | BISAC: FICTION / Romance / Contemporary. |
FICTION / Family life. | FICTION / Contemporary women. |
GSAFD: Romantic suspense fiction.
Classification: LCC PS3618.A4799 F57 2016 | DDC 813/.6—dc23
LC record available at https://lccn.loc.gov/2016027134
p.   cm.

First G. P. Putnam's Sons hardcover edition / November 2016
First G. P. Putnam's Sons trade paperback edition / January 2018
G. P. Putnam's Sons trade paperback ISBN: 9781101982297

Printed in the United States of America
1   3   5   7   9   10   8   6   4   2

BOOK DESIGN BY NICOLE LAROCHE

For Giuliana, with whom it is a privilege
to share my life every day.

For Duke, whose growth and wonder provide
a constant source of joy and pride.

For Karen, with whom I work every day and
whose support is a true blessing.

For my mom, who pushed me to
make my dreams a reality.

And for my dad in Heaven, who believed in
me even when I didn't believe in myself.

First Light

1

The envelope arrives one afternoon when I'm out in the yard raking leaves. I'm feeling pretty good at the moment, watching the street for the car bringing my wife and son home from the soccer game, wondering if Jackson got to play, wondering if he got to score. He's been riding the bench all season, watching his friends get more playing time, and it's been bothering him enough that he's added extra practices and workouts to his routine, running suicide drills at the stadium, lining up kick after kick in the fall twilight. I've been practicing with him in the evenings and on weekends, videotaping him so he can watch his form. A dentist appointment that morning kept me from actually making it to the game, but I've been thinking of my son all day as I scrape up leaves, red and brown and gold, wondering how it went. If he still didn't get to play, or played badly . . . I know how disappointed he'll be.

I remind myself that Jackson is a bright and loving kid who does well in school, who has plenty of friends, who is pretty much as well adjusted as any parent could hope. If he doesn't get to play in the soccer game today, so be it. Worse things have happened.

The leaves crackling underfoot remind me of the crunch of snow in the dead of winter. For a minute I'm back in the Yukon, in the woods with the snow falling all around, listening to Kerry's slow breathing, watching her chest rise and fall. It's a memory I have often—when my wife crawls into my arms at night, when our son sits between us on the sofa at home to watch a movie together or read a book. I remember praying for another breath, then another, then another. Praying for her, for us, to live, and thinking, *I'm not strong enough for this. I'll never be strong enough.*

My breath catches, and I freeze for a moment, remembering. The truth is that we almost didn't happen, Kerry and Jackson and me. If we hadn't been saved. If we hadn't survived. Then a siren blares and I remember where I am, what I'm doing. The ordinary world fits itself around me again, safe and calm and familiar.

The mailman pauses on his afternoon route to hand me the mail. Behind me, the house Kerry and I bought and renovated seven years ago sits in its rectangle of mown grass, stained-glass windows glint-ing red and gold in the sun. Down the street I can hear the kids at the playground, their voices rising on the afternoon air like a flock of birds. I get a glimpse of Lake Michigan through the trees, sea green and icy cold even on such a hot day. Along the shore there are kids biking and playing volleyball, whizzing by on skateboards, soaking up every moment of sun before the long, cold Chicago winter that's coming, and I think that maybe Jackson and I will join them, once he gets home.

But when I flip through the mail and see the envelope with the Denali Airlines logo on the cover, I know immediately what's inside. I don't need to do any math to know that this year marks the tenth anniversary of the crash; I feel it every time I look at Jackson, his gangly limbs, his big feet and hands. Like my wife and me, he's a survivor, though he doesn't know it yet.

I sit down on my front steps with the envelope in both hands, turning it over and over, almost afraid to open it. Finally I slit the top and take out the card inside, also printed with the Denali Airlines logo: a blue mountain backlit by a setting red sun. I read: *You and your family are cordially invited to be our honored guests at a ceremony honoring the victims and survivors of Flight 806 . . .*

"Dad? Are you okay?"

It's Jackson. He and Kerry are home from the soccer game, but I didn't hear them pull up to the curb. I didn't hear anything except the roaring in my ears.

I look up into the face of my son, so like his mother—large, light-brown eyes; a mop of thick auburn hair that he's forever refusing to cut; the same high, freckled cheekbones; the same wide mouth. He's always been a good kid. Good-hearted, level-headed, if a bit on the sensitive side, with a tendency to mope. Like me.

I think, *It's time. He deserves to know.*

For a minute I consider throwing the invitation away, pretending it never came, but that's not a serious option. There are a hundred reasons why we should be at that memorial service, the most important standing right in front of me.

"Dad?"

"I'm fine, buddy," I say. "I'm just looking at this invitation that came in the mail."

Behind him Kerry sees the envelope and freezes. She, too, knows what it means.

"Invitation? Like to a party?" asks Jackson.

"Sort of. I was thinking maybe you and me and your mom should take a trip."

Jackson's face lights up. "Like, where?"

I can see by the look on his face that he's equating the word "trip" with "vacation"—Disney World, maybe, or California. Someplace warm, near the ocean, with a nice sandy beach and warm blue swimming pool and maybe a water slide or two. He isn't thinking about snow and isolation, the deep cold woods of northern Canada. He isn't thinking about memorials to the dead. His life, until now, has been fairly uneventful. A fact his mom and I have tried very hard to preserve.

Jackson grabs his skateboard from the front porch and is doing a few simple tricks along the sidewalk while we talk, taking a bit of a tumble when he trips trying to flip the board over. "Helmet, please," his mother reminds him for the millionth time. He groans and takes the helmet out of the trunk of the car. Soon he'll be a teenager, and getting him to listen won't be so easy. *No*, I think—*it has to be now*. While he might still be willing to open his ears and his heart and hear, really hear, what we have to say.

"I was thinking we could take a drive up to Canada. To White-horse," I say. "There's something happening there soon the three of us are part of."

I can feel Kerry tense up, but Jackson is oblivious to his mother's fear, and mine. He scrunches up his face. "Whitehorse? Is that a real place?"

"It's a city in Yukon Territory. Near Alaska."

"Oh." His face falls a little bit. "It sounded like a town in *Dragon Age* or something. I thought it would be something cool."

"It's a real place, all right. Your mom and I have been there before."

He looks intrigued. This is new information to him. "When?"

Kerry glances at me. We both knew this day was coming. Maybe not today, but soon. She says, "Before you were born, honey."

He's looking at me sideways now, his brown eyes full of skepticism, even a touch of annoyance. We almost never talk about our lives before he was born, though I know he's curious. He asks us, sometimes, the story of how we met. "At work" is all we've ever told him. "We worked together, and then we fell in love and decided to get married." He's never pushed the issue, though I've often wondered when he would ask for more details, when we'd have to tell him the truth and nothing but the truth.

Jackson says, "Did you say we're going to *drive* there? Isn't it, like, a million miles from here?"

"Four days' drive, maybe five." There is no way, absolutely no possibility of getting Kerry on a plane, not to mention me. Driving is our only option.

He groans. "Five days in the *car*? For *fun*?"

5

"Not exactly for fun," I say. "It will be educational."

That word "educational" is Jackson's personal bête noire. He doesn't like museums or historical sites, any of the things his mom and I have tried to interest him in whenever we use that word. He hears "educational" and thinks "boring." But I have something in mind for this trip that will make driving imperative, beyond our fear of flying. And it will be educational, just not the way he thinks.

I want Jackson to see. To *know* the place, and what happened to us there. I want him to taste the air in the Yukon, ride its roads, see its towns and its hills. I want it to be as much a part of him, his life, as it is Kerry's and mine.

"There's a ceremony of sorts. A memorial for the victims of a plane crash. We should all be there."

"A memorial for a plane crash? Why?" He drags out the last word, filling it with all the pre-teen skepticism he can muster.

"We were on the plane when it crashed," I say.

I've imagined saying the words for so long, practiced them so many times, that the words are halfway out of my mouth before I realize it, but Jackson only looks at me and laughs, a kind of incredulous chuckle. Like he thinks this is another one of my weird dad jokes, as silly as the time when I taped a picture of a mallard to the low ceiling over the basement stairs and told him to "duck" when he went downstairs. He doesn't realize I'm serious. "No, really, Dad. What's going on?" He looks from me to his mom and back. "A plane crash? Like, for real?"

I catch Kerry's eye. We've talked about this moment so often: when we will tell him, how we will. We've been close to doing it already a number of times the past few weeks but just haven't been able to make ourselves do it. Now her look says, *Are you sure about this?*

I'm not, not at all, and I know she isn't, either. Still, she says, "For real."

A hundred tiny emotions flit across his face—anger and confusion and fascination and fear. Finally he settles for curiosity. "Why didn't you ever tell me?"

Kerry steps up and puts a hand on his shoulder, though I can see his posture tighten, almost as if he wants to throw her off but is not able to bring himself to do it; he's at that age when he both wants and resents his mother's reassurances. "It's complicated," she says. "But we think maybe you're grown up enough now to understand."

He narrows his eyes at her, still skeptical. "But only if we go on this trip, right?"

"I know it doesn't sound like fun," I say. "But I think we should be there."

Already I'm planning. Four days in the car, maybe five, would be just enough time to talk to Jackson. We need to be able to talk to our son, to have his full attention, away from video games and soccer and math homework, away from his friends and the city and all our familiar places and distractions. We need him to listen. To hear us.

"Dad," he says, "can't we go to Disney World instead? Or at least the beach?"

"This is more important, buddy. This is someplace we need to be. I promise you, this is something you'll always remember."

"You always say that, and it always ends up being so *boring*."

He's not accepting it, but at least he's not fighting me too hard. It will be okay, I know it. "What do you think? Want a snack?" I ask, putting my arms around him and leading him inside the house, the dog panting at his heels.

"Sure," he says. "But nothing healthy. No kale. I hate that stuff."

I laugh. "I wouldn't dream of it."

By the time we've got the car packed, the mail stopped, the house buttoned up for the time it will take to drive to Canada, attend the ceremony, and come home again, we're all worked up into such a state of anxiety that even the dog seems glad to see us go, dashing off her leash at the kennel without so much as a backward glance. Jackson cries a little on Sasha's neck, turning his face away so I won't see his tears. "She'll be happier in the kennel than in the car with us, buddy," I tell him. "We'll be back in no time." He turns his head away again. He's having trouble believing that his mom and I are taking this trip for anyone's benefit except our own, and I don't think he's entirely wrong about that.

We climb in the car, and soon we're on the highway heading out of the city, past deep-dish pizza parlors and Vienna Beef stands, merging into the stream of cars on the Kennedy heading north toward the Wisconsin border. Traffic is terrible, the cars thick and slow-moving, like minutes ticking on a clock. A few days out of town, away from the crowds and noise, will be a relief. But then I remember the quiet of the forest and the snow in the Yukon, the sound of the wind in the trees, the bitter cold that seeped into my fingers and toes, the fear, and I remember. This isn't a vacation: Kerry and I nearly died out there. She spent a week in the hospital after, myself more than two. She still suffers migraines and memory loss from the injuries she sustained in the crash. She still has nightmares sometimes, though in the mornings she says she doesn't remember what they're about. In some ways, I think it's better. There are parts of the story I wish I could forget, too.

As we head north, the Chicago streets give way to a stream of beige suburbs, the white hulks of malls, the green tracts of forest preserves and subdivisions, the houses growing farther and farther apart until suddenly we're out in the country, in the open spaces of farmland and dairy pasture, the stubble fields brown in the fall light. Here and there a cloud of dust announces the presence of a combine harvesting the last of the corn, and every few miles a handpainted sign declares "Pumpkins for sale!" At each one, Jackson begs us to stop and buy a pumpkin, forgetting we won't be home for weeks, that there is no more room in our Toyota for anything after packing three suitcases, a cooler of snacks, and Jackson's collection of books and games.

"Maybe on the way back, buddy," I say. I've taken the first shift, thinking Kerry will want to take the lead—she's his mom, and much of the telling of it should come from her—but I catch her eye across the car. The night before, she'd told me she was ready, that it was time. "I'll be glad to get it over with," she'd said, pulling out the old black journal, the only thing she'd brought back with her from the Yukon. I'd glanced at it, and she said, "It will be a relief to talk to him about everything, finally."

Now neither of us can bear to begin. It should be just like ripping off a Band-Aid, I think—one quick tug and you're done. Maybe we should wait for Jackson to ask a question. But no, that's no good, we might be waiting until we get back home again and the trip will be over.

Kerry makes a choking noise in her throat, and I shoot her a quick look of sympathy. It isn't easy, this business of dredging up the past. I realize with a tiny jolt that the black journal is in her lap. I didn't even see her take it out.

"Don't feel like you have to say everything at once," I say. "Begin at the beginning."

"I can't."

"One of us has to. We're going to want to stop for the night in an hour or so."

She squeezes her eyes shut. "It's too hard."

"You were always good at stories," I tell her. "Why is it so hard now?"

"There are big parts of it I don't really remember. And what about the rest? All those things we only learned about afterward, in the hospital? I don't know if it's enough."

"What you don't remember, I do. The parts we didn't see firsthand, we'll have to describe as best we can, as they were told to us."

"It feels weird. Speaking for people who can't speak for themselves."

She knows what I'll say next, because I've said it before, more times than either of us can count: *If we can't speak for them, then who can?* We are the living witnesses, the survivors, but we've always known this story belongs as much to the dead as to the living. We owe it to them to tell their story as truthfully as we can.

She rubs the cover of the black journal and gives me a wan smile.

"Don't worry," I tell her. "We're in this together."

She reaches over and takes my hand, gulping in air. It's clear I will have to begin. Looking into the rearview mirror at our son, who's reading a book, I say, "Hey, buddy. Jackson. Your mom and I want to talk to you a minute." He leans forward, between the two front seats. "Do you remember your mom and me saying something about a plane crash?"

I can feel him sit up a little, pay more attention. "You said you'd tell me all about it on this trip. You said I was old enough now to understand."

"Maybe he's still not ready," Kerry says, so quietly I wonder if Jackson hears.

I reach over and grab her hand, feeling how badly it's shaking. "He is."

"Understand what?" He furrows his brow. "Like secrets?"

Secrets. The one word we were being so careful to avoid. "Not exactly. But parts of the truth we were waiting to tell you when you were old enough."

"So . . . secrets, basically." The kid is too smart for his own good sometimes.

His mom looks at him, then at me. "They might seem like secrets, but we don't think of them that way. It's just some things we've been waiting to tell you when the time was right. Grown-up things, I guess you could say."

I've rehearsed this speech over and over on nights when I couldn't sleep, starting when Jackson was a baby curled in his crib. *You have to understand,* I always start, in my imagination. *We all thought we were going to die. Some of us* did *die. And the things we did in order to live . . . none of it will ever be completely understandable to someone who wasn't there. But I have to try to make you see why it matters. Because if I don't, then what was it we were trying so hard to live for?*

Next to me, his mother takes a deep breath and blows it out slowly. Her face is white. "Mom," Jackson says, "are you all right?"

She fixes a smile onto her face and says, "I will be, honey."

Outside the windows the miles of corn and the little farms go by, the cows chewing their cud in the fields. Tomorrow we'll cross over into Canada, leaving behind the familiar world. There can be no more excuses, no more delays. Let him know that everything we did was for him, and why it all matters so much, still.

Every child deserves that. To know. To understand.

And so we begin.

2

It was December, two weeks before Christmas, and Daniel Albrecht could not remember the last time he'd been warm.

Listening to the groan of the hotel-room heater trying to keep up against the cold, as well as the constant hiss of the channel changing as his fiancée flipped around looking for the news, Daniel burrowed under the comforter. Kerry put her cold feet on Daniel's leg, making him yelp and pull away from her. "Hey!" he said. He rubbed the spot on his calf where she'd warmed her toes. "What did I ever do to you?"

"Come on. I'm miserable here."

"We're all miserable here," Daniel said. "Don't make it worse than it already is."

"Please? I'll let you watch football."

"No way," he said. She stopped her channel-flipping at ESPN for a moment, but as soon as she put down the remote, Daniel picked up her frozen feet and rubbed the warmth back into them. "Wow, they *are* cold."

"That feels good," she said, lying back and closing her eyes. "Do you know what time it is?"

They had been in Barrow, Alaska, for nearly two weeks, and in all that time they had not seen the sun—two weeks spent pummeled by snow and freezing wind, working twelve-hour days entirely in the dark, never knowing if it was eight in the morning or eight in the evening. Daniel looked out the darkened window at the street beyond—at the flat, low buildings of Barrow, at the flakes of snow tapping restlessly on the window—and said, "Around ten at night, I'd say."

"What day?"

"Monday. Give or take a week."

Daniel and Kerry were both part of the crisis-management team at Petrol, Inc., the world's biggest oil company. Two weeks before, an explosion on one of the company's oil platforms off the Alaska coast had killed three workers and spilled two hundred thousand gallons of crude oil into the pristine waters of the Beaufort Sea. The CEO had dispatched the crisis-management team to Barrow before the bodies had even been recovered. The team's job: shut down the leak, help the families of the dead employees settle their affairs, offer the company's assistance to the local authorities to clean up the mess and minimize the environmental impact, and handle the company's public image in the media.

All that was easier said than done when the crisis was happening in Alaska in December, the darkest month of the year, and one of the coldest. Daniel was director of operations for the crisis-management group; his job was to get the leak shut down and the spill cleaned up, a job that was proving difficult because of a colder-than-usual cold snap in the area. Conditions for sending the submersibles down to the seabed, to the source of the leak, were bad—the waves rough and frigid, topped by sub-crushing floes of ice on the surface, murky with oil and silt below, making the descent dangerous at best. Daniel felt he couldn't risk their people in these conditions—it could mean further loss of life. Daniel told his boss they would need to wait until conditions improved before sending their people down to the sea-floor to clamp the leak. "I'll send my guys down when it's safe to do so," Daniel had said, "and not before. We don't want more bodies in this situation."

Daniel's boss, Bob Packer, had *humphed* into the phone, clearly disagreeing with Daniel's assessment, but at the time, he'd been back in Chicago, keeping track of the situation from afar. A day later, almost like clockwork, he'd flown in to oversee the operation in person, and every day since then Daniel had felt him growing restless, wanting to get the job done and get their team out of there. Every minute the mess wasn't contained cost the company money, not to mention kept the leak in the public eye.

And Bob Packer was not a man who took no for an answer. The mercurial senior VP of the crisis-management department famously blurred the lines between his personal and business lives. Extremely competent, accomplished, and driven—"driven to insanity," Kerry liked to joke—Bob had headed the department for twenty years. For the last two of those, Daniel had traveled with him all over the world, from the Middle East to the Gulf Coast to the

North Sea to the Alberta tar sands to Alaska and everywhere in between. Not once, in all that time, had he ever seen the man relax. Bob never stayed in the bar to have a beer with his team after hours, never offered a word of encouragement or congratulations on a job well done. The joke around the office was that he didn't sleep, either, that he was really some kind of vampire, feeding on corporate earnings reports. He was famously quoted as saying that he'd taken the job at Petrol because crisis management was the only real challenge left in the corporate world, and Daniel didn't exactly disagree with him—he'd taken the job there himself, after all—but the longer Daniel worked under Bob, the more he wished that he'd retire and let someone else take over the department. He was well past sixty, though, and showed no signs of wanting a quiet retired life.

"Because his wife won't let him," Kerry always said. "She doesn't want him around any more than the rest of us do."

And Daniel had laughed even though he felt sorry for Bob's third wife, a pretty but dull woman he'd met exactly once at an office party. She'd looked miserable the whole time, staring off at the ceiling while Bob talked business with every person in the room and ignored her. Just last month, a *Forbes* headline had declared Bob "Married to the Job," a piece that had become required reading among his employees. Twice divorced, working six days a week, more than three hundred days a year, Bob Packer demanded as much perfection from his team as he did from himself. The fact that other people didn't want to live on such a schedule never seemed to enter into his thoughts.

ESPN went to commercial, so Kerry started flipping channels

again. As the director of the media-relations team, she managed press inquiries for the company during a crisis, acting as a go-between for the senior executives and various media outlets. She and her people monitored the media coverage of the event and worked to influence the way the story was being told to keep up the company's positive image.

"Where's the damn newscast?" she muttered, still flipping. "I can never keep the hotel channels straight."

Daniel looked over at his fiancée, wearing fleece pajamas now and two layers of socks, her red hair soft on her shoulders, makeup off so that all her freckles showed. It was so different from her workday look, the pencil skirts and killer heels, her hair tied up in a neat if somewhat severe twist to keep it out of her face, though since they'd been in Alaska she'd been wearing heavy coats and sweaters and boots. He leaned over to kiss her, trying to distract her from thoughts of work. She turned to kiss him back, but then just as quickly she turned back to the TV, and Daniel sighed. God help the man who came between Kerry Egan and her work. There was a reason Bob Packer had hired her, after all.

Media attention on the Beaufort spill had been quiet so far, and Daniel knew that fact was making Kerry a little nervous. Either she and her team were doing their jobs extremely well, or events were about to blow up in spite of her best efforts—the company name smeared across the 24-hour cable-news screens, the newspapers, the snarky news Web sites. If that happened, the media coverage could very quickly go from bad to disastrous, and Kerry would have her hands full in a hurry. He supposed he could understand her concern: the longer it took him to get his people down to the sea-floor to stop the leak, the harder Kerry's job became. It did sometimes put something of a damper on romance.

So far, though, coverage of the explosion had been limited to an occasional mention of the bare facts on a couple of the 24-hour cable-news networks in the States, a third-page headline each in the *New York Times* and the *Washington Post,* and only fifteen seconds apiece from two of the four major network broadcasts. The international press was tougher, offering a few more detailed and critical pieces on the possible causes of the explosion and the damage to the local ecosystem. None of this was unusual.

What *was* unusual was that the Russians were starting to make serious noise about the environmental impact of the oil spill so close to their own coast, and taking their case to the international media—the BBC, Al Jazeera, Reuters. Daniel knew Kerry was worried that the trouble for Petrol was really just beginning, that the longer the crisis went on, the more reporters would start digging around for an angle. If the families of the dead men started going around the company to talk, if the Russians started making more noise to further some of their own causes in the court of public opinion, reporters could start landing in Barrow by the dozens from every country and continent, and then she and the rest of the team would be stuck in Alaska through New Year's at least. And Daniel knew that Kerry wanted very much to be home for Christmas this year.

Her mother was bugging her about the holidays, as usual, asking why Kerry had to work such long hours, why wasn't she ever home with her family, and when were she and Daniel actually going to set a date for the wedding? Though she wouldn't say so, Daniel knew all these things were weighing heavily on her.

Daniel glanced over at her face—brow furrowed, deep in thought—and wished he could get her to turn off the TV for the night. But one of the producers from a Big Four newscast had told her they were finally running their piece on the Petrol accident that night. Since Kerry had put the producer in touch with Bob himself for the piece, she wanted to see the angle they were going to take on it.

When she hit on the right channel at last, Kerry put down the remote and sat up, paying no attention to the fact that Daniel was still rubbing her cold feet while the deep-voiced and smoothly tanned anchor discussed the president's latest poll numbers and his battles with Congress.

Daniel rubbed her feet more vigorously. "Hey," he said, "I thought we said no work tonight? That we were going to spend some serious time together tonight?"

"I know, babe, I just want to see this one story. It should be on any second."

"How romantic," he said. He pushed into the soft spot in the middle of her foot with one knuckle, but Kerry couldn't take her eyes off the broadcast, waiting to see how the story was going to go.

Now the news switched to a story about a plane crash in Taiwan, citing the number of survivors and discussing the possible causes of the crash—human error or mechanical malfunction? Kerry squirmed with impatience all through that story and the next one, too, about new FDA regulations of chicken farms. "Why do producers always make you wait until the end of the show to get to the part you care about?"

"Better for ratings."

"Aren't you clever," she said.

The broadcast went to commercial break. The newscast really was waiting until the last minute this time to get to Kerry's story. She turned to look at him. "I saw you through the window earlier, when I was walking back to the hotel. You were on the phone. What did Bob have to say?"

"How'd you know it was Bob?"

"Because you looked pissed off. When you got off the phone, you threw it down and gave it the finger."

He chortled. "Yeah, well. He was telling me I have until midnight to get those submersibles to the bottom to shut down the wellhead or he'd find someone else who would. I keep telling him it's too dangerous to send people down in these conditions, and he told me he's already got my replacement picked out . . ." Daniel sighed and said, "You know how he is."

"I know how he is, all right."

"How about you? How's it going from your end?"

"He promised Judy we'd be going home in two days," Kerry said. Judy Akers was Kerry's deputy director and best friend. She'd been complaining about wanting to go home almost from the moment they'd stepped on the plane to Alaska. Nothing was to her liking—the cold, the dark, the food, the work.

"And you don't think so."

"No. I think the Russians are going to start making noise soon, and then this whole thing is going to blow up. No way Bob will let us go then."

"Can't I get you to turn that thing off and kiss me already?"

"Soon," she said.

When the news came back on, the anchor immediately launched into the piece on the Petrol spill, staring dramatically into the camera while he read the feed from the teleprompter next to a picture of an oil platform on fire. Kerry sat up straighter. Daniel sighed and dropped her foot.

"Now a report from Alaska, where three employees of Petrol, Inc., died last week in an oil-platform explosion above the Arctic Circle," said the newscaster. "The wellhead was damaged in the explosion, leaking nearly a million gallons of oil into the Beaufort Sea and threatening the fragile ecosystem near Prudhoe Bay."

"Hmm," said Daniel. "They got the numbers wrong on that one."

Kerry sighed—she'd have to call them to issue a correction tomorrow, but the damage would already be done.

The anchor continued reading. "Efforts to close the wellhead and stem the tide of oil flowing into the ocean have been hampered by frigid weather and the fact that the area is completely dark twenty-four hours a day between November and January."

The photo of the burning oil platform switched to a video of Bob, his prominent brow furrowed, his thick gray hair standing up bushy from his forehead. He was still, at sixty-seven, imposing and attractive, with the build of the football player he'd once been. His face wore his usual expression of outrage barely masked.

The anchor went on reading. "Because of the location of the leak so close to Russia's Siberian shore, authorities in Moscow are monitoring the situation closely and threatening to take action if the situation isn't resolved. Petrol Senior Vice President Bob Packer, however, said today that the company expects its submersibles to reach the ocean floor by midnight tomorrow to repair the damaged wellhead and stop the flow of oil into the sea, although the platform will be shut down for several weeks to complete repairs and investigate the cause of the accident. Now to Sacramento, where the—"

Daniel turned off the TV. "Well, that certainly explains some things," he said. He shook his head and laughed. "He can say anything he likes to the media, but I can't wave my magic wand and make it safe for my people."

"Still, could have been worse," Kerry answered.

"Much worse."

Already he was feeling better. Daniel slid his hand slowly up her leg, his fingers pressing gently on the back of her knee, the length of her thigh, and pulled her toward him. She sighed and pulled his head down toward her. God, he loved her, and now, with her body warm beneath him, her lips parting gently . . .

Just then the room's phone rang, loudly, making them both jump.

"Hello?" Kerry asked. "Hi, Bob. Yes, we were just watching it. Sure. Here he is." She held out the receiver for Daniel, who groaned a little and put it to his ear.

"I'm glad you were watching," Bob was saying. "You can see the pressure we're under here. We need those submersibles to the bottom, pronto."

"Sir, there's no way we can get it done on the timetable you suggested in that broadcast. You know that. Our people will be in danger, and I think it's a mistake to jeopardize more lives until conditions are better. You wouldn't want to lose a submersible crew . . ."

Kerry threw him a worried look.

"Conditions aren't going to get any better for weeks. Maybe months," Bob said, his voice clipped. "The longer this goes on, the worse the mess is going to be for all of us. You heard what the Russians are up to. I don't want to get the White House involved here. The environmentalists are already screaming for blood."

"But the water is so murky the submersibles can't navigate—"

"Put extra people on it if you have to."

"Extra people aren't going to do any—"

"Soon as it's done, everyone can go home, you included. Kerry can start breaking down the command center tomorrow. I've already told Phil to start tying up any of his loose ends."

"You did." Daniel looked at Kerry, who rolled her eyes.

"Yes. So I want you wrapping things up tomorrow yourself and getting ready to get on a plane out the day after. I think the cost of keeping our team up here is outweighing the benefits at this point. Corporate is making noise about how much we spend on food and hotels, and we don't need more media attention up here than we have already."

"Respectfully, sir, I feel we shouldn't rush through this operation—"

"You've hardly been rushing, Daniel."

"What I mean is that the situation could go south in a hurry—"

"The only thing I want going south in a hurry is our team, and that all hinges on you and your people. You have a job to do. I suggest you get out there and do it."

Daniel held very still and didn't answer, as if he could avoid the task by not acknowledging it. It was wrong—the whole thing was wrong. Bob knew it. He knew he was risking everything by pushing the team to do more than they were safely able to accomplish, just as he always did. He didn't care how it got fixed or how much danger it put everyone in as long as he got the results he wanted. As long as Bob could go to the board and brag about the team's performance, he'd risk anything.

"Two more days and we're all out of here," Bob said. "Tell Kerry. In the morning, she and Judy and I are going to have breakfast with Phil. He wants to put together one last press release on the things the company is doing for the families of the victims, setting up a scholarship fund . . ."

A feeling like desperation—or maybe it was resignation—sank down through him like submersibles to the bottom of the deep black sea. *You sonofabitch,* he thought. *You devious, rotten sonofabitch.* He hung up the phone.

"Well," Kerry said, "so what's the good news?"

Daniel murmured, "He says you and Judy are supposed to meet him and Phil for breakfast first thing in the morning to go over one last press release before we leave."

Kerry gave another frustrated groan and flung the covers over her head like a child saying she was too sick to go to school. She would not relish breakfast with Phil Velez, the director of the third leg of the crisis-management team—human resources. Kerry thought he had all the sparkling wit and personality of a compliance memo.

"Is that all?"

"Not quite. After you meet with Phil, Bob wants you to break down the command center and get everyone ready to go home. He says the trip is costing the company too much money. He wants us on a plane in two days."

"Two days? Is that even possible?"

"You know Bob. He'd make it rain out of a clear blue sky if he could figure out how."

"That's why he's the senior VP. What about the bad news?"

"Bad news is he's insisting the leak is fixed by the end of the day tomorrow. Which means I better get on it now."

"You can't!" Kerry exclaimed, sitting up and clutching the blankets to her. "You've already been working all day. You told him it was too dangerous. *He can't make you do this!*"

Daniel sat up and flung his legs over the edge of the bed. "He can. He already did. I don't have a choice."

"You do," Kerry said. "You could always quit."

"Not now. Those guys," he said, looking out the dark windows, thinking of his team—the sub drivers, the sailors, the engineers who reported to him—"they need me. I can't let them down, not now."

"You don't have to go yourself. You're the director of operations. So direct someone else to do it and stay here."

Part of him recognized the wisdom of this idea, but he couldn't do it. He couldn't let someone else do a job he wasn't willing to do himself, no matter how tempted he might be. Daniel's father, who'd been a steelworker in the Indiana mills, had always said that the best foremen he'd had were guys who'd come up from the mill-works, who knew what it meant to work for a living, who weren't above putting their own backs on the line. His father had never let someone else do a job he could do himself. No—Daniel had to get it together, get the job done and get everyone home safe. It was his father's voice he heard in his head: *Keep your eye on the ball, Daniel. You take your eye off the ball for even just a second and someone could die.*

He gave a heavy sigh, then stood up and starting putting on his warmest clothes once more—thermal underwear, then jeans, then snowpants, then a thermal undershirt, fleece, down coat, earmuffs and a fleece hat—and he stuffed two pairs of gloves in his pockets for good measure.

"How can I make those guys go back out there if I'm not willing to go with them?" he asked. "It's not right, Kerry. If they go, I go."

Kerry watched him perform this familiar ritual and sighed. "It's nearly eleven o'clock. It's fifty below out there. What do you think you're going to be able to do?"

"Whatever it takes." Daniel looked at her from under his layers of wool. Already he could feel fatigue stiffening his limbs, a yawn stretching the back of his throat, but he would never be able to sleep warm and comfortable knowing his guys were out in the cold Arctic night without him. He'd be up all night anyway; might as well try to be useful.

"You heard Bob," he told Kerry. "I'm going to single-handedly save the company from disaster and get the team home for Christmas."

"You're not Superman. You can't conjure a heat wave or calm the seas with a flick of your wrist."

"I'll think of something," Daniel said, leaning down to kiss her forehead, patting the pockets of his coat to make sure he had his satellite phone, his emergency charger and his hotel key. "Sleep tight, babe. I'll see you in the morning."

"Hopefully," she muttered as he turned to go.

"Hopefully," he said, and then he was out the door once more, into the cold.

3

When Kerry Egan woke to the sound of knocking at the door of her hotel room the next morning—or what she assumed was morning; the clock on her cell phone said seven, but evening or morning she couldn't tell in the darkness—Daniel was still gone. She rolled over to see his side of the bed still empty, still cold. He'd been out in the frigid weather all night long, and a sudden jolt of worry squeezed her. She didn't like wondering where he was.

Another knock at the door. It was Judy, coming to collect Kerry and head downstairs for their breakfast meeting with Bob Packer and Phil Velez. Still half-asleep, Kerry shuffled to the door, keeping the blanket wrapped around herself. Judy looked nauseatingly cheery for seven a.m., her tousled blond hair recently washed and styled, makeup on, neatly dressed. In contrast, Kerry felt like she'd been punched in the face; her eyes felt swollen, her mouth so dry she could barely swallow. The constant cold and the chugging of the heaters gave the inside of the hotel a hellishly dry quality. She gave a theatrical groan and flung herself back down on the bed.

"What's the matter?" Judy asked. "The prospect of breakfast with Phil doesn't sound too appealing?"

"It's not Phil. I could be having breakfast with George Clooney this morning and I would still hate it."

"If you were having breakfast with George Clooney, I'd hope you'd take a shower at least."

"I'm not sure I could muster the energy even for him."

Judy gave an inelegant snort. "One of these days you'll discover you're really a morning person, and *then* I'm going to remind you of this moment."

"Not likely. Please tell me that's my coffee in your other hand."

"It's your coffee in my other hand." Judy handed over the cup and looked at the bed, the blankets still undisturbed on Daniel's side. "Bob strikes again?" she asked.

"Of course," Kerry said. "He used last night's broadcast to make sure Daniel gets the leak fixed on *his* time line. Nothing like announcing success to the whole world to make sure it happens."

"He's the boss," Judy joked, sitting down next to her on the bed. "Come on, get in the shower. We're supposed to be in the diner in fifteen minutes."

Bob preferred the food in one of the local diners to the restaurant in the hotel, which meant going outside, which meant boots, coats, scarves, gloves, every inch of exposed skin covered to stave off frostbite. Just then, Kerry couldn't face the idea of going outside into the cold even one more time—it was just too much. She sat up next to Judy and said, "You're sure there's no way of getting out of it?"

"Not if we want to still have jobs when we get back home."

She groaned. "Can't you tell Bob I'm sick or something?"

"Like that's ever worked."

"You could tell him I'm pregnant. That I'm on my hands and knees puking my guts out, and you have to stay here and tend to me in my delicate condition."

Judy appeared to think that over for a second, then shook her head. "He'd probably ask to see the stick you peed on."

"I'd be willing to try if it meant I could get another hour in bed."

Something nagged at the back of Kerry's mind, some little thing she needed to give her attention to. Her period—*was* it late? In all the crazy crush of the past few days—not to mention the incessant darkness—she'd lost track. She picked up her phone and looked at the date: the tenth of December. Her calendar said she should have gotten her period no later than the fifth. A quick jolt of adrenaline shot through her. She was never late.

Judy's phone buzzed briefly. She looked at it and said, "That was Phil. Says he's got us a table and to come on over when we're ready."

"Isn't he the early bird, though?" Kerry said, though she could think about nothing except getting her hands on a pregnancy test. The pharmacy wasn't too far away, but she had the meeting with Phil and Bob before she'd have time to pick up a test, much less take it. She decided to temporarily banish the question from her head. No sense freaking out yet. It was probably a fluke.

"Come on," Judy said, "quit complaining and get in the shower."

A few minutes later, Kerry bundled up in her heaviest things to brave the outside temperatures—heavy down coat, fleece-lined leggings, waterproof knee-high boots, knit hat, scarf and gloves—feeling like she was the one headed down to the bottom of the sea instead of Daniel, and this time without a submersible.

The thought of him out in the cold all night made her afraid. She wished he wouldn't let Bob goad him into taking such terrible risks. His sense of responsibility to the people who worked for him was admirable, and she understood he was still living by his father's philosophy of leading from the front—but he didn't always have to take on *every* duty himself.

"All right," she said, mumbling to Judy through the layers of clothing, "let's go."

They pushed open the door and stepped outside, struggling up the street toward the coffee shop where Phil and Bob would be waiting for them, and for the hundredth time she wished they'd been able to rent snowmobiles, apparently the preferred form of winter travel in Barrow. At least there would be hot coffee and food when they got there, she thought, even if it would be dark all day.

The one thing Kerry really wanted at that moment, with the snow blowing in her eyes and the streetlights overhead throwing a feeble glow on the dim street, was to watch the sun rise up over the eastern horizon, just for the space of a breath. A glimpse of orange on the horizon. After nearly two weeks in Barrow, she was longing for even the slightest hint of sunshine, for any reminder that the world would not always be drowning in darkness. She found herself staring at the edge of the horizon and thinking, *Please. Please, just a glimpse.*

Sometimes, near the middle of the day, if the weather was clear, the sky would lighten, turn blue, a phenomenon the meteorologists called "polar twilight," but there was never any real sun, never a beam that broke the horizon and fell across the frozen ground. It was too close to the winter solstice. The sun wouldn't rise for real here for another five weeks.

"When I get home," Kerry said finally, "I'm never complaining about Chicago winters again."

"That's what you said after Newfoundland," said Judy. "At least Bob says we're going home tomorrow."

"That's what he'd like you to think," Kerry answered, "but if Daniel can't get the leak shut down, it won't matter what Bob says."

"You really think Bob would lie to my face?" Judy asked. "About going home?"

"I think he'd sell his own right hand if he thought it would be good for the company," Kerry said.

Judy stopped in the middle of the street, frowned theatrically at Kerry and said, "I'm not hanging around you anymore if you're going to be such a downer."

"What are friends for?" Kerry answered, and they both gave a laugh. "Come on, let's get there before we freeze to death."

They stepped aside to let a couple of snowmobiles blow past, pausing in front of the brightened windows of a house strung with white Christmas lights, caribou bones and whale bones making up part of the family's fencing. What fortitude it must take to live here year-round, Kerry thought, stopping to watch the family matriarch load more wood into the stove in the middle of the room in which four children were gathered, playing a game at the kitchen table. What kind of resilience did a person have to have to live in a place where the air was never really warm, where there were no roads in and out, where Taco Tuesday at the local Mexican restaurant was the biggest weekly event?

"I suppose I shouldn't complain so much," Kerry said at last, watching the youngest kid throw the dice and land on Boardwalk. "At least we *do* get to go home again. Sooner or later."

"I thought you promised Daniel he could build a summer home overlooking the Beaufort Sea. I bet it's beautiful here in the summer."

Kerry couldn't see her face, but her best friend's voice was definitely full of mirth. "Could you imagine going all summer *without* darkness, too? Waking up at two in the morning, and it's still light? I don't know what would be worse."

Judy smiled, but shivered. "Bob would love it. He'd work us year-round."

Kerry sighed. "You're probably right."

Then the squat, flat-roofed form of the diner rose up out of the snow to meet them, all the windows ablaze, the sign outside a rising sun made of gold and blue neon, shining the only real light in the December darkness. Kerry paused for a moment and saw Bob just inside the front door, pacing back and forth with the phone to his ear. His face, already red from anger, turned nearly purple for a moment, and he shouted something into the phone. She knew without even hearing the conversation whom he was talking to and what the gist of the conversation was—Daniel still didn't have the leak shut down.

Judy looked where Kerry was looking. She knew who was on the other end of the line, too. "Bob's got him working early."

"You mean late. Very, very late."

Judy looked at her through layers of wool. "We could always quit," Judy said, looking up to where Bob paced behind the window. "The whole lot of us, in protest."

Kerry had suggested the same thing to Daniel just the night before, but she'd known even then it wasn't a real solution. "Fat lot of good that would do. He'd replace us with cheaper workers, and the board would give him a raise as a thank-you."

"You could always go back into journalism," Judy said.

Kerry snorted. "You think I could get a *real* media job after working for the enemy? No way. I'd be kryptonite."

"Not to mention you like it," Judy said. "No matter what you try to pretend, you're good at what you do. You can't be that good at it and not love it."

Kerry shook her head, half-pleased. The truth was, she *was* good at it—sometimes better than she wanted to be. Anyone could manage the corporation's image in good times, but she felt it took real ingenuity to be able to spin a disaster, to stem the inevitable tide of criticism and turn it to the company's advantage. Kerry had a knack for feeding the media feel-good humanitarian stories of dramatic rescues, or communities banding together to serve the families of the victims, anything to keep the attention off the disaster itself. It was her specialty, the humanitarian story—she was known for it. Give Kerry Egan a mess, and she'd dig around until she found the story within the story, the best possible angle. Spinning garbage into gold, or at least that was what Bob always called it. She was proud of that ability, but the truth was, there was something in it that shamed her, too. That made her feel she could have done more, something nobler, if she'd only tried harder.

Once upon a time Kerry had looked forward to a promising career as an actual journalist: a degree from Northwestern and a prestigious summer internship at a big national print newsweekly, which she'd hoped would set her up for her eventual career as an investigative journalist. Hard news—the kind that would really challenge her personally and professionally. She'd wanted to be Diane Sawyer; she'd wanted to be Christiane Amanpour, jetting around the world to talk to business leaders and prime ministers, taking on the powerful, the corrupt. She'd wanted a Pulitzer Prize.

But between the one-two punch of recession and the rise of Internet news, ad revenues and subscription numbers across all media platforms had plummeted, and the magazine had been forced to cut its staff to the bone, letting half the newsroom go just as Kerry was crossing the stage in Evanston to collect her expensive degree. When she went back to New York to the magazine's offices that summer with her résumé in hand, applying for an entry-level position, she was told how sorry everyone was, how much the editors liked her work, but the news business was bad all over and they just couldn't take on new people when they could barely support the ones they had left. The magazine had gone out of business entirely later that year.

Faced with a mountain of student-loan debt and unsure what else to do in the meantime, Kerry had come back to Chicago and taken a job answering the phones in the Petrol media-management office, thinking it was just a summer job, thinking that eventually she'd find a better position and get back out into the real-news world when hiring picked up again. No one was more surprised than she was when Bob assigned her a press release on a new spill cleanup project the company had developed to be more environmentally friendly, or when the story had received major press coverage, coverage that got her noticed at the company. Bob told her she was a natural and started giving her more and more responsibility, at first small things like minor press releases about plant upgrades, then she moved on to more important projects like annual earnings reports, announcements of mergers and acquisitions, even international development deals, working her way up and up until she was director of the toughest department in the company—the crisis-management media team.

It wasn't an easy job, but she doubted she'd have been happy if it were. What was harder than making the company look good in the middle of a colossal failure, after all? She had a better paycheck than she'd ever have had working in print journalism, which was practically dead anyway (or at least that's what she told herself). Who wanted to do media management for a breakfast-cereal company, a garbage-bag company, after working at a place like Petrol? How much challenge could there be at a job where she'd be writing press releases hawking the features and benefits of a toothpaste? No— part of her liked the challenge of managing crisis media for a company as public and controversial as Petrol. Bob knew she liked it, and he'd used the possibility of a promotion to vice president— dangling the ultimate in golden handcuffs—to chain her permanently to her desk at corporate headquarters.

But that didn't mean there wasn't still a part of her that would have liked to be on the other side of the equation sometimes. Who knew what would have happened if she'd quit Petrol after six months like she'd originally planned, living on ramen and cheap beer and using all those reporting skills for which she'd paid so dearly for their intended use? She imagined what it would have been like if she'd been the one interviewing Bob on the newscast the night before instead of the one calling the network to issue corrections on the number of spilled gallons. She imagined chucking it all, telling Bob where he could stick his paycheck and his weekend house in Aspen. It was tempting, today more so than ever.

But no. That ship had sailed long ago. She'd chosen her path and now had only to walk it as well as she could. Plus there was Daniel to think about.

Before they'd met, Kerry's personal life was a mess: random blind dates and Internet dates that never led anywhere, even once an ill-advised drunken hookup that ended in a scary stalker situation. She was never in one place long enough to meet someone and develop a real connection, not when the company had her jetting off to Dubai one week and Newfoundland the next, all the corners of the earth where the company's oil platforms churned up crude from beneath the earth's crust. She couldn't even get a dog, much less maintain a relationship with a man, when she was traveling for work nine months of the year and putting in ten-hour days at the office the rest of the time. She liked to joke to Judy that her longest relationship was with the coffeemaker in the break room.

That had all changed when Daniel was hired. Always the center of attention in every room, the guy with the infectious laugh and the winning personality, Daniel drew people to him like fire to oil. He'd surprised Kerry first by making work fun, then by making *her* more fun when he was around.

She remembered the first time she'd spoken to Daniel on a flight of mostly Petrol employees heading to Gulf Shores, Alabama, one fall afternoon nearly two years ago. She'd been lucky enough to score an entire row to herself; she'd been looking forward to stretching out, taking up the whole armrest and reading the newspaper. It was a dreary afternoon in November, the day before Thanksgiving, rain blurring the windows. The mood in the plane was equally gray; no one on the team wanted to be away from home over the holiday. Halfway through the flight, though, she'd looked up from her copy of *People* to see the new guy, Daniel Albrecht, using the intercom for an impromptu stand-up routine, apparently in an effort to raise the team's spirits. "Just in case we go down, there are some things you need to know about me," he'd said. "Mostly that I've seen every episode of *Gilmore Girls*. Twice."

Someone yelled out, "That's it? My teenaged daughter has seen them all at least a dozen times."

Daniel grinned, pointed at the responder and said, "You win the prize Thanksgiving turkey!"

Kerry watched this, bemused, and then called, "All right, then. What else you got?"

Daniel looked at Kerry with a sheepish expression, then said, "I dominate games of *Risk*. I'm a big believer in taking up position in southern Europe and winning the whole thing from there. Let's see, um. . . . I secretly love Renaissance fairs and amusement parks. I once ate an entire anchovy pizza in one sitting. My mother still calls me Danny. What about you, Kerry? Anything you want to tell us about yourself?"

She shook her head no. Everyone was looking at her.

"You sure? No skeletons in your closet?"

Kerry shook her head again, but she was smiling—she didn't

realize he'd known her name. She didn't have the gift of making people laugh, but she'd always admired people who did. Who weren't afraid of laughing at themselves, most of all. After a succession of boyfriends who'd taken themselves very, very seriously, she was starting to see how charming it might be to be with someone who didn't.

Then Daniel started calling people up one by one for their own most embarrassing confessions, keeping them all laughing so hard they were wheezing. When he'd finished and started back to his seat, she'd stopped him. "I didn't know you were such a comedian," she'd said. "If you ever get tired of crisis management, you can always find work as the opening act for Louis C.K."

"No way," Daniel said, waving his hand in dismissal, "he can open for *me*." Kerry cracked another smile. Despite herself, she couldn't stop staring. The large brown eyes, a shock of chestnut hair a little longer than strictly necessary, wide cheekbones surrounding a mouth always curling at the edges into humor—how had she never noticed until now how good-looking he was? Had she ever really seen him before?

Daniel had looked from her face to the empty seat next to her and back. "What'd you do? Scare off your seatmate? Was he easily intimidated?"

"By what?"

"You. You always seem to be so . . . intense."

Kerry smiled. "I'm not *always* intense," she said, though she knew she gave that impression; she sometimes deliberately cultivated that impression. Maybe now was the time to relax a little. She moved her purse off the seat next to her. "Want to join me?"

He looked surprised, but sat down with a big smile, his arm brushing against hers. They'd talked the entire way to Gulf Shores, trading stories about their childhoods and drinking glass after glass of red wine until, for the first time in a long time, Kerry was sorry to see the flight end. At the gate they'd stood up to deplane, and Daniel had offered to help her with her carry-on. "Let me give you a hand with that," he'd said, pulling it down for her and pretending to fall over from the weight—Kerry refused to check her bags, and so her carry-ons were a marvel of engineered packing—and she'd laughed so long and hard at the shocked look on his face and his clowning that she'd actually gone too far and hugged him—he was tall and thin, wiry like a basketball player, his skin surprisingly cool. And after throwing propriety to the wind so early in their relationship, she told him later, how could she possibly have refused when he asked her to dinner that night?

They ate alone at a quaint little place in Gulf Shores with a view of the Gulf. Over crab cakes and more wine, Daniel had confessed that he'd been secretly trying to get Kerry to talk to him for weeks, that he'd noticed her first when he'd come to the department for his job interview a couple of months back—he'd passed her office and caught her eye for just a moment, an event Kerry definitely didn't remember—and something about the redhead in the pencil skirt and librarian hair just had him riveted. "I thought, *That's the kind of woman I'd like to know better. A lot better.*"

"The kind who's intense?" she said.

"Exactly," he said, pouring her another glass of wine. "To see how intense she might be in other ways."

He kissed her for the first time that night, after walking her back to her room and catching her at the door before she could lean down to insert her keycard and say good night. His mouth had been firm and soft, searching but sweet, as he'd reached up and pulled out the pins that held up her hair, letting it fall over her shoulders and into his hands. She'd told Judy the next morning that either it had been too long since she'd kissed anyone or else he was really, really good at it, because they kissed for at least twenty minutes in the hall of the hotel before someone walked by and embarrassed them into stopping.

Judy had feigned being scandalized. "What would have happened if no one had walked by?"

"I don't know," Kerry had said, feeling her face reddening. "I've never dated anyone at work before. I don't quite understand what the rules are. Is this a mistake? It's a mistake, isn't it?"

"Not when he's that cute."

Trust Judy to not take the whole thing so seriously.

After that, she stopped worrying about whether dating a co-worker was a bad idea or not. On that first trip, they spent nearly all their free hours together, sitting on the beaches of Gulf Shores, Daniel finding a moment to kiss her in the corridor before lunch, between phone calls in the evening.

When they got home to Chicago, they immediately ran away together for a long weekend in the Upper Peninsula of Michigan, where Daniel said he had a cabin. It turned out to be less a cabin in the woods than a high-end log house with a loft and a stone fireplace and a view of Lake Superior. They spent the weekend kayaking and hiking in the woods, ignoring Bob's constant texts and voicemails and claiming later there'd been no service so far north.

It was a life Kerry had never really experienced before—so remote, so far from city life and its noise and its messiness—but she was surprised to find she loved it, or at least she did with Daniel, who fancied himself something of an outdoorsman. He had learned to sea-kayak and was taking sailing lessons; he hiked in the Hiawatha National Forest on a few occasions, he told her, with only a sleeping bag and a lighter. His big plan, he said, was to make enough money to retire at forty-five or fifty, move up to the Lake Superior cabin full-time and have a family. Lying next to him with the fire burning down in the fireplace, she could see herself there, too, raising a gaggle of kids, maybe writing that novel she'd always dreamed about, bundled up in heavy wool socks and carrying around enormous cups of tea in mugs she'd made herself. She could have a garden. She could get away from Petrol and city life and the choices she'd fallen into rather than decided upon.

Before six months were up, they'd moved in together, arguing over decorating choices and whether or not they should get a cat, spending their free weekends canoeing the Wisconsin River or going apple picking in Door County. Daniel never let her take her job, or herself, so seriously that she couldn't get out of the office once in a while, have a life of her own. He fought for private space for the two of them, not just with her but with Bob, too. "We work to live," he always said, "not the other way around."

They were perfectly happy. Kerry was thirty-four and knew who she was, finally, and what she needed to make a life for herself. She had the company by day and Daniel by night, and she'd always thought she'd have been quite content to go on that way forever.

But now, standing in the snowy Alaska street looking through the window at Bob screaming abuse down the phone, knowing her fiancé—who'd been out in the dangerous cold all night—was likely on the receiving end of his tirade, Kerry was starting to think the time for a lifestyle change might be coming sooner than she'd anticipated. Bob was putting Daniel in danger this time, and the people who worked for Daniel. Bob had risked people's lives before, but what if this was the moment he pushed everyone just a bit too far? If his insistence on having his way really did cost additional lives? She could spin lots of things, but if Bob caused a crisis that didn't need to happen—Kerry wouldn't be able to spin that. She wouldn't want to.

She watched through the window as Bob regained control of himself, his face turning from purple to red to a shiny pink, hanging up the phone with one meaty thumb. Then the old man disappeared back into the warmth of the diner, where Phil was already waiting at a corner table for the two women to arrive. Kerry could see him tapping out something on his phone with a stylus, then set it down.

In a moment her phone beeped: Phil had sent her a text. *Are you on your way?* it said, and Kerry felt her annoyance level leap into the red. *I don't need you checking in on me,* she typed, her finger hovering over the Send button. Then she changed her mind and deleted the text.

The director of human resources had long been a source of irritation to Kerry, though she couldn't always put her finger on why. Enormously secretive about his personal life, with a dry, uneven sense of humor that could flare up or die off unexpectedly, Phil was an enigma to everyone around the office, sometimes personable and funny, sometimes unexpectedly cold and aloof, especially to Kerry. Even Bob had noticed and remarked on it from time to time. Fortyish, with thick dark-brown hair and small brown eyes framed by a pair of square no-rim glasses, Phil had a way of never quite looking her in the eye when he was speaking to her, as if something about the sight of her caused him pain. There were times when she'd catch him staring at her when she was in the middle of a presentation or asking a question, and then he'd look away, his mouth turned down. Or he'd brush past her in the hallway at Petrol without even saying so much as hello or nodding his head.

The truth was that Phil had made it clear, from the first day he'd met her, that he didn't think much of someone her age and experience leading the media-relations team; it had literally been the first thing he'd said to her, that she didn't look old enough for her position. She'd been shocked and hurt, especially when Bob had felt the need to defend Kerry's record, but she'd made up her mind to try to win Phil over on her own. For the first few months they'd worked together, she'd done everything she could to at least earn his respect. She'd gone out of her way to highlight his projects to the media, to get his buy-in on important projects. She'd been her most charming, her most hardworking and impressive. None of it mattered—Phil Velez never warmed up to her, no matter what she did. Eventually she stopped trying.

"Give Phil a break," Judy always said whenever Kerry complained that he had all the personality of a wet herring. "The guy's got it bad."

This was Judy's favorite theory—that Phil was awful to Kerry because it made it easier for him to dismiss his feelings for her—but Kerry knew her friend was wrong. "Not for me, he doesn't. Anyway, he's married."

"You don't know that."

"The man wears a gold wedding band. I don't need a detective agency to tell me what that means."

Judy wouldn't be swayed, but Kerry knew better. From their very first meeting, Phil had made it clear he thought Kerry wasn't good enough: Not for her job. Not for the company. Not for him.

Fine by me, she'd thought, and written Phil off as a hopeless case. They were co-workers, but they didn't have to be friends.

Now she could see Phil at the table, scribbling on his tablet with the stylus again, frowning down at it. He was wearing a jacket and tie even here, despite the crazy temperatures and blowing snow, making him look like a substitute teacher on a bad day. Kerry had a momentary image of herself turning around and walking straight back out, returning to the hotel, packing her bags, gathering her fiancé, and catching the first flight back to Chicago.

Kerry squared her shoulders. "Come on," she said to Judy, "let's get this over with. Afterward, if we survive, I'll buy you a drink."

"Deal," Judy said, her voice still muffled by her scarf. "At least there's plenty of ice."

4

As the two women came into the restaurant—stamping their feet and stripping off their hats, gloves and scarves—Phil Velez could see Kerry was upset or maybe irritated about something, her eyebrows pinched together, mouth turned down just slightly as she looked at him, as if she'd smelled something bad. Then she caught sight of Bob and composed herself, her brow smoothing, her mouth turning up again at the corners, and by the time she and Judy sat down across from Phil at the table, Kerry appeared herself again—self-possessed, alert, polite—although just barely. Somewhere underneath that calm exterior, he could sense a hidden irritation. Something had set her off, but what?

"Good morning," she said, shrugging out of her parka and letting it fall on the back of her chair. "We made it."

Bob waved to the waitress for a warm-up. "Was there any doubt?" he said.

"Phil just sent me a text asking me to check in," she said. Her brow furrowed once more.

So it was Phil's quick text that had irritated her. A familiar sense of dread rose in his belly as he watched her take out her Moleskine notebook, square her shoulders and give a little sigh. Her dislike of Phil was always there in the background, a little static in the air between them. Usually he managed to ignore it, except for days like this one, when they needed to work together so closely. He should smooth things over with her.

"I wasn't asking you to check in," he murmured. "I only wanted to know if you were on your way."

"Exactly," she said, and before he could respond, she tapped her stylus on her tablet and said, "Shall we get to work?"

"Yes, let's."

Phil picked up his own tablet, reminding himself that Kerry was angry at Bob, not him, that she was using Phil as her personal scapegoat because she couldn't take it out on the real object of her frustration. Well, he wasn't here to make friends. He had never wanted to make friends among his co-workers at Petrol; that was the whole point of taking the job.

It was only about three years ago that he'd joined the crisis-management team at Petrol, after a day of intense interviews with Bob Packer and upper-level human-resources executives. He'd never forget his first impression of Bob, how the man had come in twenty minutes late for the interview (deliberately, Phil figured out later), how he'd sat on the edge of his desk instead of behind it, how he'd leaned in very close to Phil's face, smacking his hands across his pants as if he were brushing dust from them, and asked exactly one question: "So. Why should I give you this job?"

Phil could remember very little of the initial answer he'd given Bob that day—something about the challenge of working in a high-pressure environment, of helping the hardworking employees of Petrol under the most difficult of circumstances, etc., etc.—but he remembered very well the sight of Bob leaning backward against the desk, his big hands gripping the edge, and the distinct feeling that Phil was about to be shown the door. Everything about Bob's body language was broadcasting the fact that the interview was going badly, and Phil knew it; the man had heard these kinds of canned answers before, and this one was no different, no better. It was disingenuous at best and dishonest at worst. Phil was a human-resources professional, for God's sake; how could he forget everything he knew about giving a great interview when *he* was the one on the other side of the desk?

By the time Phil realized neither of them was talking, there had been a good ten seconds of silence. Finally Bob asked, "Is that it?"

All the air seemed to go out of the room. He would lose the chance at this job if he didn't say something true, and say it fast. And he *did* want this job, wanted it more than he'd been willing to admit to himself until that moment. Wanted it for reasons that had nothing to do with money or helping others or work-life balance or any of the other bullshit he'd just been spouting off.

Would a man like Bob understand the truth, though? That was the question Phil kept asking himself.

"No," he said finally, looking down at his shoes. Then, realizing that was exactly the wrong thing to do, he looked up, straight in Bob's eyes. Bob was waiting for something, something that would catch his attention and make Phil stand out among the dozens of other people who'd applied for the job. Some leverage, maybe. Phil decided to give it to him.

"I don't just *want* this job," Phil said, "I need it. I need it very much right now."

That got Bob's attention. Now the old man narrowed his eyes, looking at Phil with greater interest. "Need it why?"

Having opened up that much, Phil knew he had no choice but to go straight to the heart of the matter. "I—lost someone recently. My wife. She died very suddenly last year. Ovarian cancer. Since then I've found it nearly impossible to go to work at my old job. It's just— too much familiarity." He was nearly choking on the effort to say this much, but he couldn't stop now, because he was sensing in every change in body language and facial muscle that he was saying exactly the kind of thing that Bob Packer liked to hear. That need, more than loyalty, was a thing Bob valued in his employees. "Everyone at my present job knew my wife, and having to face them, face their pity every single day, it just—it—"

He was getting emotional, the one thing he'd promised himself he wouldn't do. He could feel the color rising to his face and looked down at the floor. He didn't like talking about his wife with anyone. He didn't like anyone to see him lose his composure, much less the powerful senior VP of a company he hoped to work for.

Phil took a breath, composed himself again, and said, "I need a change. I'm looking for a place where I can go back to being anonymous. Where I don't have to talk about my wife with anyone who knew her and knows what happened to her. I almost don't even care where it is, to tell you the truth."

It was risky, this strategy. Bob Packer was still staring at him, not speaking, using one of the oldest tricks in the book—stay silent and force the interviewee to fill the gaps in the conversation, thereby forcing him to reveal more of himself than he might have otherwise.

Phil lifted his chin. "And, frankly, I'm looking for a place where I will have more work than I can ever do in one lifetime. I want to be busy so I won't have to think about anything else."

Now Bob spoke again. "And you think this will be the place?"

"Why not? You need someone who doesn't have a life. Someone who can be at your beck and call 24/7. I'd not only be willing, I'd welcome it."

"Is that so?" Bob said, the outline of a smile flickering at the corners of his mouth. "You think you can really run away from your problems by coming to work for me?"

Phil had choked out a single word: "Yes," he said. He realized, to his horror, that his hands were shaking.

"Well, if that's the case," Bob said, "I think we can work together. Welcome to the team."

Phil had nearly wept. "Thank you, sir. You won't regret this."

"I'd better not."

Phil reported for duty that first day with an enormous sense of relief. Although he knew Bob Packer owned him after that interview, would ask for the moon and expect to get it, the job still offered a fresh start, a chance at forgetting his old life. The big glass Petrol Tower on Wacker Drive couldn't have been more anonymous, more coolly corporate, and as Phil entered the sliding doors and gave his name to the security guard, he sighed audibly. It was exactly the way he'd imagined it: no one looked at him out of the corner of an eye; no one stopped to ask him how he was doing, gave him a nod of barely repressed pity, or lowered their voices into a whisper when he walked by. Not a single person here knew about the days he'd broken down in tears at work, the wreck he'd been at Emily's funeral, which had been populated with hundreds of Phil's co-workers. No one even so much as glanced at him. Not a single person here, except for Bob himself, knew that Phil had even been married, much less that his wife had died in agonizing pain, hardly able to recognize him at the end. He was totally and completely anonymous, which was exactly what he'd wanted when he applied for the job.

So when he stepped out onto the thirtieth floor of Petrol Tower, Phil was feeling like he'd truly be able to disappear into the job. He could be a useful member of the team, not a man whose emotions had crippled him on a near daily basis for the last year. He wanted to be all about the work, and nothing more.

He was feeling so great about the decision to accept the position at Petrol, in fact, that when he arrived in Bob's office that morning, he had been completely thrown off by the sight of a young woman sitting across from Bob's desk. Kerry Egan looked like a kid—long red hair done up tightly in a knot at the base of her neck, neat gray skirt and white blouse, a long silver necklace around her neck, towering heels. He got the impression of a young woman trying on her mother's clothes. A very young, very beautiful woman.

He'd been so thunderstruck he'd paused in the doorway and taken a moment to compose himself, feeling shame over his attraction to any woman who wasn't Emily, and discomfort when he realized the young woman was there because they'd likely be working together. If that was so, why hadn't Bob included her in the interviews in the first place?

Because Bob Packer was a man who didn't need, or want, other people's buy-in on his decisions, that's why. He'd been there for an hour and he knew that much about the man already.

She'd stood, welcoming Phil to the team as Bob made introductions. "Glad to hear you're joining us," Kerry said. "You must have a strong disposition; Bob usually scares off our potential new hires."

She'd reached out her hand to Phil, but he didn't take it right away, afraid as he was that his palms were sweating. *This* was the director of media relations? For a minute he could feel the color rising to his face and tried to get hold of himself. He was determined to be businesslike and professional in his new position, like he'd told Bob. Nothing more.

She was still holding out her hand, so Phil wiped his hand on his pants and took it, shaking it once, loosely, and then letting go as quickly as possible. "Nice to meet you," he said. "Bob says you're the youngest director in the company. I can see he was right. You don't even look like you're thirty yet."

"I'm thirty-one. Does that surprise you?" she asked.

He felt himself beginning to squirm. He found looking in her eyes distinctly uncomfortable, as if she were the sun, and decided to focus over her shoulder instead. "Maybe a little. But it's great," he stammered, and then said again, "I think it's great. Looking forward to working with you."

"Kerry's our ace in the hole," Bob said, putting a beefy hand on her shoulder. "Been at Petrol nearly a decade now, isn't that right? She's proved herself time and again to be the best in the business."

Phil had watched Kerry's face burn and realized he'd made a cardinal error. He knew better than to comment on a co-worker's age or appearance; what was *wrong* with him? Nor did she like her boss defending her against the new guy's fumbling. It was his first day, his first hour, and already he'd gotten off on the wrong foot.

Phil mumbled something about needing the washroom and then excused himself. Later that day, he'd heard Kerry in her office complaining about him to Judy Akers. What was Bob thinking, she'd said, bringing a guy like that onto such a tightly knit team? Who hired an HR director who had zero people skills, who made a critical HR error the minute he opened his mouth?

He'd been so ashamed of himself that he'd done everything he could to avoid direct contact with her. In her presence he was always carefully professional, never asking her questions about herself or crossing the line into anything the slightest bit personal about his family, his home life. No one wanted to hear about his dead wife anyway, the dark thoughts that crowded his head whenever he had a free minute to himself. At first, Kerry had tried to win him over, seeking him out for his ideas, offering to brag him up to the media, but the sight of her caused him so much pain those first months that he could never bring himself to be much more than polite. "Thank you, but I don't think this is the right time," became his constant refrain with her.

Eventually she'd gotten the hint and started keeping him at arm's length, coolly professional in the hallways, at office parties, on the road; she was never rude, but never warm, either. The fact that he couldn't keep his eyes off her didn't help: more than once she'd caught him staring, and that little frown would tick at the corners of her mouth. Phil's sense of helplessness seemed bottomless. He'd come to Petrol to erase the mistakes of the past, and instead he'd made a whole host of new ones.

He started thinking he was simply not fit to be around other humans. He should just do his job and keep his mouth shut, keep away from any distractions and do what he needed to survive, nothing more. His wife was dead, and his future along with her. Any happiness or hope he'd felt was long gone, and everyone would be better off, Kerry included, if Phil kept to himself.

He threw himself into work, took on extra projects and longer hours, anything to keep him at the office as long as possible. He sold the house in the suburbs he'd shared with Emily and got a new apartment downtown. He never socialized at work, never went to lunch or out for a beer. He kept his head down, his mouth shut and his mind occupied. If he kept himself busy, he wouldn't have time to think about anyone, especially Kerry Egan.

For the most part, he was successful, too—except when they were all on the road together. Then it was harder to stay away from her, but he did what he could, avoiding her at dinner, holing up in his hotel room whenever he wasn't immediately needed. It would be easier that way to ignore the way he felt whenever he looked at her: dizzy, like he'd just looked over the edge of a very tall building.

Then there was that trip to Gulf Shores. Phil remembered the plane ride and how the new guy, Daniel Albrecht, had done his little stand-up routine for the whole plane to hear. Then Daniel sitting down casually next to Kerry, the two of them laughing together.

Phil had been sitting a couple of rows back, and he'd been over-whelmed with jealousy at the ease Daniel had with her. Despite all his efforts to the contrary, he'd have given anything to chat with her so amiably, have her look at him that way. The only emotion in Ker-ry's face whenever she spoke to him was annoyance.

He'd spent three years trying to disappear into his work, and it wasn't enough. It was easier back in Chicago, where he could be anonymous at the end of every day, but when they were all forced to spend time together on the road, Phil was always uncomfortably aware of her, of her perfume, of her laugh, of the physical presence of her, and felt that same small tightening in his throat. He shouldn't be attracted to her, he thought. He didn't have the right. His wife was dead, he reminded himself, and Kerry was going to marry Dan-iel. Better for them all that way.

Now Kerry and Judy were sitting across the table from Phil, who looked down at his tablet and wished for the thousandth time that the very sight of her didn't turn him into a stammering mess.

She's a beautiful woman. She's smart and accomplished. Why shouldn't you be attracted to her? It was his dead wife's voice, Emily's voice, he always imagined in his head in those moments, her teasing putting him immediately at ease. *You're not dead, are you?*

Phil shook his head; Emily always had had a way of understand-ing him, even when (especially when) he didn't understand himself. It wouldn't do to think of her now, sitting in a diner in Barrow, Alaska, in the middle of a workday. Emily was gone, and Phil had work to do. He picked up his tablet and bowed his head.

Bob had already taken his heart pills and eaten his protein bar, the same breakfast he ate every morning. Phil ordered a bowl of oatmeal and more coffee, while Kerry asked for yogurt and bananas, possibly the most expensive meal she could have ordered in a place where perishables had to be flown in daily. Judy ordered a muffin and coffee. "Now, we're doing what this morning?" she asked.

"Last things," said Bob. "Phil says he's got a little humanitarian story for you two to pitch before we get out of town. Something about a new program Phil's developing to pay for the son of one of the victims to go to college."

"Sounds promising," said Kerry, not looking at Phil as she poured cream in her coffee. "Let's hear it, then."

But before Phil could get started, Bob stood up, pulled out his phone and excused himself. "Pardon me," he said, "but I think I have some calls to make. I'm sure you all can handle this without me?"

"Sir, we'd really appreciate getting a quote from you for the press release," Judy said.

"Don't you want to weigh in on the value of the program, all the features and benefits, et cetera?" Kerry asked.

"I'm sure you can handle the et cetera without me," said Bob, not looking up as he scrolled through his phone. "This is Phil's baby. He can tell you all about it. Make up a quote for me—you know the kind of thing I always say." Then Bob was pushing buttons on his phone and walking away. Phil heard him say, "Daniel."

Kerry looked up at the sound of her fiancé's name, staring after Bob as he walked toward the door. She seemed to be only dimly aware that, next to her, Judy and Phil were already going over notes for the press release, getting the facts about Phil's scholarship program, deciding where and how to pitch it.

She was still watching Bob's back when Judy poked her shoulder. "Hey," Judy said. "Earth to Kerry."

"What?"

Judy touched her friend's shoulder again and said, "Are you going to chime in, or am I on my own here?"

"I'm sorry," she said, looking back toward the entrance of the restaurant, where Bob was gesticulating at the phone. "I've got a lot on my mind right now."

Phil felt himself staring again and looked down at his tablet. "It's natural to be worried," he said.

"I'm not worried," Kerry started. "I'm furious."

Phil cleared his throat and said, "Daniel's a big boy. He can take care of himself."

"I *know* he can take care of himself," Kerry snapped, rounding on him, her voice cracking with emotion. "Bob has no right to take chances like this with people's lives. *You* don't have to be so flippant about it, either."

He coughed and looked over at Judy, who looked as surprised as he did, and said, "Let's not get personal here, Kerry. Let's keep this professional—"

"*I was keeping it professional.*" She started to say something else, then stopped herself and threw up her hands. "Oh, hell. I'm sorry, Phil. This isn't about you." She blew out a deep breath and said, "Can you two please excuse me? I have some calls to make, too."

Phil stood up from the table as Kerry got up to go. There was a crease of consternation between her eyebrows. "Of course," he said. "I'm sorry, Kerry. I didn't mean to give you the impression that I—"

"Don't worry about it," Kerry said. "I shouldn't have gone off on you. You didn't do anything wrong; it was my fault." She looked at Judy and said, "You got this?"

"Go on. I'll fill you in later."

She grabbed her coat and bag and headed out the door. Phil watched her go, listening to the blood rush through his ears. She'd never blown up at him like that before. He found the experience far more uncomfortable than he would have liked to admit.

Now there were just the two of them left at the table in the diner. "She's marrying someone else," Judy said, stirring sweetener into her coffee and looking at the place where Kerry had gone. "You aren't making things any easier on her. Or any of us."

"I don't know what you mean," Phil said, picking up his tablet once again, but the words were swimming before his eyes. "I don't have any kind of a problem with Kerry. I never have."

"Of course you don't," Judy said, letting out a sigh. "Now, where were we again?"

5

Daniel had just hung up with Bob when his satellite phone rang again. "Babe?" Kerry asked. "What's going on? I heard Bob call you."

Daniel put a hand on the wall to steady himself against the movement of the ship. Outside the bridge, the subs were just coming back up to the surface after a long night underwater. The waves were rolling underneath them, spray lashing the deck just outside the window, and Daniel could hear the voices of the sub crew over the conn as they maneuvered into position below the ship.

"Well," he said, his voice thick with exhaustion, "we got the leak fixed finally. Got the subs down to the bottom this morning and got the wellhead clamped. The guys are just coming back aboard."

"And everything's okay there? No one's hurt?"

"It was a long night," he said, though that was putting a nicer face on it than he would admit—just getting the subs in the water had been two hours of hell, and one of the ship's crew was being treated for frostbite on his hands—"but it's all fixed, and now the cleanup can start. Tell everyone we're going home tomorrow. For real this time."

"And you?" she asked. "You're okay?"

"I will be, when I get warm and get some sleep," he said.

"I could kill Bob," she said, "keeping you and those poor guys outside all night in those temperatures. He's lucky you didn't all freeze to death."

"I don't want to think about Bob or even hear his name right now. I told him if he ever pulled a stunt like that again, I'd quit on the spot."

"No wonder he was so angry."

"I don't really care if he was." One large wave rolled the ship from side to side, met with shouting by the crew. "Meet me at the room later? I want to pick up where we left off last night."

He could practically hear her smiling. "You sure you have the energy for that?" she asked.

"You better believe it."

She laughed. "See you in a few."

He hung up the phone, feeling every bone in his body ache, feeling exhaustion settle into his legs, the small of his back. In a couple of hours he'd be back at the hotel in Barrow in bed with the woman he loved. He'd make love to her and afterward they'd fall asleep together, and he had no intention of leaving his bed again until it was time to go home to Chicago.

When Daniel arrived back at the hotel at last, Kerry was waiting for him. He opened the door to his room to find that she'd opened a bottle of wine, turned the heat all the way up and burrowed under the blankets, so that when Daniel dropped his wet, frozen clothes on the carpet and crawled under the covers beside her, the only thing he encountered was Kerry—naked, warm and ready to pick up where they'd left off the night before.

"Well," he said, his cold feet brushing against her leg, "looks like it's your turn to warm me up for a change. You up for it?"

She pulled him down to kiss her. "Of course," she said. "Fair's fair."

At nine the following morning, the crisis-management team of Petrol, Inc., arrived in the terminal at Anchorage International Airport to catch their connecting flight back to Chicago. The hard part was over, Kerry thought—the flight from Barrow to Anchorage on the 737 had been rough in parts, the wind shuddering the wings at takeoff and landing, but nothing serious enough to do more than make her look up for a moment in surprise. There was a big storm coming inland from the Pacific—a giant typhoon moving up from the southwest—but the pilot had said the rough takeoff was par for the course for a flight over Alaska, so no one had panicked.

Still, when Kerry saw the lights of Anchorage below them as the plane came in for its landing, she was immediately relieved. They were below the Arctic Circle again, and in a few hours they'd be home in Chicago, where even in the winter the sun came up for several good hours, and going outside didn't require covering every inch of exposed skin. She was watching the monitors in the terminal as the weatherman reported seasonal temperatures of 29 degrees in Chicago, with a light wind off the lake bringing a few flurries to the city and south suburbs. After two weeks of bitter cold in Barrow, such a forecast sounded practically like summertime.

Outside the windows she could see the clouds gathering, the weather moving northeast from the sea toward Anchorage. On the Departures board, a few West Coast flights had been canceled—Seattle, San Francisco, Portland—but so far the flights to places farther east were still listed as "on time." She was eager to get going; the storm sounded bad enough that if they got grounded, they might be stuck in Alaska for several more days. *Please, please*, she thought. *I just want to get home.*

She still hadn't told Daniel about the pregnancy test she'd taken the day before. After leaving the diner, she'd gone straight to the pharmacy, bought the test and taken it back to her hotel room. When only one little pink line had appeared on the stick, she had been enormously relieved. When she looked again five minutes later and there were *two* little pink lines, she'd had to grip the edge of the sink to keep from falling over.

She'd wanted to tell Daniel when he first came in. She'd thought about it, even had the pregnancy test on her nightstand all ready to show him. But he'd been so cold, so exhausted, that after they made love he'd fallen immediately asleep. She'd lain awake half the night, worrying about how to tell him. Then the morning came too early, and in the rush to pack up and get to the airport, they hadn't really had time to talk.

"Hey," Daniel said, poking Kerry in the ribs. "You awake?"

"Mostly," she answered. "I was thinking about home. A lot on my mind right now."

"Me, too," he said. "I was thinking about taking the rest of the day off. Maybe an early dinner. What do you think?"

"Hmm," she said, distracted. Taking the day off sounded nice, but it was hard to see how she'd manage it. She took out her phone and checked her e-mail: two messages to answer from reporters, and four voicemails, three of which were from her mother. Then she looked at her calendar: two meetings next week, a doctor's appointment she might need to reschedule. In a few hours they'd be home, in their condo with the view of the lake. Kerry was thinking of the things she had to do: pick up the dry cleaning and the mail; call her sister about their mother's upcoming birthday; e-mail the president of the condo association about a leaking water pipe. And those were just the non-work-related things she had to take care of. In the five hours it took to get home, she wondered, what might go wrong at the office? What if the White House decided to get involved in the company's dispute with the Russians? What if that pushy reporter from Reuters decided to run that environmental-impact story she'd been dancing around all week? What if the company's people in Barrow couldn't get the leaked oil properly cleaned up?

And what if Daniel wasn't thrilled to find out he was going to be a father? What would she do then?

"I don't know," she said. "Maybe it would be nice just to stay home."

Daniel took the phone out of her hands and turned it off. "Why don't you give the list a rest for a little while?" he asked, and handed it back to her. "There's something I want to talk to you about."

She tried to keep her voice steady and asked, "What's that?"

"The wedding."

That spring, he'd surprised Kerry on her birthday with a helicopter ride over the lake and a diamond ring he'd offered her with a view of the city below them. He'd held out the black velvet box with the glittering diamond inside, and it had taken her several seconds to realize what she was seeing, what Daniel was doing as he took her hand and slid the ring on it. Through the noise of the helicopter and the roaring in her ears, she barely heard him ask the question, barely heard herself saying, "What? Wait, what are you saying?" and making him repeat it again. She'd said yes, of course. Wholeheartedly yes. It was a wonderful surprise, she told him that night—she hadn't suspected a thing.

But since then they'd had trouble trying to figure out a date for the ceremony. Their work schedules were notoriously subject to last-minute changes and disruptions—crises by their nature being unpredictable—so to every request for a two-week window off sometime the following year, Bob had said no, no, I need you then, there's too much to do, I can't have you both gone at the same time.

"It's going to be a little difficult for us to get married otherwise," Daniel said to him once.

Bob had only laughed and said Kerry and Daniel should have a quickie ceremony at the courthouse one afternoon with a few friends and take their honeymoon sometime later, when they had some downtime. "That's what I did," he boasted. "And you don't hear my wife complaining."

"Of course not," Kerry had said later on, when Daniel told her what Bob had said. "Bob's wife isn't allowed to speak in public."

For a little while they had dropped the subject. There should be a lull in the fall, they'd thought at first—then the fall had been unexpectedly busy. Maybe a Christmas wedding, they'd thought, and then there was the trip to Alaska. Even if they started planning the minute they got back home, a spring wedding would still be difficult to arrange, with dates for churches and reception venues hard to come by, not to mention any number of disasters that might happen on any date of their choosing. They'd given up on the idea of a honeymoon right after the ceremony, even, but still Bob had refused to let the rest of the team handle things in Kerry and Daniel's absence if something should come up. *If they could manage without you, they wouldn't be assistant directors,* was what he'd told them, his shoulders shrugging inside his twelve-hundred-dollar suit.

So no date had been set so far. In the last few weeks, Kerry had noticed Daniel getting restless about the subject, bringing it up more and more as a sore spot when talking about Bob—often as a joke, though Kerry could always sense the irritation behind the lighthearted words. In all the work they'd had to do over the Beaufort spill, she'd stopped worrying about it until Daniel brought it up while they sat in the airport terminal, waiting for their flight to be called.

"What about the wedding?"

"I think it's time we get serious about setting a date."

"Oh," she said, her head swimming. At the moment the wedding sounded like one more problem she was going to have to deal with. She didn't really feel like digging into *that* hornet's nest, along with everything else.

"You sound surprised."

"I am," she said. "Have you been talking to my mother again?"

"She loves you," he said, picking up her left hand and kissing the diamond on her third finger. Apparently he *had* been talking to her mother. "She'll feel better when it's official. I'll feel better."

"My mother wants the big church wedding so all her friends can see us."

"There's nothing wrong with a big church wedding."

"There will be if we can't settle on a date. I'm just so tired of people asking us when we're actually going to go through with it." *Not to mention the fact that now I'll need to buy my wedding dress in the maternity section.*

"So," she said, forcing a smile, "think Bob will relent on Memorial Day weekend, if we ask him now? Want to give it a shot while he's still in a good mood?"

Daniel looked over his shoulder toward the spot where Bob sat talking on the phone again. "I don't think he's ever going to let us plan ahead. He's made that pretty clear."

"So, what, then? You want to elope? Head to Vegas and come back with the deed done already?"

"No, I really want our families there."

"So what do you have in mind, then?" She looked around the terminal, full of her co-workers and friends. *Home. I'll tell him at home, when we can be alone. It's just a few hours. I'll feel better then. More calm.*

Daniel grinned at her, his teeth flashing white, the corner of his mouth turning up the way it did when he was pleased with himself for figuring out the answer to a sticky problem. "Let's have a flash-mob wedding."

"A what?" Kerry asked. She didn't quite understand what he was saying.

"I saw some guy arrange it for his fiancée on YouTube. They showed up at a mall in L.A. and the groom had the whole thing set up for the bride as a surprise."

"A mall? That's *so* romantic."

"We don't have to do it in a mall. Look," he said, rubbing her engagement ring with his thumb, "we can't reserve a space because we can't get Bob to give us time off. So let's not take time off. Let's just show up someplace where we'd love to get married and get married there. Have the guests show up, the florist, you and me in our wedding clothes, and get married wherever we like on whatever day we choose."

"If you're kidding——"

"I'm not," he said, his face losing its usual look of barely restrained amusement and settling finally on the expression he'd worn the day he proposed to her——serious, adoring. "I want to marry you. I'm tired of waiting."

Kerry was picturing it now: their family and friends gathering in the lobby of the Field Museum, maybe, or maybe the observation deck of some massive skyscraper, everyone watching, a minister in hurry-up mode before they were all thrown out by security, their family and friends in on the planning, everyone laughing, everyone hoping they could pull it off in time. It could be fun. It could be a little bit precarious, a little bit dangerous——and if there was something Kerry lived for, it was rising to a challenge.

Not to mention the wedding would take place well before the

baby was born. *Don't get ahead of yourself, Kerry. One problem at a time.*

"What do you say?" Daniel asked. "Want to?"

She laughed and leaned over to kiss him. "You're crazy," she said, "but I love it. Where should we do it?"

It would have to be someplace a crowd of people could get into and out of, at least for twenty minutes or so, Daniel said. It would be winter in Chicago, so anyplace outdoors was off the table. Daniel suggested the Art Institute, which Kerry liked—they could get married in front of the enormous Seurat painting, maybe—but then she suggested the observation deck of the Hancock building, which Daniel liked even more. The views of the city below, the green curve of the lake, the lights of Navy Pier. "We can get married in front of the whole city," he said. "I love it!"

"I love you," Kerry said. So it was decided. When they got home, she'd start making phone calls—but not to the condo association president. She'd need to send invitations, hire a florist, find a minister willing to do something this crazy . . .

"What date should we pick?" she asked.

"What do you say about January first?" Daniel said.

"New Year's."

Kerry was still feeling the blood rushing in her ears when the flight attendant came over the loudspeaker. "Good morning, ladies and gentlemen," she said. "In a moment we'll begin boarding passengers for Flight 806 to Chicago . . ." Their flight was leaving on time after all; in just a matter of hours they'd be back in Chicago. Back home.

Just for a second she pictured herself holding the baby, Daniel's baby, and she nearly cried right there, in line for the flight home, hugging her arms around herself. Maybe it wasn't planned, maybe it wasn't the best possible timing, but surely if two people could make it work, they would.

"So what do you think?" Daniel asked. "Should we go for it?"

"I can't wait," said Kerry, pulling her carry-on behind her. "Let's get going."

6

By the time the plane was heading down the runway, the snow was falling fast and thick and the wind was rising, a low guttural lurch that shook the plane from side to side as the engines picked up speed, that shuddered the metal fuselage as the wheels left the tarmac. From his seat in the emergency-exit row, Daniel could see the clouds closing in as they climbed higher and higher in the sky above Anchorage.

"Thank God," Kerry said when they were airborne. "I was afraid they were going to ground us."

Daniel took out a magazine he'd bought at the airport. "We're lucky. In a few minutes we'll be up above the storm, and then we'll be home."

"Good." She seemed distracted, or maybe it was just tired. Daniel picked up her hand and kissed it.

When the pilot did come on the intercom, he only said that although there might be a little chop ahead during the first hour of the flight due to the bad weather coming in from the Pacific, he expected the rest of the trip to be smooth sailing. "Still, please keep your seat belts fastened while you remain in your seats," he said. "Wouldn't want any of you to bump your heads if we experience some sudden turbulence, and enjoy the rest of the flight."

Kerry leaned against Daniel's shoulder and drifted off. She seemed genuinely excited about the flash-wedding idea, if a little surprised, and he was pleased with himself for coming up with it, pictures of Kerry in her wedding dress flitting through his head. God, she'd be so beautiful. She was so smart and capable, the kind of woman who made *him* feel smarter and more capable just because she loved him. He'd never had much luck with women before he met her; he'd had a string of bad relationships with women who couldn't deal with the fact that Daniel was always on the road. They were always calling, demanding he check in at all hours of the day and night. He'd finally given up on finding someone who wouldn't need to be reassured constantly of his affection for her, who had her own mind and her own life and wasn't afraid to live it. At least until he met Kerry, who'd knocked him over not just because she was beautiful, but because she didn't need him to tell her he loved her every moment of every day. She knew that already, and knowing it made it more true than just saying it ever could.

That thought was like a wedding vow: she knew that he loved her, and her knowing that made it real again and again. That would be what he would say to her on their wedding day.

He kept picturing the surprise on the faces of the people at the Hancock Observatory, the laughter of their friends and family, who would be in on the scheme, all of them getting away with something. Kerry's mother wouldn't like the flash-mob idea—she had visions of the family church decked out with flowers, all the neighbors and relatives in attendance—but she was so eager for Kerry and Daniel to make it official that she'd get over her disappointment before long, he was sure of it.

More important than all of that was the idea that they'd be together for good, finally, just the way he'd always wanted it. Jobs might come and go, friends would drift in and out of his life, but Kerry was the only thing Daniel had ever really wanted for himself. He couldn't believe his own good luck that she wanted him, too.

A sudden lurch of the plane jolted him upright. He sat up and looked out the window, where the clouds closed in around the plane, thick and gray.

He didn't have the slightest idea where they were; the northern provinces of Canada were mostly a mystery to him. Were they over Yukon Territory, the Northwest Territories, maybe Alberta? It could be any of them. He knew a little about the Alberta tar sands because Petrol had an operation there, but as to anything else, he was totally mystified. He looked to see if he could catch a glimpse of a town or a road, but below them there was nothing but thick, dark-gray banks of cloud, closing in around the plane, condensation clinging to the clear surface of the window.

As he watched, he could have sworn he saw the condensation beginning to freeze. No, he was sure—the water on the window was turning into crystals. But that wasn't supposed to happen. They'd been sprayed with deicer before they'd left the airport. He remembered it distinctly, because the captain had shut off the air for a few moments while the crews worked outside, to keep the passengers from breathing in the chemicals. It should have been enough to keep ice from forming on the plane's surface. Except there was definitely ice forming on the window.

Then a stream of thin gray smoke was coming from the engine on the left wing, a little at first, a wisp like a smoker exhaling. Or was it even smoke he was seeing? He couldn't be sure. The air here was so heavy with clouds and snow that the so-called smoke might be just a bit of condensation gathering around the engine, a little bit of water in the air coalescing around the jet intake.

The grayness thickened and grew darker, blowing out from the engine and behind them in a long sputtering stream. The longer he looked at the engine, the more he was certain that what he was seeing was smoke.

"Umm," he said to Kerry, "that doesn't look so good."

She opened her eyes and looked out the window, to see what he was seeing. "What—?"

Then the engine burst in a sudden eruption of sparks and yellow-orange flame. The plane lurched to the left and shuddered as great quantities of heavy black smoke started pouring out of the engine.

"Oh God," Kerry said, clutching the armrest. She caught Daniel's eye, and he saw his own sense of dawning fear on her face.

Around them a general murmur went up, mild at first (the word "turbulence" rumbled its way through the cabin a few times), then more alarmed as people leaned over to look out the portside windows of the plane at the flames and smoke over the wing. The plane made a sudden turn and banked wide to the right, turning back the way they'd just come.

Near the front of the cabin, one of the flight attendants was picking up the intercom and saying something to the pilot on the other end, then looking at her co-worker across the aisle. There was fear on their faces. Then the flight attendant came over the loudspeaker: "Ladies and gentlemen," she said, and Daniel could distinctly hear the nervous crack in her voice, "as you probably noticed, we are experiencing some engine trouble. The captain has shut down the affected engine for the time being, but we still have two more engines, both in good working order. We are not in any immediate danger. However, as a precaution only, the captain is turning around to make an emergency landing in the city of Whitehorse. If you could please remain in your seats with your seat belts fastened, we would—"

Another lurch, this time to the right, as the right-hand engine erupted now in flames. Somewhere in the cabin someone screamed. Daniel watched the flight attendant pick up the intercom once more, heard her say something frightened to the captain, though the words weren't clear. Daniel reached over and grabbed Kerry's hand. "It's all right," he said, as much to himself as to her. "We're all right."

"Ladies and gentlemen," said the flight attendant, "the captain says we are going to have to make an immediate emergency landing. He asks that you all assume the brace position, with your feet flat on the floor under your seat and your heads against the seat back in front of you. Please look to the front and we will demonstrate the proper positioning—"

The plane lurched again, the last engine screaming under the strain of keeping the aircraft aloft; from somewhere Daniel heard someone reciting a "Hail Mary" and realized it was Kerry, her eyes shut tightly, her mouth moving in a whisper around the words she'd learned long ago, as a girl in Catholic school: "Hail Mary, full of grace, the Lord is with thee . . ."

I don't believe this. I don't believe this is happening. They were inside the clouds, sinking fast, the ground invisible below, mist and ice whirling past the darkened windows. Like being blind.

The flight attendant continued, "Place your hands on the seat back over your head, one hand holding the wrist of the other arm. If you cannot reach the seat back in front of you, tuck your head forward over your knees—"

Another lurch. Out the window, Daniel could see the clouds break; the ground was very close now, getting closer. What alarmed him the most was the realization that there was nothing down there, nothing but wilderness. Not a house, not a road, not a light— nothing. They were in a damaged plane going down in the wilderness of far northern Canada in the middle of a December snowstorm.

"Please remember the location of the emergency exits. Those of you seated in an exit row are reminded that you have agreed to aid all passengers in exiting the aircraft safely. Once we've come to a complete stop, please exit the aircraft in an orderly fashion . . ."

Exit the aircraft in an orderly fashion? Is she serious? It would be pandemonium, assuming they even survived, not to mention that there was no shelter, no help anywhere nearby. The inside of the aircraft was likely to be the only safe place for them all down on the ground in this weather. None of them would really have the first clue what they were dealing with.

The treetops were getting dangerously close now, the earth bunched into hills that had seemed low from the air, now rising in humps like the backs of elephants covered in white snow and dark trees. The sky was low, the wind high, snow coming down heavily all around them. It would be cold out there, bitterly so. And no warm hotel to hide in when the cold got to be too much. Even if they survived the crash, they were going to be desperately, life-threateningly cold.

I can't believe it. I can't believe this is happening.

The flight attendant had said the captain had radioed their position to Whitehorse. Daniel had no idea how far away the city was, but as long as someone knew where they were, he thought, it would be all right, they'd spend a few hours inside the plane, it would be all right, it will be all right.

Next to him Kerry was still whispering her Hail Marys. "Hold on," Daniel murmured to her, leaning forward to brace himself against the back of the seat in front of him. "We'll get out of this."

"I love you," she said. "Remember that. I love you so much."

"We're going to be okay, Kerry. I promise you."

"I love you, Daniel," she said, her voice shaking. "Say it back to me."

"Don't. Kerry—"

"Please."

He clutched her head against his shoulder and said, "I love you. More than anything."

The hills were close, then closer, tops of the trees were just below them, thick and black and heavy with new snow. The wings of the plane were brushing the treetops, the engine whining, people around them praying and breathless with fear. *Our Father, who art in heaven, hallowed be thy name . . .*

Then the world exploded.

A loud crash, then a sudden, violent lurch. The sound of tearing metal. The feel of cold on his back, wind in his hair, cold down the neck of his shirt and around his ankles. Then darkness.

The plane had broken; he was vaguely aware of light and air behind him, and the sound of screaming. A child was screaming, and not just a child, but the entire plane was screaming as they waited for the ordeal to stop, while Daniel could manage nothing more explosive than a gasp for air.

Everything rattled. The walls, the seats, his teeth. Everything.

Any minute now. Any minute now and we'll stop.

The air went white with snow. Braced as he was against the seat in front of him, his head down, Daniel could see nothing at all but his own knees and swirling snow, his black leather oxfords next to Kerry's knee-high boots. The sight of Kerry's feet reassured him even more than the child's continued screams. She was still there, Kerry was still there beside him.

Hang on, hang on, hang on, hang on . . .

But the plane didn't stop. He didn't dare look up, didn't dare do anything except hold on and breathe. They jolted and bounced, the overhead bins popping open and luggage falling down around them, the sound of tearing metal and plastic and people crying out all around them. Something heavy fell on his head—a suitcase, someone's carry-on—and something else small and hard. He was wet and cold and sticky, as if liquid had fallen on him. Someone's drink, maybe.

Beside him he heard Kerry say, "Oh shit, oh shit," as their seats lurched and loosened. Then the seat pulled free from the floor and flung Daniel and Kerry forward into the seat backs in front of them, dumped over like rag dolls in their plastic chairs, his whole body thrown forward, then backward as the plane suffered one last massive jolt and came to a sudden and violent halt.

Finally they came to rest in a heap on the floor of the plane, battered and bruised and panting as if they'd just finished running a marathon.

But he was alive. Of that, he was certain.

Daniel could hear nothing but the roaring in his ears, his limbs trembling with a rush of adrenaline. They were still strapped into their seats, surrounded by loose pieces of clothing, suitcases, shoes, plastic cups, shredded pieces of metal, oxygen masks, bits of Plexiglas window, foam insulation, and the heavy feel of the suddenly cold air, the snow greasy around their feet. Around them they could hear people crying and calling to each other, the Petrol team members and the passengers they didn't know. One woman was calling frantically, "Zach? Zach, where are you? Zach, I can't see you!" while Daniel fumbled around his waist for the strap of his seat belt, lifting the buckle up and off, gasping for air. He hoped beyond hope that Zach was not the boy he'd heard crying, who wasn't crying anymore.

"Kerry," Daniel murmured, touching his belly, his ribs, his arms and legs. Nothing seemed to be broken, though his knee ached where he'd hit it against the seat back, and he couldn't seem to catch his breath or stop himself from shaking. "Where are you?"

Nothing.

"Are you all right?"

No answer. He felt like he was falling, like the earth was not at all solid under his feet. Kerry was hurt—maybe badly. He needed to get the heavy seats off them. Daniel braced his feet against the carpeted floor of the plane and pushed upward until the seats fell backward, away from the spot on the floor where Daniel and Kerry had landed. For the first time he could breathe. He could see Kerry lying on her side on the floor of the cabin, curled up into a fetal position, still in one piece, as far as he could see, though there was blood coming from one corner of her mouth, and she had the beginnings of what would probably become a fairly sizable bump near her right temple, about the diameter of a quarter.

His first thought was that it could have been worse. Much, much worse.

He wouldn't think of all the things that could go wrong with a head injury: concussion, hemorrhage, memory loss, mood swings, loss of motor function. All his years working in crisis management had given him plenty of experience with head injuries. He had to get her awake, get her talking, and the sooner the better. But he wouldn't think about the worst-case scenario, not yet.

"Kerry," he said. "Babe. Look at me."

"Unnnnh," she said, which didn't exactly fill him with relief.

"Kerry, wake up. Open your eyes, Kerry. Look at me."

As he stood over her, trying to wake her from what he hoped was only a faint, Daniel felt more helpless than he ever had in his life. He brushed her loosened hair away from her face, revealing her bruised and bloodied mouth, twisted at the corners in a grimace of pain. Anything could have hit her temple in the crash—flying debris, the arm of the chair as it came loose, a cell phone. It didn't matter what it was; she needed to open her eyes, look at him, recognize him, speak to him. She had to be all right. They were supposed to be getting married in a little more than two weeks, for God's sake.

"Kerry," he said again, her name sticking halfway up his throat.

Her eyes fluttered and opened, but they were glazed, fixed on nothing. She swiveled her head around to look at him, and he was relieved to see that her neck, at least, wasn't broken. What he feared was not the snapping of bones, which would heal, but the breaking and bruising of her mind.

"What happened?" she asked. "How long have I been asleep?"

"You weren't asleep," he said, touching the side of her head where the contusion was. "You hit your head in the crash. You passed out for a minute. I'm worried you may have a concussion."

"Oh." At least she wasn't particularly upset.

"How do you feel?"

"Dizzy. A little bit dizzy. And tired." Her eyes fluttered closed again and she said, "God, I could go right back to sleep."

"Don't sleep, Kerry," Daniel said, the relief he'd felt a moment before fading. She had all the symptoms of a rather serious concussion, and God only knew when help would arrive. "Kerry, don't go to sleep." He helped her sit up against the wall of the fuselage, gently rolling her head back and forth between his hands to check the movement of her neck. "Does anything hurt?"

"A headache. And my mouth hurts. I think I banged my mouth on something," she said. He looked up to see her mouth streaked with blood, her teeth red with it. "I think maybe I broke a tooth."

"You did. Two of them, it looks like." The bottoms of her two front teeth were ragged and bloody, giving her expression a vampirish quality, and he reached up with the tail of his shirt to wipe the blood away.

Just then the flight attendant came rushing down the aisle, checking on each passenger in turn. She stopped at Kerry and Daniel and said, "Are you two going to be all right? Can you walk?"

"I think so," Kerry said, her voice still slower and thicker than usual—he could tell she wasn't thinking clearly. "Do you need us to get out of the way?"

"We need to get the emergency exit open," Daniel said, standing up. "Get all these people outside to safety."

The flight attendant gave him a strange look and said, "Are you kidding?" She nodded toward the back of the plane.

Daniel stood and looked up over the tops of the seats: the cabin was nearly unrecognizable. Many of the seat rows had pulled free and were lying willy-nilly around the floor, along with vague dark shapes: a drink cart that had come loose from the galley near first class and rolled backward into the aisle, airline pillows and blankets, coats and bags from the overhead bins. Every single oxygen mask had been released from the ceiling and now hung like empty IV bags in the air over the survivors, vaguely sinister and medicinal. After all the years he'd listened to flight attendants tell him how to put on an oxygen mask in the event of a loss of cabin pressure, there'd been no time in the crash to do so.

Around him people were crying, people moaning the names of friends and loved ones, people begging for someone to help them. "Please," someone cried out from the front of the plane. "Please, I'm stuck."

But the thing that really caught Daniel's attention was the fact that just two or three rows behind them the entire rear half of the plane was missing. The fuselage had broken off just behind the wings: there was nothing back there but a gaping hole where the tail of the plane had been, and snow and wind blowing down the length of the cabin. Daylight was illuminating the back portion of what was left of the cabin. Daniel could make out the shape of a pine tree, broken halfway up its length by the impact of the plane, standing not ten feet away from the place where he stood. The snow was several feet deep and still blowing in hard.

The crashing noise, the jolt. The entire back end of the plane had hit something and been sheared right off.

"My God," Daniel said.

"Daniel," Kerry was saying as she struggled to her feet, "help me open the emergency exit. We need to get these people out of here." She was yanking on the handle that would open the exit, her voice edging higher.

"We don't need the emergency exit," he said. "Look." And Kerry turned to look in the direction he was facing, the gaping hole in the fuselage of the plane, wires and bits of plastic and metal hanging down over the hole, letting in the cold air from outside.

She made a gurgling sound in the back of her throat. "The fuel," she said. "If it blows up, if we explode—"

He exchanged a look with the flight attendant, who said, "The pilot dumped the fuel before we landed to minimize the fire hazard. Standard procedure. I'm asking those who aren't seriously hurt to help those who are. We need to move quickly now."

"Aren't we evacuating?" Daniel asked. "Wouldn't that also be standard procedure?"

"Under the circumstances I don't think that's a good idea. It's too cold out there. If we haven't had a fire by now, we're not having one at all. Please," she said, "if you could help some of the hurt passengers, I would really appreciate it. We need all the help we can get right now."

"I'll do what I can," Daniel said.

"Thank you," she said, and kept moving, checking on passenger after passenger.

Kerry was scrambling toward the hole in the back of the plane, her eyes glazed with pain and fear and Daniel didn't want to think what else. "We need to get out of here," she gasped. "I can't— I can't—"

He grabbed her by the shoulders. "Listen," he said, "the inside of the plane is the only shelter we have out here. We need to stay put."

She was shaking her head, but she said, "If there's a fire, an explosion—"

"I know you're scared," he said, "but it's not safe outside right now. We'd freeze in minutes." He could see the panic in her eyes still. "I need you to calm down. Calm down and stay put. Can you do that?"

"I—I don't—"

He held her by the wrists. "Can you please trust me? Can you believe that I would never do anything to put you in harm's way?"

She put her head down, letting it fall into place in the middle of his chest. He could feel her heart rate slow and steady under his hands. "Okay. Okay, I trust you. Of course."

With Kerry calm, Daniel looked ahead to the first-class cabin, but he didn't see Bob or anyone else they knew. There were dark shapes among the chairs and debris: bodies, some still moving sluggishly, some very still. Here and there a bright stain of blood.

He looked away, gulping air, fighting back a sudden surge of nausea. He'd seen bodies before, most recently at the accident site in Barrow—in his job he couldn't avoid seeing them—but the line between life and death was too thin just now.

They'd lived. They'd lived, but maybe not for long.

He gripped the overhead bins and held on until he felt steady again. He couldn't fall apart. If this were a Petrol accident, if he were in charge here, what would he do in these circumstances? Plan, prepare. He'd make lists, choose a course of action and begin trying to undo the worst of the damage, as much as he could.

People always had to come first. He took a quick mental inventory of all the Petrol people who'd been on the plane with them out of Anchorage: Bob was in first class in the front of the plane, of course, but then there'd been Phil Velez, and himself and Kerry, a couple of people from Daniel's team, an assistant coordinator on Phil's team. Who else?

Judy Akers. Kerry's best friend usually sat near the last row when she could—she always said she liked to be close to the rear galley, where she could stand up and walk around a bit on long flights. He was sure that was where she'd been sitting, but now the tail of the plane was completely gone.

"Kerry, where was Judy sitting?" he asked, staring at the hole in the back end of the fuselage.

"In the back, the same as always," she choked, looking in the direction he was facing. "Oh my God. She's gone. *Where did she go?*"

"She has to be with the tail section. Wherever the tail landed, we'll find her, I'm sure of it."

They should look for their missing people and tend to the injured. The most important thing was to keep Kerry awake as long as possible. A person with a concussion could go to sleep and never wake up again: Daniel had seen it happen before. She *had* to stay awake.

Just then, as if in answer to a question he hadn't asked, there was a gasp from the row behind them: someone was hurt. "Uh," said a voice. "Help me. I can't breathe."

"Phil? Is that you?" Kerry said.

Phil Velez had been sitting two rows behind them, just at the point at which the fuselage had broken. Daniel had assumed he'd been one of the passengers lost in the crash, but now here he was, lying on the floor of the cabin clutching his belly.

Daniel pulled the leg of a chair off him. "What's wrong?" Daniel asked.

In the dim light Phil looked green. "I'm not sure," he muttered. His voice was ragged from the effort of drawing breath. "Something slammed into me. Maybe it was the leg of the seat, I don't know."

Daniel knelt down near Phil. "Where did it get you?" he asked. "Is there any blood?"

"Knocked the wind out of me. Still hurts." His voice was sharp with pain.

"Can I look?"

Phil nodded, letting his still-clenched hands fall to his sides. Carefully Daniel lifted the tail of Phil's white shirt, looking for blood, a puncture wound, a sign of immediate trauma. The skin just beneath his belly button was a little discolored, pink around the edges and turning purple in the center, but the skin was unbroken at least. He might have internal damage; Daniel couldn't tell by looking.

"Can you stand?" Daniel asked.

"I think so. Maybe. Let me try."

Phil grabbed hold of a seat across the aisle and pulled himself to a standing position, breathing heavily, still clutching his belly. Daniel felt a nagging sense of unease as he looked at the other man: what if it was an internal injury? Daniel was no doctor. He knew some basic first aid, and that was about it. Phil was on his feet at least; that was a good sign.

"What about you two?" Phil asked. "You all right?"

"We're okay, mostly. I think Kerry has a concussion, but she's up and talking. I need to keep her awake."

"A concussion?" Kerry said. "Is that what this is, the headache?"

The fact that she was asking that question—that she wasn't thinking entirely clearly—made the last shred of doubt fade away. "I don't know that for sure, babe. I think so. You need to see a doctor."

"I don't feel so great, either," Phil said, but he managed to give her a halfhearted smile anyway, the lines on either side of his mouth deepening involuntarily. "You don't have any aspirin in your purse, do you, Kerry? Ibuprofen maybe?"

"I don't remember. I don't think so," she said.

"You shouldn't take any aspirin or ibuprofen," Daniel said. "If you have any internal bleeding, the pain meds will just make it worse."

"Do you think I have internal bleeding?"

"I hope not."

"Great." Phil eased himself into an empty seat nearby, plainly hurting, but there was nothing Daniel could do for him at the moment.

The rest of the surviving passengers were slowly coming to their senses as well, checking themselves for injuries and picking up what few belongings they could find. For the most part they were unnaturally calm, Daniel thought, moving around the cabin like zombies, or maybe it was only the shock of finding themselves still alive. The only real noise came from a woman a few rows ahead scrambling over her seatmate and Daniel himself to get at the door in the fuselage to Daniel's left, yanking on the red lever that should have released the mechanism, but it wasn't working. "Let us out!" she screamed.

She was wild, completely panicked and irrational, so it didn't do any good when Daniel pushed her off and said, "We don't need the goddamn emergency exits, lady! We could fit a circus in here!"

Still, the woman pushed and pushed, clawing at their faces, their bodies, until finally Daniel had no choice but to shove the poor woman off of himself and his fiancée, back toward her seat.

She sank back down into what was left of her seat, sobbing into her hands. "Let me out. I need to get out," she muttered, over and over, and though Daniel sympathized with her—he was beginning to feel the same wave of giddy panic coming over him as the adrenaline rush of the crash and the immediate aftermath started to subside—it was slowly dawning on him that none of them would be alive for long out here if they didn't get their act together soon.

Now Kerry was reaching into the open overhead bin and rummaging around for something. "We need to go look for Judy," she was saying. The crying woman was screaming now, asking people why they weren't leaving, why was everyone just sitting still? Daniel could feel the tension in Kerry, the rising panic, could see her hands shaking. He had to keep her calm. If they were going to get out of this alive, they were all going to have to stay calm.

"Kerry. Talk to me, babe."

Her head snapped around. "I—" she started, and he realized how terribly pale she was. "I'm sorry. I'll be okay in a minute."

He touched her hands, which were icy cold. He hoped she was not going into shock on top of everything else. "You sure?"

"I think so. I'm just c-cold." She touched her temple with one finger and looked around at the plane, the passengers, everything. "I can't believe this is happening."

He moved into the aisle to find a blanket, the coats they'd stashed in the overhead bins before takeoff, the giant parkas they'd worn every day for two weeks in Barrow. His own black one was still in the overhead bin, but Kerry's purple one was missing. A quick glance around the floor showed him that it was nowhere in sight. Probably it had been flung out of the plane when the tail ripped off.

He took a green parka no one had claimed and wrapped it around Kerry, rubbed her freezing hands between his own, and asked, "Is that better?"

She nodded, shivering, but in a minute she started to look a little better. She asked, "Can I call my mother?"

It took a minute for Daniel to realize that she was making what was actually a reasonable request. His satellite phone. He hadn't even thought about it.

He felt around in the pockets of his jeans, the back of the seat where he'd been sitting, the pockets of his coat. The satellite phone, the one thing that might really have been useful in this situation, had been in the front pocket of his shirt, the last he remembered. Now it was gone—lost, along with Kerry's coat and half the plane's passengers. His regular cell phone was in the front pocket of his jeans, of course. He took it out and swiped the screen. Zero bars. Of course.

She gave him a bleak look. "It's gone, isn't it?"

"I'll look for it. It has to be here somewhere."

He went through the debris on the floor, crawling around on his hands and knees. He bumped into the body of an older woman of maybe sixty, lying on her side in one aisle, her neck broken, and gave a little gasp, squeezing his eyes shut until his pulse quit hammering in his chest.

He flung aside magazines and books, barf bags and bits of wire and loose screws, but he didn't see his phone anywhere. It had to be outside somewhere. He had to look for it, and the others, the people who were missing.

Finally he stood, uncertainty hardening into decision. "I'm going to go look for Judy," he said. "She might be hurt."

"You can't leave me here alone!"

"You won't be alone. Phil's here." She gave him a look that said exactly what she thought of asking Phil Velez for help in this situation. "I know, but someone has to go," he murmured in a low voice. "Wouldn't you rather it was me? Someone who knows Judy and cares about her?" Kerry nodded reluctantly, yes. "I'll look for the phone while I'm at it. Get us home before nightfall."

"That sounds good."

He glanced at her legs—Kerry was wearing only a skirt and tights and black suede boots made more for fashion than warmth. She was going to be hypothermic very quickly unless they found her coat or some clothes. Her carry-on would have something that would help keep her warm. Jeans, pajama bottoms—it wouldn't matter. She had to get warm, and the sooner the better.

She wasn't the only one. There was a whole plane full of passengers who would die soon if they didn't get themselves bundled up. A whole plane full of passengers, and not enough help to go around.

If he could find the sat phone, he could call for help. The search teams could follow the phone's signal straight to the crash site.

"Phil," he said, keeping his voice low, "I want you to do something for me. I need to look for my satellite phone. While I'm gone, can you look for Kerry's bag? Make sure she finds something to put on her legs?"

"Why can't you look for it?" he asked.

"I'm going back to look for the tail. See if I can help the others. My phone might be out there somewhere."

Phil glanced at Kerry, frowned and said, "Maybe I should go look for our people. You should be the one to stay here with her."

"You're hurt; you need to stay. Come on, Phil, I wouldn't ask you if I didn't really need you right now."

Phil would never make it through the kind of snow Daniel was seeing out the back of the fuselage—in places it looked waist-high. Phil's face still had a greenish cast, and Kerry was pale and shaky. Daniel was worried about leaving either one of them in this state, but someone had to go and find the tail, and the rest of the Petrol people, and if possible the sat phone. Right now there was no one else.

"Someone needs to keep Kerry awake," Daniel said. "Phil, help her look for her carry-on. It can't have gone far."

"All right," Phil said. "I can keep her company for a few minutes. It won't kill me."

Daniel caught just a glimpse of the grim look on Phil's face. The other man looked as if Daniel had asked him to swim to the bottom of the sea and cap a wellhead with his bare hands. But Daniel needed to find their people and help them, if he could. Keeping everybody alive was the only thing that mattered now.

The white moon of Kerry's face, looking very vulnerable and young, floated toward him, and he kissed her, grasping her cold hands. Then he said, "I'll be back as soon as I can, I promise."

"Wait, Daniel," she said.

He looked up. Her mouth was set in a grim, determined line. "What is it?" he asked.

"Find Judy. Please find her. Please help her. She could be really hurt."

"I will. I promise you, babe. I'll do everything I can."

"Daniel?"

"What?"

Her voice quavered. "If Judy's dead, don't tell me, okay? I don't want to know."

7

Whatever you do, don't let Kerry fall asleep. If she falls asleep she might not wake back up again.

Daniel had implored Phil to keep Kerry conscious one last time and then left the broken fuselage, struggling out the opening and into the deep snow outside. Phil thought about going after him into the teeth of the storm, anything except staying here inside the broken plane with Kerry, waiting for something to happen. Waiting for rescue, for help. Something.

What could he do to help Kerry, to help any of them? Really, what could he do? He felt helpless, almost the way he'd felt in those months when Emily's cancer had eaten away at her, when he'd sat by her bedside night after night and wept. If there was one thing he believed with conviction, it was that small talk was no good in situations like these; he should be *doing* something. He couldn't just sit here and hope everything would turn out all right in the end.

He realized that Kerry was saying something to him. "What?" he asked her.

She blinked slowly and said, "I asked if you'd seen a coat no one is using."

"Oh." He looked around and spied a coat on the floor, a black trench coat that wouldn't do much for the cold, but she put it on over the green parka Daniel had given her. Smart, he thought—the trench would add an extra layer and partially cover her legs, too.

"Have you seen Bob yet?" she asked.

Phil looked up. Where *was* Bob? "I haven't."

"Maybe we should go look for him. He could be hurt." Her voice was slow and thick, as if she were speaking through molasses. Daniel had said she might have a concussion, which is why he'd wanted Phil to keep her awake. Phil didn't know anything about concussions, but he suspected what she really needed was a doctor, not a human-resources director whose presence she barely tolerated. Still, he'd do what he could for her and anyone else he could find.

Phil had to admit that he hadn't so much as thought about the senior VP in the minutes since the crash. Bob Packer was such a force of nature himself, so much larger than life, that he seemed nearly indestructible. It hadn't even occurred to Phil to think Bob might need the help of mere mortals like him.

But Kerry was right; they should have seen Bob by now. They should check to see where he was. "I'll go," Phil said. "You stay here. Stay here and rest."

"I'm coming with you."

"Is that a good idea? Daniel said you got a pretty good bump on the head. You should probably take it easy for a little while."

"If I sit here much longer, I'll fall asleep."

She got unsteadily to her feet, but Phil resisted the urge to take her under the elbow, although with anyone else that's exactly what he would have done. He was never quite sure how to act around her, what would upset her; his natural instincts always seemed to be wrong in her case.

Instead, he said, "Are you sure you're going to be okay? We don't have to go and look for Bob, he's probably capable of taking care of himself."

She gave a dry little laugh and looked down at her feet, still clad in knee-high boots, and then up into his face as if she were pleading for something. "Thank you," she said, her voice earnest for a change, devoid of its usual layer of sarcasm, "but maybe I need something to do right now. I think it might help to move around a little."

He looked into her face, pale and bloody around the mouth. He didn't have so much as a bandage or a painkiller to offer her, nothing but the fact of his presence, which didn't feel like much under the circumstances. In the inside of what was left of Denali Flight 806, Phil Velez and Kerry Egan were more than co-workers—they were survivors. They could find a way to help each other. They *should* help each other, their past history be damned.

"All right," he said. "Let's go find Bob and see if we can help. Better than sitting here feeling sorry for ourselves."

She gave him a wan smile and started up the aisle toward first class, Phil following at her heels, the two of them picking their way through the debris. It was cold inside the fuselage, getting colder minute by minute. Outside, the storm that had brought them down was still howling, freezing bits of snow coming in now and again on a gust of wind, stinging at his eyes. Ahead of him he could make out the shapes of people moving around, looking for their missing loved ones, their few possessions. Everyone was nearly silent, speaking in low whispers or not at all, either in shock or because speaking too loudly would disrupt the fragile luck they'd had so far.

Surely help was on the way already. Before the crash, the flight attendants had said the pilots had radioed back to Whitehorse, and Phil had to believe them, had to trust they were right. Surely there were people on the way to them already—this was the twenty-first century, after all. Planes and people didn't just disappear, not anymore. The plane's own radio signals would bring the rescuers to them. By the end of the day, maybe a little longer, rescue crews would be reaching them, bringing food and blankets, transporting them out of this mess. All they had to do in the meantime was not die.

With this thought comforting him, Phil followed Kerry's progress up the length of the fuselage to first class, where a dim emergency light still shone over the broken cockpit door. The seats here had piled one on top of the other just as they had in the main cabin, though it was quieter here, still; the passengers were all either dead or had already evacuated. The body of one of the pilots was visible through the broken cockpit door, his head turned at an unnatural angle; his neck was broken, his eyes still bright.

Phil yelped and jumped back. *Jesus.* But there had been a co-pilot, right? There might still be someone alive in there.

Steeling himself, Phil stuck his head inside the cockpit door, hoping, but the co-pilot lay slumped over the control panel, a patch of blood above one ear. "Hey," Phil called, still hoping, but neither of them stirred. The instrument panel was smashed in, covered with blood and stinking of chemical fumes. The cockpit had apparently taken the worst of the impact.

"What are you doing?" Kerry asked from behind him.

"Checking if the pilots are alive."

"Are they?"

"No." Phil turned away from the cockpit and the dead men inside, gulping deep gulps of air and blinking, trying to focus. He'd seen too much death for one lifetime.

Kerry was hanging on to the overhead bins in first class, calling, "Bob? Are you all right? Are you here?"

A voice growled, "I'm right here, damn it. Stop shouting."

"Where? I don't see you."

The small first-class cabin consisted of only three rows of seats, two on each side, that had all come loose from their moorings and slammed forward into the front row, bunched one on top of the other like the folds of an accordion. Most of the people who'd been sitting there had already left, following the surviving flight attendant, but one man was still standing in the aisle, looking for something in the mess on the floor, scowling at Phil and Kerry as though they were personally responsible for the crash. But Bob wasn't visible. They had heard him quite clearly, but they couldn't see him.

"Down here. Under the seats."

Bob had been sitting in the very first row, as was his wont, so that when the plane stopped abruptly and all the seats had kept up their forward momentum, he'd been trapped underneath, not to mention underneath the people who'd been sitting there and half the luggage in the overhead bins as well. He was a big man, but even Bob Packer was no match for a plane crashing into the side of a mountain at high speeds.

He didn't sound like he was too badly hurt, just pissed off.

"What can we do?" Kerry asked.

"You can get these damn things off of me for starters."

"Hold on," she said, bending down. "I'll try."

Together Phil and Kerry pulled two carry-on bags off the pile and set them aside, then bent to tackle the tangle of airline seats. The top set came loose fairly easily, though it was heavy, and they were able to push it out of the way with a little effort. The second and third rows of seats, though, were tangled together like old wire coat hangers, and every attempt to pull them apart left Kerry winded and Phil gasping, the spot under his belly button throbbing painfully. A bruised muscle—that's probably all it was—but it hurt like hell. Even bending over was taxing him.

They fell back for a second, groaning. "What are you two doing?" Bob snapped. "This isn't a coffee break."

"We're both hurt. Not too badly, but it's making us move a little more slowly."

"Hurry up. I'm folded up like a newspaper and my legs are cramping."

When they'd both caught their breath, they knelt down again, pulling and pushing, Phil with his left arm, Kerry with both, and

Bob from underneath, and slowly the three of them got the last of the heavy seats off. Bob came to his feet like an enraged bull.

He brushed off his clothes and straightened up with the air of a man gathering what was left of his dignity. "Where the *hell* is that flight attendant?" he snapped. "Isn't it her job to get everyone out safely? She went right on past me."

Phil was thinking that the flight attendant—the only crewmember he'd seen alive—had bigger problems on her hands than searching for a single missing passenger, but he knew better than to say so. Bob was not a man who was good at seeing the world through any perspective but his own. The old man was already huffing and sweating; the last thing they needed just then was a purple-faced 220-pound former linebacker giving himself a heart attack.

"Are you hurt?" Phil asked.

"No thanks to that pilot," Bob said. "I think he was trying to kill everyone aboard. Seems like he nearly succeeded." Then he seemed to notice for the first time that the back half of the plane was missing. "Jesus," he said. "It's worse than I thought." He looked first at Phil, then at Kerry, and seemed to realize that there were just the two of them there. "Where's Daniel?"

"He went to look for the others," Kerry said. "He'll be right back."

"That's a relief. Glad to know someone's doing something useful around here. What else are we doing?"

"The flight attendant and Daniel said we should stay inside the plane," Kerry said. "It's too cold to go outside."

"So that's it? We're sitting around waiting for the cavalry to arrive?"

"We should do what we can to help," Phil said. "Check the rest of the plane to see if anyone's hurt. Gather up whatever clothes and blankets we can find. Food and water, too."

"First we need to find our own people."

"Daniel's working on that," Kerry said. She was trying to stay calm, but Phil could see she was looking over to the place where the two dead pilots lay, behind the cockpit door. Kerry's breathing was getting heavier, her expression frozen. "Everyone else was in the tail section. They—they might be hurt."

"Here," Phil said, helping her down into a nearby seat, "you should sit down. I don't want you to fall over."

"I'll be all right," Kerry said. "I just can't stop thinking of Judy and the others."

"Sit down before you fall down, Kerry," Phil said, more firmly now. "You're still hurt."

"I can't even help my best friend. She could be dead. They could all be dead, and—"

"It's okay. They'll be fine," he said. "We made it. They could have made it, too."

"You think so?"

"Of course. I'll bet Daniel comes back with them in ten minutes."

She leaned against the bulkhead and closed her eyes. "I hope you're right," she said. "God, I can't believe this is happening."

Behind him Bob was cursing his lack of a cell-phone signal (had he really thought there would be one out in the middle of the Canadian wilderness?) and was working himself up into a lather about how disorganized everything was: where was the crew? Someone needed to take control of the situation, he was saying, someone needed to get on the horn with the control tower and find out who was coming and how far away they were. "Someone needs to give us some goddamn answers," he muttered, shaking his beefy head back and forth.

Bob pursed his lips and tilted his chin at the smashed door of the cockpit. "Can we get in there to use the radio?"

"Everything's pretty smashed up."

"So you haven't even tried?"

"If you're so keen on doing something," Phil said, "you could give Daniel a hand finding the rest of our people. I'll stay here with her." He inclined his head toward the place where Kerry sat. "I promised to keep her awake until Daniel gets back."

Bob looked toward the missing rear of the plane, where the other passengers were searching for coats, hats, gloves. "Good thinking," he said, patting Phil on the shoulder. "You keep an eye on things here. I'll be back with some answers." He stopped to find himself a jacket and then disappeared out the back of the fuselage, following Daniel's tracks in the snow.

Phil watched him go with an enormous sense of relief. The old man was alive and kicking, all right. And Kerry and Daniel, too. My God, were they ever lucky. A few bumps and bruises were nothing compared to what could have happened. They'd survived a *plane crash*, of all things. They'd lived, an idea that seemed more and more improbable the longer he thought about it. They should be dead. They should be, but they weren't.

"You're smiling?" said a woman standing in the aisle behind him. "I can't believe you're smiling right now."

Phil looked up in surprise. He hadn't seen her standing there, much less realized that he was smiling at the moment. "I'm sorry," he said. "I almost can't believe it. That we're still alive."

"Not all of us," she said, looking in the direction of the cockpit door. "I heard you just now. You really think the people in the tail are all right?"

"I don't know. I hope so. Some of my co-workers were sitting back there. A couple of our people have gone to look for them."

She looked at the snow accumulating out the back of the plane and shook her head. "I don't envy them that job."

"Me neither."

She had a bustling, focused energy that reminded Phil of a mother hen gathering up her chicks, though all she seemed to be doing was searching for her belongings amid the wreckage. Probably no taller than five feet, with short black hair threaded with gray and a deep cut over one cheek that was bleeding down the side of her face, the woman made him think of the native Alaskans he'd met in Barrow, the Petrol employees, the shopkeepers and restaurant owners who seemed to view the Petrol crisis team as something to be both resented and embraced simultaneously. "Why were you headed to Chicago?" she asked Phil.

"Going home. We'd been dealing with that oil-rig accident up in the Beaufort Sea the past couple of weeks. You?"

"Catching a connecting flight. My mother's been in the hospital in Cleveland for two months now. They don't think she's going to make it. I'm trying to get there in time to say my good-byes, but I suppose this means I'm going to miss my connection."

He knew he was supposed to smile at that, but he couldn't bring himself to do it, not over such a subject, not now. "What does she have?" he asked.

"Congestive heart failure. They were hoping to buy her a little more time, but . . ." She trailed off.

Phil was silent for a moment, thinking about Emily, about hospital beds and constant doctors and the people who came in at the end to say whatever they had left to say to her, say their own good-byes, her friends and family. He'd driven her to see some of the doctors in the Cleveland Clinic himself before the end, too, though Emily had known no one would be able to help her. She'd known, but Phil had insisted anyway, saying they had to do everything they could to save her. They had to try everything, he'd said, because he didn't know how he'd go on without her. He couldn't fathom it.

No one can ever try everything, she'd said to him. *I can live with ending like this, Phil. I just hope you can learn to live with it, too.*

"I'm sorry," he said now, not quite able to keep his voice even.

She shrugged. "I might still make it. You never know how long people are going to be able to hold on in these situations."

She was remarkably calm about it, almost businesslike. Phil didn't know what to make of that. He simply said, "I hope you do make it. For your mother's sake, and your own," and left it at that.

She thanked him, then went back to climbing over the debris, trying to reach the bin over her head.

"Here," Phil said, standing up immediately. "Let me help you. What are you looking for?"

"My coat."

Phil reached up and started pushing things aside, looking for the woman's coat. There were two carry-on bags in the way, so he started pulling them out, thinking of the things in there they could use until rescue crews arrived. He might find sweaters, socks, pants. Food, even.

The first bag came out no problem, and he set it down next to him in the aisle, but the second bag, which must have weighed a good fifty pounds, came free and pushed Phil back into the seat behind him, falling into his arms so heavily that he felt the spot in his belly throb painfully. *Just a bruise,* he thought. He coughed, and the spot throbbed again. What if Daniel was right, and he had some internal injuries? What would happen then?

He set the bag down and returned to search through the overhead bin for the lady's coat, finally coming across something puffy and soft in the far corner. "Here you go," he said weakly, handing the coat down to her.

"Thank you so much," she said, wrapping it around herself and pulling the hood up. "That's better."

"Thank God we were coming from Alaska and not Hawaii, right?" Phil said, his breath short.

"If we were coming from Hawaii we wouldn't have crashed in a snowstorm," the lady said. She was watching him, her face full of concern. "Are you all right?" she asked. "You don't look so good."

"Something hit me just about here," he said, touching the aching spot on his belly. "A chair leg, I think. It's still a little sore."

His fingers found the spot and halted just a millimeter away from the place where the pain began, felt where it wasn't just the skin but whatever was underneath that felt tender. He tried to remember which organ went on which side of the body in that spot. Bladder?

Large intestine? Either way, something he needed. He gave a little gasp and sat back down heavily in a seat.

"Ah," said the lady, her voice falling in sympathy, "you shouldn't have been helping me, you should be taking care of yourself. I'm sorry."

"No, no," he said, "it's okay. You need your coat. I may have overdone it with that last bag, is all. I'll be all right."

"Here," she said now, with the air of someone used to being obeyed, "let me take a look at that. You might have some internal bleeding."

"That's what my co-worker said. Is that bad?"

"It's no picnic. But I could be wrong." She grimaced. "I'm an ER nurse, or was, before I got married and had my kids."

She stepped over a piece of metal debris into the aisle, stooped next to Phil and lifted both his coat and the edge of his shirt the way Daniel had done, feeling around in the tender place just under his belly button. Her fingers were gentle but insistent, and soon she found the most tender spot. He gasped and squirmed, the pain intensifying—for a moment he saw stars, the insides of his eyelids going bright with them—but then she was done and pulled his coat back around him again.

"Hmm," she said. "I wouldn't be able to tell without a scan, but you definitely have a bruise. I can't tell if there's distention—it's too soon—but if there is, you might have some internal bleeding."

"Anything I should worry about?"

"Well. You should definitely take it easy. I wouldn't go running off after your friends." She looked around the mess inside the plane, the other injured people. "There's no puncture wound at least. Still, if there's internal bleeding it won't be easy to spot. You should be looked at right away, and by a doctor. With any luck they'll find us right away and we can *all* get looked at by a doctor."

"Did you see this kind of thing often? When you were a nurse?"

"Oh. You know." She shrugged, and her eyes flickered away from his for a moment, giving him the impression that she wasn't being as truthful as she might like under the circumstances. "Now and again. Sometimes the kids in my village would have hockey fights, the occasional fender bender, that kind of thing. Usually nothing too serious."

"But I'll be okay?" Now she was making him nervous. In his experience, medical professionals only told you about half of what they knew, revealing the rest only on a need-to-know basis.

"I don't see why not," she said. "But I'll feel better when I hear those rescue helicopters coming."

"Thanks," he said, but his anxiety didn't lessen at all. "What's your name?"

"Beverly. What's yours?"

"Phil. Thanks for your help, Beverly."

"No problem, Phil. Say," she said, her forehead wrinkling in concern, "is she doing all right?"

He turned and saw Kerry lying with her head against the bulkhead—her eyes were closed, her mouth open slightly, her breathing deep and regular. *Damn.* He was supposed to be keeping her awake. He'd turned away for one second, and she was out cold.

Now he knelt beside her and shook her gently. "Kerry," he said. "Kerry, wake up, you're not supposed to go to sleep now. Come on, open your eyes."

Kerry stirred but did not open her eyes. That couldn't be good. He looked up and saw the dark-haired woman watching him.

"Do you know anything about head injuries, too?"

"A bit. Did she get clonked by something?"

"I think so. I didn't see."

Beverly knelt down next to Kerry and rolled the unconscious woman's head back and forth between her hands, touching her scalp with careful fingers until she came to a spot over Kerry's right temple where there was a slight discoloration. "Hmm. I don't like that. Is this the first time she's lost consciousness?"

"I don't know. I was sitting behind her."

"Miss?" Beverly asked in a loud voice. "Miss?" She looked back at Phil. "What's her name?"

"Kerry."

"Kerry, I need you to open up your eyes *right now* and look at me," the woman said in that same authoritative tone, the one she must have used on concussed hockey players at home in her village. "Come on, now."

No answer.

"What happens if she doesn't wake up?" Phil asked, wishing for the first time that Daniel were here.

"Let's worry about that when it happens," said Beverly, leaning Kerry's head forward over her knees. The former nurse was tiny but surprisingly strong, and Phil found he was intensely grateful to have someone there who seemed to know what she was doing. "Right now I need you to help me get her awake."

"What do I do?"

"Talk to her."

He watched Kerry's head rolling back on her neck, the limp feel of her arms under his hands. She looked like she was already dead, and Phil felt a pain in his belly that had nothing whatsoever to do with his injury.

Kerry, don't you dare die on me now. Please wake up.

"Kerry, can you talk to me? Come on, now. It's important."

Daniel will never forgive me. I'll never forgive myself.

He looked outside to the snow, the wind, the whiteness on the hills, the other survivors milling around the back of the plane like zombies. Too many of them were bleeding, limping, crying, freezing. Too many of them were dead. They were all going to freeze to death out here, even Kerry, who was still wearing nothing on her legs but tights and a thin trench coat. Daniel had asked Phil to help her find her bag. Where was her bag? He shoved aside one carry-on after another, looking for something familiar, until he stubbed his toe on the massive suitcase he'd pulled down from the overhead bins when he was helping Beverly look for her coat. It was Kerry's, of course; her name was written in blue ink on the little tag. He nearly laughed, looking at it, then pulled it open and found a pair of fleece pajama bottoms inside. Perfect—just what she needed to keep warm.

"I need to tell you something, Kerry. You're never going to believe it."

She didn't move, didn't answer. He could keep her body warm, but he didn't know how to heal her mind. He tugged the pajama bottoms over her legs one by one, his eyes blurring.

I can't do this again. I can't watch you slip away.

But none of that mattered—his fear, his love. Kerry Egan had never been his to lose.

8

Twenty below zero—that's what the temperature gauge had said on Daniel's sports watch before it froze up. Dangerously cold, not made any better by the storm, which was sending icy winds down the spine of the continent, increasing the wind chill by ten degrees, maybe twenty. Daniel tried to remember what the forecast at the Anchorage airport had said, how long the storm was supposed to last—two days, three? Four, God forbid? Truth be told, he hadn't been paying enough attention, he'd been so wrapped up in making wedding plans with Kerry. Already, that morning—those plans—seemed like a very long time ago.

He wouldn't let himself think about anything except what needed to be done. He could feel that same strange giddiness welling up in him, threatening to come out as laughter, and he choked it back until it was little more than a coughing sound. Not that anyone was nearby to hear it at the moment: he was alone on a hillside among the broken trees and wreckage, a couple of hundred feet above the nose section of the plane and climbing, where the only sound was the roar of the wind in his ears and the pulse of his blood. He wouldn't give in to hysteria. There was too much else at stake.

The snow stinging at Daniel's eyes and mouth and nose, burning his face and hands, brought him back to earth. It wasn't normal snow but granular, like bits of ice, tiny snowballs that had melted and refrozen in the subarctic air, hanging in heavy clouds over the landscape. No wonder the plane's engines had failed if this was the stuff that had gotten inside them.

The weather—that was the primary problem. If the weather was ugly enough to bring down a passenger jet, it would be far too ugly for rescue helicopters and small search planes. How many times had he dealt with something similar at Petrol? Weather was almost always a factor in a rescue operation, especially in the world's remote places. Even now, there were probably teams of folks in Whitehorse assembling rescue crews, scouring the air for the signal from the jet's emergency transmitter. He seriously doubted there would be flights in the air searching for the site of the wreckage, though, not while the storm still raged. At Petrol he'd waited days, weeks, to send his people in to clean up a situation if it wasn't safe for them. Daniel and the rest of the passengers might wait hours or even days out here before help arrived, days in which people would die if they didn't plan, prepare. It was nearly impossible for a passenger jet to disappear completely in this day and age—these big planes had enough instrumentation and electronics to run a small city—but even the most sophisticated electronics wouldn't help them if Mother Nature decided not to cooperate in the rescue effort.

He thought of the crisis-management people at Denali Airlines and felt a grim kind of connection to them. He knew exactly the kinds of phone calls they were making, the kinds of plans they had in place for situations just like this. He knew the kinds of hours they'd be putting in to find the missing plane and passengers. And he had an idea of how he could do his part.

The first part of his plan was to find the missing passengers, the ones who'd been in the tail of the plane when it broke in half, and keep everyone together and alive until help arrived. The second part involved looking for a bit of high ground from which he might spot a town or a road or even, if he was really lucky, pick up a cellular signal. There might be a town or village nearby, someplace that might have emergency-rescue crews, snowmobiles, trucks with four-wheel drive, even a small trauma center. Or barring all that, a telephone, a CB radio. Something.

He was cursing the loss of the satellite phone. Its battery would last maybe an hour or two in this cold, nothing more. If he could find it, he could use the emergency charger, but finding it in the snow would be like looking for a single drop of water in the ocean. The regular cell phone would be their best bet, as long as they weren't too far out of range.

But first, the missing passengers. He could only hope that the people in the tail section had been as lucky as the people in the front of the cabin, and that most of them—no, all of them—were still alive. That he could help them somehow.

It was slow going through the snow and the cold. The landscape around the crash site was hilly, gently sloping in some places but steep in others, heavily wooded with fir trees, and between the trees and the snow coming down thick, it was difficult to see more than a hundred feet or so in front of him. He knew he was going uphill by feel more than by sight, through snow nearly past his knees in places, covered with a crust of the stinging bits that were still filling the air, but light and soft underneath—none of that heavy, wet stuff that fell during winters in Chicago and turned the roads to slush, at least.

He was following the depression in the snow gouged out by the front of the plane where it had skidded down the hill for several hundred feet before coming to a violent halt against a low outcropping of rock. The snow was not quite as deep in the depression, so Daniel followed it like a road, knowing it would lead him to the rear of the plane and whatever he might find there.

After just a hundred feet or so he was already fatigued, stopping every few minutes to catch his breath. The muscles of his thighs and calves already burned. He should have snowshoes for this, or skis, but fat chance he had of finding any. If Judy or the other Petrol employees were alive, they might be seriously hurt and needing help; by now they'd be close to hypothermic. If the tail section had broken off cleanly just behind the wings, as appeared to be the case, the tail might have slid to a stop the way the nose had, like a sled going down a hill, coming to rest against a tree or boulder. Yes—it was just possible for Daniel to believe that when he found the tail section, he might find there were people still alive in it.

He lifted his head to look around, take stock of his surroundings and catch his breath. Here and there along the trail there were bits of debris—suitcases, airplane seats, foil packages of pretzels and cookies. A hole in the snow contained a plastic water bottle, which he stopped to pick up, followed by a can of ginger ale and another of tomato juice. Soon his pockets were stuffed, and he made a mental note to gather all the food he could find on the way back. There wouldn't have been much food on the plane, but there'd be enough, perhaps, to last a day or two out here if they were careful.

No satellite phone, though. He wasn't that lucky. The damn thing could be anywhere.

He passed bits of the plane's hull, pieces of aluminum blackened by smoke and dented almost beyond recognition. He passed a yellow inflatable life jacket and several loose oxygen masks lying like dead fish on a beach. Already these artifacts were being buried by the new snow coming down in the storm; in a little while, most of the debris would be invisible from the air, a thought that definitely gave him pause until he remembered the emergency beacon, the electronic signal that all planes carried along with its pinging "black box." The plane could be at the bottom of Hudson Bay and air-traffic controllers would still be able to find them—assuming the emergency beacon was still working.

He kept going up the slope, his breath coming harder and harder. At another deep hole in the snow he stopped to look. Always he looked for something that he might be able to use, if not now, then later on. A carry-on, he thought, or maybe a piece of a wing they could use to close up the back of the nose section, shelter them from the wind.

Instead what he found was the body of a man, his head nearly severed, the wound raw around the neck and shoulders. The snow splashed with bright-red blood. Snow was falling right in his open eyes and mouth, into his nose.

Daniel startled, taking three quick steps back and stumbling into the deep snow, which he fell into up to his ears. Daniel had seen dead bodies before, plenty of times, but for some reason the sight of this one was too much. All these people who just wanted to go home, just wanted to finish their work and get home to their families, all these people who had been so glad to know they weren't going to be snowed in at Anchorage. They'd practically cheered when the plane had taken off. And now—and now—

He put his head in his hands and wept for all the people who would be late home, or not at all.

And what about Kerry and Phil and me? What if we don't make it home, either?

Stop feeling sorry for yourself, Albrecht. It won't help you out of this situation.

When Daniel was calm again, he pushed himself to his knees and crept toward the depression. He didn't want to look again, but he had to make sure the body wasn't that of someone he knew. Looking down into the man's open mouth and his eyes, which were a light greenish brown, Daniel had a sudden feeling of vertigo, as if he might pitch forward into the hole himself, never to be found. The dead man was looking directly up at the sky, not at Daniel after all. Seeing nothing.

But what Daniel really couldn't stop looking at was the angle of the man's head, thrown back two or three inches from the neck, ex-

posing bits of blood and bone and sinew. The head was still connected on the left side by a bit of skin and muscle. Daniel gulped air
and looked away as quickly as he could, already knowing that for
the rest of his life the image of the man's head would appear to him
behind his closed eyes.

He stood for a second, shivering in the snow, wishing he had
something to cover the man with, a blanket at least, and he spent
maybe a minute looking around for one. The wind howled around
his ears, almost like it was screaming. He stopped, his hands clench-
ing and unclenching, and then realized it was stupid: if he found a
blanket, he should use it to help the living. There would be time to
mourn the dead later, when they were safe again. He left the dead
man where he was and kept going.

The smell of broken pine branches and the ozone tang of new
snow came to him, along with jet fuel and— yes, he was sure of it
now—a bit of oily smoke. Through the haze of the storm he could
just make out a thin black column coming from a deep depression in
the snow, which turned out to be one of the plane's massive engines.
It sat at the base of an ancient fir that had probably grown unmo-
lested in the Yukon soil for two hundred years before Denali Flight
806 came dropping out of the sky. Now the tree was broken perhaps
a third of the way up its length, the spar toppled over on one side and
oozing the smell of turpentine, while beneath it the round engine
emitted that single mournful thread of black smoke and the acrid
smell of burning jet fuel.

He was close to the crest of the hill now, a rocky outcropping of
gray stone jutting toward the sky. Likely it had been the hill itself
that had broken off the tail section. The plane had been struggling

to maintain altitude, dragging its tail behind it. When it fell, the top of the ridge had probably sheared off the tail section, sending it backward down the hill in one direction, the front pitching forward in the other.

At the top he should be able to get a better view of the land around the crash site, as well as any remaining bits of the plane. About fifty feet from the crest of the hill, the depression in the snow left by the nose section came to an abrupt end, marked by a sudden profusion of debris, including several rows of airline seats. Some still had bodies strapped to them.

He checked each one, feeling sick. He called, "Hey there. Hey, anyone hurt?" No one stirred. If they'd survived the crash, they were dead from exposure already. None of them were wearing coats. None of them were Judy or the other missing Petrol employees.

He checked one or two for a pulse—nothing—and left them where they were for now. There would be time to tend to the dead later, while the business of the living was still urgent. He kept going, up and up.

At the top, the trees thinned a little, the clouds still thick as the storm gathered itself. Finally Daniel stood on a piece of bare rock at the top of the hill and looked around.

He was standing on the ridge of a hill as stony and broken as the spine of an ancient beast only half-buried. The other side of the hill fell away steeply toward the thin trickle of what Daniel guessed was a creek, a thin frozen white line limned by trees of deep green. The hills on the other side of the valley were rockier than the one he stood on, more sparsely treed, but everywhere there was snow— snow on the ground, in the air, on the trees, in his eyes. Snow everywhere, and more falling by the minute. And not even the smallest hint of a town, a road, an electrical line.

He didn't really have any hopes of being within range of a cellphone signal in all this wilderness, but still he took out his phone and held it up, waved it around in the air in the hopes of seeing those little bars jump. Nothing. Out here the phone was nothing more than a bit of electrical junk, a hunk of metal and wire that would be useless to him when his battery ran down. He did have his hand-crank backup charger, but that would only provide an hour or two of useful battery life. For emergencies only. *And what is this if not an emergency?* he thought. It was a bit of luck that he had such a thing, that he hadn't lost it in the crash. His only bit of luck, so far.

So much for looking for a town this way.

Maybe the other direction, then. If the plane had finished its turn and was facing west when they crashed, instead of south, like he'd first assumed, then Whitehorse would be in the opposite direction of the way he'd just come. The nose of the plane would be like an arrow pointing the way back to civilization. It might be worth checking out anyway.

Down below he could see the trail the nose section had made as it careened down the hillside, the broken tree trunks, the pieces of the wings, the dead engine, and the nose itself, surrounded by a few black dots moving slowly—the rest of the living passengers gathering up what supplies they could find.

He hoped Kerry was all right. She and Phil would look out for each other at least. If only she hadn't lost consciousness in the crash, if she hadn't hit her head. If he'd taken the seat in the bulkhead instead of her . . .

There was no point in what-ifs now. He'd do what he could for all of them, starting with the people in the tail.

Daniel turned back to face the narrow, desolate valley on the opposite side of the hill, searching through the gloom, looking for a piece of the fuselage. Instead he saw mostly debris.

Then he saw it: the tail section lay maybe fifty feet below the crest of the hill, held from sliding farther down the opposite slope by several large fir trees. Unlike the nose section, it was a twisted heap, a mass of crushed aluminum that bore such little resemblance to the jetliner it came from that Daniel's hopes sank. It looked like nothing so much as an old piece of notebook paper that someone had crumpled up and thrown away.

No one moved around the tail section, no people sat huddled for warmth or companionship like they did around the nose. No footsteps showed that anyone had come out. It looked like a tomb.

He didn't want to go down the slope toward them, but he couldn't go back without looking, without knowing if Petrol people were inside. Right now, in this moment, it was still possible to think of them whole and alive, maybe trapped, maybe hurt, but still alive. He wouldn't know for certain until he looked inside. Schrödinger's cat wasn't dead until you knew it was dead, and in order to know, you had to look. He'd appointed himself this task, and he must see it through now.

He looked around for a path that would take him safely down to the wreckage, maybe a hundred yards below the spot where he stood. A rope would have been ideal in this situation, if he'd had one, or maybe a sled. A sled could get him down there in seconds, let

him rest his aching muscles, not to mention it might be helpful, if he
did find people alive, to have something he could use to haul them
back. He thought longingly of the sleds and dogs the hunters in Barrow had used, not to mention the snowmobiles that had whizzed up
and down the streets of town. It had seemed strange, even exotic,
their first day in town, that people traveled the streets of Barrow by
snowmobile; later he'd seen the practicality of it. Now he'd have
given anything he owned for a snowmobile. Come to think of it,
he'd give anything to be back in Barrow, which was positively a beacon of civilization compared to the place he found himself in now.

What could he use for a sled? The piece of wing was too big and
heavy—he'd never be able to lift it by himself—but he was thinking
one of the plane's seats might do the trick.

He scrambled back down the slope to the place where there was
an empty seat in one of the rows that had fallen out of the broken
fuselage. He didn't want to think about why it was empty; at the
moment, he was simply glad it was there. He took hold of the seat
back with one hand, braced the seat bottom with his foot, and tore
for all he was worth. A few violent tugs and the seat back came free.

At the crest of the hill, Daniel set the seat back down on the top
of the snow and set himself on top of that, feet-first, like a kid on his
first snow day—except that this was for necessity, not thrills. A few
pushes and he was sliding across the surface of the snow toward the
tail section of the plane, the twisted hulk of metal in which his
friends and co-workers lay waiting, alive or dead.

Fifty feet or so from the tail, Daniel put his feet out to stop his
descent, digging in hard with his heels and grabbing hold of a low

branch to pull himself to a stop. He stood up, his hands shaking, and set the seat back against the trunk of a white birch, taking in the scene in front of him.

The tail had hit more than the crest of the hill when it had broken off; it must have crashed into half the trees on the slope, which had punched in its sides like a loaf of bread dough. It was a misshapen lump of a thing now, barely recognizable except for a blue circle of paint still partially visible in the midst of the wreckage. One of the rear exit doors had popped off and gave a dim view inside of darkness and metal. No bodies, at least. The front of the tail section, where the cabin had broken in half, was turned away from Daniel, facing downhill. All the windows dark. No movement.

"Hello?" he called out, hating the sound of his own voice. It was too loud in that still place, in all that silence.

Daniel took a breath and put his head inside the open rear door. The dark clapped itself over his eyes like a mask; he could see the vague outlines of the rear galley, but nothing else, until his eyes adjusted to the dark. He had to be sure there were no survivors, that there was no one else left to help, before he could think of returning to the nose and to Kerry. He'd told her he'd look for her friend; now he was afraid to find her.

"Hello?" he said again, barely above a whisper, then cleared his throat and said, "Is anyone hurt in here? Does anyone need help?"

Silence. Somewhere a blast of wind cleared an overhead branch of snow; Daniel heard it fall with a soft *whump*. Small clicks and groans and settling noises came from the wreck, but no voices. The air had a tang of metal and smoke Daniel could taste in the back of his throat.

"Is there anyone alive?" he called again, not expecting or even hoping for an answer this time. "Does anyone need help?"

Then the sound of a voice breathy with pain. "Yes," it said. "Please, help me."

The voice was a woman's, and suddenly Daniel had visions of Judy trapped beneath seats and suitcases and other bodies, unable to move. "What's your name?" he asked.

"Kecia. I'm one of the flight attendants."

"Is there anyone else in there with you, Kecia?"

"There's another woman here. She's trapped under the seats. She says her legs might be broken." Kecia's voice hitched, as if she were wincing. "There was a man calling for help a few minutes ago, but he stopped. I think he might be dead."

Two passengers alive, maybe more. It was better than he'd been hoping for just seconds ago.

"Hold on," Daniel said. "I'm coming in."

He pulled himself up into the open doorway that led to the rear galley, where the smell hit him even more strongly: the black smell of smoke, the metallic tang of blood. He resisted the urge to cover his nose while his eyes adjusted to the dark inside the tail section. He'd need both his hands for this.

Slowly the shapes inside the plane turned into things he recognized. The ceiling and far wall of the rear galley had collapsed, leaving the small space strewn with cans of soda and boxes of food still wrapped in cellophane that had fallen from their cupboards. A black suitcase with a popped zipper had rolled backward into the galley and exploded its contents in the middle of the floor, including a tube of toothpaste and several pairs of black boxer briefs that now lay atop what turned out to be the body of a male flight attendant, already cold. Daniel snatched his hand back from the man and stuffed it in his pocket. *Steady, now.* There would be more bodies inside, surely, and at least two people he might be able to help, as long as he didn't fall apart.

"Where are you?" he asked the darkness inside.

"Here," said Kecia, her voice close now. "Just a few rows up."

He moved forward into what remained of the cabin, the darkness easing a little as his eyes adjusted further. He had to duck down low—the ceiling had collapsed in places, the plastic bins hanging open and leaving the aisle crammed with bags, clothes, even a laptop that Daniel had to pull out of the way before he could move up the aisle toward the sound of the woman's ragged breathing, her voice saying "Here" over and over. As he moved forward he could hear another woman's voice, muffled, crying, "I can't—I can't breathe." Somewhere else, the soft sound of someone coughing wetly.

"Are you there?" asked the first voice. The flight attendant, Kecia.

Daniel answered, "I can't move very quickly, but I'm coming."

He passed the lavatories and moved into the main cabin, or what was left of it. The seats here had bunched together in the crash the same way they had in the nose section, but in the opposite direction—toward the back. They were smashed together so tightly Daniel could hardly see that there *had* been rows, once upon a time. He thought with envy of all the equipment and people he'd always had at his disposal at Petrol, the power tools and vehicles and first responders. This situation called for all of that and more.

"You're in the back row?" he called out.

"Fourth from the back," said the woman's voice. "I sat down in an empty seat when we started to descend."

"That was smart," Daniel said, tossing someone's smashed iPad behind him so he could keep moving. He wanted to keep the woman talking, keep her conscious. "See, you were lucky."

"Unh," said Kecia, gasping. "If you say so."

"Are you in pain?"

She gave a noise that was half gasp, half grunt. "Yes. A lot of pain. My arms are smashed between the seats." She took a shaky breath. "I can't move them. I'm completely stuck in here."

"I'll see what I can do," Daniel said. *Keep talking. Just keep talking.* Inching toward her little by little. He passed a pair of feet and reached out to touch them, but they were cold. He snatched his hands away again.

"Are there others with you? The pilots? Amber and Dave?"

"The pilots' names are Amber and Dave?"

She gave a near-laugh. "No, those are the other flight attendants. The pilot's name was Alan, I think. I don't remember the co-pilot."

"I think the pilots are dead," Daniel said, not wanting to tell her also about the dead flight attendant in the rear galley just then— Dave, probably. "The front of the nose section was smashed up pretty badly. We landed on the other side of the hill. I had to climb a long way to get here."

"Nose section?" Kecia asked. "The plane broke apart?"

"You don't remember that part?"

"Honestly, my eyes were shut the whole time."

He'd reached her now; he was kneeling on the floor right beside her, where she sat in what was left of the row of seats. She must have put her arms up to shield her face when the seats started flying at her: one arm was bent back at the elbow, a horrible angle that nearly made Daniel sick to see. The weight of the chairs and the bodies in them had crushed it. Still, if she hadn't put her arms up, it was likely the seats would have gone into her face instead. She'd saved her own life.

"I remember rolling, and then the seats smashing into each other." She winced. "I didn't know why it was so cold, or where everyone else was. I guess it makes sense now. Are people in bad shape in the nose section?"

"Most of us are all right," he said, truthfully enough, and then turned to the problem at hand—how to get Kecia out from beneath the seats. "I don't know if I can get these seats off you by myself. I might be able to move them enough for you to slip out. Do you think you could, if I can get the seat up a little bit?"

"I don't know. I can try. It hurts a lot."

"I know. But you can't stay wedged in there."

"I'll do my best."

He put all his weight against the nearest seat and pushed. The thing moved only an inch or so, though he was using every bit of strength he had, and the flight attendant wailed as she pulled herself out from beneath the tower of seats and bodies. She slid to the floor and landed on her knees next to Daniel in the aisle of the plane, clutching her wounded arm limply to her chest with her good hand.

When she could speak, she looked up and said, "Thank you. I was starting to think I was going to die in here."

He looked at her arm, which was purple nearly to the wrist, swollen almost beyond recognition, and said, "Can you get back to the galley and wait for me there? I'm going to see who else I can find. I'll come help you as soon as I can."

"I think so. I'll try."

Daniel said, "I should warn you, there's someone dead in the rear galley. A man, one of the crew."

"That must be Dave," the woman said, her chin trembling as if she was trying not to cry.

"Maybe you can help me," he said. "I came here looking for some of my friends, some people I work with. A woman named Judy, who would have been sitting with two men. We all work together."

Kecia said, "I don't know about anyone named Judy, but there was another woman somewhere up above me, in one of the forward rows, I think. She sounded like she was hurt pretty badly."

"Thank you," he said. "I'll be back as soon as I can."

He army-crawled forward into the wreckage, calling out, "Judy! Judy Akers, are you in here?"

Silence, then a muffled sob came from beneath the mess of seats and luggage. "Daniel? Is that you?"

"I can't see you." He pulled at the cushions, listening for the sounds of the woman's breathing. "Judy?" He followed the sounds of weeping forward, pushing aside cushions, seat bottoms, loose shoes, dead limbs.

"Here," said a voice he recognized clearly now. It was weak, breathy. "I'm here. There's something on top of me."

He felt a sense of triumph. "Thank God. Kerry will be so relieved. Are you hurt?"

"She's . . . okay?"

"She hit her head. I think she might have a concussion, but Phil is keeping an eye on her."

"Phil, too. That's good."

Coughing, and the wet sound again. Like her lungs were full of water. No, not water—blood.

He was able to stand up, barely, in the tight space; Judy's voice was coming from somewhere near the middle of a great pile of seats that seemed to be mostly empty. He started moving debris to get to her. "Let's get you out of here," he said. "I'll take you to Kerry. She'll be so glad to see you. We're going to set up the nose section as a shelter, keep everyone warm until help comes. I've got a little sled all set up outside to carry anyone who can't walk. Just a little ways up the hill and we can slide down, just like a snow day. Won't that be nice?"

He knew he sounded ridiculous, but he felt like he needed to fill the silence while he worked pulling pieces of debris out of the aisle, while he ignored the sight of a dead woman in the seat to his right and the horror of a pale gray foot sticking out from underneath the pile. He had to keep Judy going, and himself, if he was going to help anyone in these circumstances.

"Daniel?" Judy said. "I'm hurt. Badly, I think. I can't move."

He stopped yanking on the piece of metal in his hands. "What do you mean? Are you stuck?"

"No," she hissed, as if even that much speech cost her. "I mean, yes. I—I can't feel my legs."

"From cold?"

"My face is cold, and my hands. Everything else is—gone. Like they're not there."

Oh shit.

He could see her now, pale in the dim light, and reached out to touch her face. The mouth moved. "It's me," she said.

He pulled away the body in the chair between herself and him, and then he could see what had happened: Judy had been impaled by a piece of metal, all the way through her torso and out her back. It must have severed her spine, leaving her alive above the wound, already dead below. There was very little blood, meaning the force and pressure of the seats surrounding her were the only things keeping her alive at the moment. If he tried to pull her free, it was likely she would bleed out in a matter of seconds.

He'd seen it before, once, during an accident on the El back in Chicago. A man had dropped his phone on the tracks and jumped down to grab it, but when the train came, he'd been unable to make it back to the platform in time. He'd been caught between the train and the platform, leaving him alive from the waist up, but only as long as no one tried to move him. Daniel had stayed with the man the whole time, tried to keep him talking, tried to keep him conscious until his family arrived, but he hadn't quite made it; the man's face had slowly turned an alarming shade of green the longer he talked, and less than an hour after it happened, he slipped away.

That day had been hard enough for Daniel, even though the man had been a stranger, someone he'd never laid eyes on before. This was a woman he knew well, a co-worker, a friend. His own fiancée's closest friend. Daniel would be the last person she saw, the last person she spoke to, and he was conscious now of the weight of that responsibility.

If Judy's dead, Kerry had said, *don't tell me.*

Judy was not dead yet, but she would be soon, and there was nothing he could do to stop it.

He swallowed and looked up into her face. "Hey, Judy," he said, horrified at the hearty sound of his own voice. "Funny running into you here."

"Huh," she said, and coughed again, that same wet sound. "You always could make me laugh at the worst times."

He was trying to look optimistic, yet he knew he was failing, knew he should be trying to comfort her more, say something profound, but he wasn't good at offering comfort. He wasn't a priest or a hero.

"This doesn't look too serious, all things considered," he said, glancing at her wounds quickly and then up again. "We'll have you patched up and home in no time, just you wait and see."

Judy gave him a wry smile. "You've always been a shitty liar, Daniel," she said. "I'm so glad Kerry has you."

9

"Kerry, wake up," Phil was saying. "Don't go to sleep now. It's not safe. There's a nurse here and she said you need to open your eyes."

No answer.

"Raise her head up," said Beverly. "Just talk to her."

"Come on, open your eyes. You need to listen to me now."

"Not like that. Don't bark orders at her," said Beverly, flapping her hands in exasperation at Phil's cluelessness. "Really talk to her. Let her hear your voice and know you're there."

Phil looked down at Kerry's closed eyelids, the skin so pale it was nearly blue, at a curl of red hair around her mouth, and wondered if it would make the slightest bit of difference if she knew he was there.

He felt a welling of anguish. He didn't want to deal with this again. If he hadn't been injured himself, he'd have gladly walked all the way back to Barrow rather than be responsible for another sick person, someone who might die at any moment. He couldn't do it again. He just couldn't.

"I don't know what to say," he muttered.

Beverly was reaching into Kerry's sleeve to feel her pulse. "What would you say if she was awake?"

"I don't know. I never know what to say to her. That's always been my problem."

"Tell her how you feel. Why she's important to you, that kind of thing."

"What do you mean?" Phil said, his head snapping up. "We're not a couple. I'm just her co-worker."

"Oh."

"She doesn't really like me very much. If she were awake, I'm sure she'd tell you the same."

"Sorry, I thought you were her husband," Beverly said, giving Phil a strange look. "Never mind. Just talk to her anyway. Say something that will get her attention."

Something that would get her attention. But what on earth would that be? He could tell her that a reporter for CNN was on the phone. Kerry loved her job—everyone knew that. The only other thing that ever seemed to matter to her was Daniel. They were very far from the job right now, so that left only Daniel.

He took a breath and said, "Kerry! Look at me right now! Kerry, Daniel's here, he's hurt and he needs you to help him. Come on, now."

Her eyelids fluttered but didn't open. *Damn*, he thought, *I was sure that would work.*

He wasn't exactly sure how long she'd been out—he'd only

turned away for a few minutes, maybe no more than ten at the most—but he was very sure he didn't want Daniel to come back and find her unconscious.

Daniel should have been back by now. "Kerry!" Phil shouted, loudly enough that people were turning around to stare.

He didn't want to shake her or slap her, anything that would cause her more pain, but she wouldn't open her eyes. *Open your eyes, Kerry, please.* She was shivering, a tremor that started in her jaw and spread to the rest of her, until she was a trembling, shaking mass.

"What can I do?" he begged Beverly. "She won't—"

"At least let's keep her warm until help gets here. Her body temperature's dropped. Come on, we'll get her in between us and wrap her up. Use our body heat."

"Really?"

She glared at him. "You got a better idea?"

"You're right, you're right," he said. "I just . . . This is not what I was planning on doing today."

"Tell me about it," she said, fixing him with a level look. "If we're still here by nightfall, the whole lot of us are going to have to pile together to keep warm. Now, put your arms around her like this. I'll get her from the back."

He put his arms under Kerry's and wrapped around her tightly, while Beverly did the same from the back. Kerry shifted a little, her breath metallic with the blood from her broken teeth. She was close enough that he could have bent forward a few inches and kissed her.

Daniel should have been the one there wrapped around her, not Phil. But Beverly was right—they had to get her warm, keep her warm until Daniel came back and took over.

He had to admit he did feel considerably warmer lying there with the three of them pressed together, Kerry in the middle, even with the cold wind blowing up his back. After a few minutes she stopped shivering. Still, whenever he said her name, her eyelids would flutter, barely lifting, and then close again.

After about fifteen minutes, he could feel her stirring, starting to wake. "Kerry?" he asked. He tilted his head back to look at her.

She flicked her eyes open and said, "It's you," before letting her head fall forward onto his shoulder, her red hair tangled in her mouth. He pulled it loose, and she answered with a soft snore.

"It's me."

He wasn't sure if she really *did* know it was him. He was reminded, horribly, of Emily near the end—her voice thick with pain, the sense that she was only partially there with him at any given moment, the fear that she might slip away when he wasn't paying attention. Those days—he had tried to outrun them, tried to forget, but something was always bringing him back to the months Emily lived in the dining room of their house, in a rented hospital bed, while the hospice nurses came to spend the day with her while Phil took the night shift, sometimes reading to her, sometimes rubbing her feet, which she complained were always cold. She'd been too young for cancer, too lovely, and the loss of her had been more than he could bear.

He'd failed her, failed Emily, and now he was doing the same to Kerry. It shouldn't be Phil here with her, it should be Daniel— someone competent, someone who knew how to lead. What the hell was taking Daniel so long anyway?

"Keep her talking," Beverly was saying. "Ask her how she's doing."

He steadied himself and said, "Kerry, stay awake for me. Tell me how you're feeling."

"I'm so tired," she muttered. "All I want to do is sleep. Can't you let me sleep?"

It was like talking to a child. "It's not safe for you to sleep right now," he said. "Can you talk to me for a little while? Keep me company? I could really use a friend."

"I don't know. I can try."

But then he couldn't think of anything else to say. Kerry's eyes were drooping, her face relaxing into sleep once more, her mouth pinching as if she were in pain. How much she reminded him of Emily.

Why did he have so much trouble talking to her? What if this were Emily here, now—what would he say then? He wouldn't have any trouble saying what was on his mind. With her, he never had. She had been his everything, and when she was gone, he'd lost himself. He'd lost everything she used to love in him—he'd turned into this sour, unhappy, pinched kind of man. No wonder Kerry disliked him. He didn't like himself much of the time, either.

Talk to her, Phil. She's a human being, not a bomb. It was Emily's voice, again, that he heard whenever he knew he was feeling sorry for himself, when he was having trouble coping. Emily had been the best part of himself—it was why he still missed her. She'd been the source of his courage.

He took a breath and spoke in Kerry's ear. "Did I ever tell you about my wife?" he said. "My wife, Emily?"

Kerry's eyes fluttered open again. "You're married?"

"Not anymore."

"I never knew that," she murmured.

"I don't like to talk about it much."

"What happened?" Kerry said, her mouth stretching into a wide yawn and making Phil stifle his own. "Did she dump you?"

He froze. *This is why I don't bring these things up at work. To have her make a joke, turn my loss into some kind of fodder . . .*

Grow up, Velez. Let it go for a change. It was just possible she didn't know what she was saying, under the circumstances.

He shook his head and said, "No, she died."

"I'm sorry," Kerry said, and Phil could feel her waking up for real now, could feel her attention shifting to him in ways she might never have allowed herself under ordinary circumstances. "No, I'm really sorry to hear that. What happened?"

The wall inside him threatened to go back up. He'd worked so hard to keep a firm separation between his work life and his personal life. *Church and state, Phil, church and state.*

Still, it was working, the way he was talking to her—Kerry was awake, she was lucid, she was paying attention. She possibly had never paid as much attention to him as she was at that moment.

"Cancer." He had to practically choke out the word.

Her eyes fluttered again in sympathy. "Oh God. I'm so sorry. That must have been hard."

Here was the moment he should have opened up more, said *It was*, and then recounted the whole devastating story, give her a chance to show him some kindness, connect on a level that had nothing to do with Petrol, and his job, and her job, and the things they genuinely had in common. He should have, and he knew it— but he couldn't, he just *couldn't*. How could he tell her about the nights when the sickness and the smell had overwhelmed him, made him seethe with resentment? How he'd hated Emily for being sick, hated himself for being so weak? How could he confess to Kerry Egan, of all people in the world, his most heinous crime—that when his wife had needed him most, he'd run away?

He didn't deserve Kerry's love, or anyone's. He was weak and useless—worse, he was a coward.

He stood up abruptly and left her, pacing to the end of the fuselage, feeling everyone's eyes on him, especially Kerry's. He looked out into the whiteness, at the slow zombie movements of the other survivors, and took gulp after gulp of air like a man who had just escaped drowning.

Eventually Beverly sidled up next to him, standing still for a moment and looking out at the snow. "That was a good thing you did. It worked."

"Thanks," he said, not meeting her eyes.

"Your wife. It was bad?" she asked.

"Yes."

"You're probably tired of hearing people say they're sorry."

"Yes."

"I am, though, you know. Sorry."

"Thanks. I'm glad you were here today."

She shifted; Phil could tell she was getting ready to leave him on his own. "I should see if there's anyone else who needs help. See what I can do." Beverly tilted her head to look at him like some kind of bright-eyed bird. "Don't worry, I'll be back to check on you, too, okay?"

"I'm all right. Go on and see to the others; I'll be fine."

"I'd feel better if you and Kerry both had a CAT scan and a hospital bed. But you'll be okay for the moment. Just keep your body temperature up, and rest. Keep her awake."

"You're coming back, though, right?"

Beverly turned and smiled at him. "Don't worry. She won't die between now and then." She sighed. "At least, I hope not."

She went outside into the snow. Phil stood a moment watching her, then turned back around into the darkness inside the plane.

"Beverly," he muttered to himself, "you are a real ray of sunshine."

10

"Did you find anything useful?" said a voice behind him.

Daniel had backed halfway out of the fuselage when he heard the voice, close enough that it felt like it was right in his ear. "Damn it, Bob, don't sneak up on me like that."

The senior VP was standing in the drift outside the rear door, his shaggy white head half-buried in someone's heavy black nylon parka. It was not the expensive gray wool sports overcoat he'd worn the past two weeks when they were working in Barrow, and Daniel wondered, briefly, where he'd come by it, before pushing that thought aside as pointless. What did it matter who it had belonged to originally? They would all need to find and use whatever they could to survive out here, ownership be damned.

"Our people," the old man asked, tilting his chin at the remnants of the fuselage. "Are any of them still alive in there?"

He was standing in snow up to his thighs outside the door to the rear galley, the flight attendant, Kecia, huddled in the snow behind him. She'd found a coat somewhere, too, a giant olive-green parka with a fur-trimmed hood, and sat against the metal skin of the plane with her broken arm clutched against her chest.

Daniel kept his back to them, not daring to turn around. He was feeling a little raw from his trip inside the tail, his throat tight, his face dirty with tear tracks and grease and blood. He didn't appreciate Bob showing up here like this, standing outside after it was all too late and demanding a headcount of the living and the dead like he was tallying up accounting figures. Assets and liabilities. The people inside the tail were not abstracts, not pencil scratches in anyone's accounting ledger. They were husbands, sons, daughters. Friends. But the old man would never grieve them, not in public. Maybe not even in private. *And if Kerry and I had been sitting back there*, Daniel thought, *it would have been exactly the same*.

"Who did we lose?" Bob demanded again.

There was no point in lying. "Jack Wisniewski and Doug Fraser. And Judy."

He neglected to mention that he'd sat with Judy while the poor woman suffered through her last minutes, her skin going gray, her eyes filmy, her thoughts confused as the blood leaked from her body. She'd called for her mother at the end, and Daniel had been able to do nothing but hold her hand and whisper that it would be over soon, that the pain would stop soon. "Don't be afraid," he'd said to her, though he was afraid himself. In fact, he'd never been so scared in his life.

Now Judy's suffering was over. Daniel hadn't even tried to move her; there was no point. When she was gone, he'd called out for anyone else—*Is there anyone alive in here? Anyone?*—and receiving no answer, he'd gone slowly back the way he'd come in, picking his way through the mess and outside.

He hadn't expected to see Bob there, like the Abominable Snowman, his breath puffing in the air, his hair full of snowflakes.

"How'd you get down here?" Daniel asked.

"Same way you did. I was looking for a town, a road. Can't see a damn thing in this weather, though. Might as well be walking through soup." He stood back and gave the ball of twisted metal and plastic a frown, as if it had disappointed him somehow. "What a waste," he said. "Those pilots should have turned back the minute we hit this weather. In fact, they should never have taken off in the first place."

Daniel didn't disagree with that assessment, but it was pointless to argue now about what should have been done. They'd been cleared for takeoff, and they had run into weather, and they had crashed. Now it was time to deal with problems that were still fixable.

"You're one of the flight attendants, right?" Bob was asking Kecia. "So what kind of emergency beacon does this baby have? What signals does it give off in a crash?"

She was looking at the ball of metal that had been the plane. "All commercial aircraft are fixed with an emergency location transmitter. It's fastened to the frame of the aircraft, somewhere in the tail," she said. "Usually it goes off with a sudden deceleration, like in a crash. When that happens, the aircraft is usually found in a few hours."

"What does that mean, 'usually'?" Bob asked.

"Most of the time they work the way they're meant to," she said. "The rest of the time they don't."

"So sometimes they don't work at all?" Daniel asked.

"Sometimes they're damaged in the crash. There's an antenna that sometimes breaks off in a crash. We rolled downhill for a ways before we stopped. The rolling could have broken off the antenna that's connected to the ELT."

"They're emergency transmitters!" Bob barked. "They have one job—to go off in a crash. They should *always* work properly."

"They're not indestructible. Everything on an airplane is breakable if you hit it hard enough, even the black boxes."

Daniel squared his shoulders. "Is there any way to know if the ELT is working properly now? See if the captain set it off, or if it went off automatically?"

"No," she said. "The signal's monitored by satellite from space, and on the ground by VHF signal. We wouldn't be able to pick it up without a radio. The only VHF I know of is in the cockpit, and if there's no power . . ." She shrugged.

"Maybe it would have some lights or screens, something to show us it was working. Do you know where it's located?"

"They're mounted as far back as possible on the frame of the aircraft. You'd have to be able to get under the skin of the plane somehow and into the far end of the tail." They all turned and looked at the ball of metal that used to be the plane's tail and tried to imagine how they might pry it apart to get at the frame. "It's a bright-orange metal thing. Looks a little like a car battery."

"Shouldn't we look for it?"

"We can try, but there are no guarantees."

"I don't want to go back to the rest of the passengers with a 'maybe.'"

They took a few minutes to search the crash site, going slowly through snow that was deepening at every moment. They circled the back of the plane and looked for holes that might let them inside the tail; there were a few small ones the size of a fist, nothing big enough to admit a full-grown man. Daniel shaded his eyes and looked inside. It was dark in there, but he thought he could see, just barely, something bright orange and boxy. There were no lights, no displays to show that it was working. He had to assume it was damaged.

He felt his hopes sink. "We're not going to be able to rely on the ELT. Anything else?" he asked Kecia. "There's something in the black box, too, right?"

"Right. It emits a signal, too, so rescue crews can find it, even underwater, but they have to be in range, maybe within ten or fifteen miles. And usually there are ELTs on the life rafts."

"That makes sense. So the life rafts can be found even in the middle of the ocean." Daniel thought for a second. "We might want to activate those just to be sure. Are there any life rafts in the tail, do you think?"

"There should be several just inside the exit there. I can show you where."

She shuffled toward the open door once more and guided Daniel to the place where the life rafts should have been stored, but the cover on the storage unit had broken off in the crash—the life rafts were missing.

"I don't understand," Kecia said. "They should be here. I checked them myself before we took off."

Daniel reached his hand inside the dark hole where the life rafts should have been and felt around. Nothing. Probably they'd been flung out into the snow, along with half the rest of the contents of the plane. He looked around him at the expanse of whiteness, the twisted metal of the tail, the copious debris trail that the plane had left as it rolled down the hillside. The life rafts could be anywhere. The three of them could search, but it would likely take all day, and darkness would be falling in an hour or so.

"It was just a thought," said Kecia, gazing out at the white expanse with a hopeful expression on her face. "I think we can safely assume the black box is working even if the ELT didn't go off. If they do a sweep of the area looking for pings, they'll find us eventually. Assuming we aren't too far off course, that is."

"That might be a big assumption," Daniel said.

"I hope not. We had started to turn back when the second engine went, so we might be out of the usual flight path, but hopefully not too far out. The captain said it was less than an hour back to Whitehorse."

"Is that a hundred miles? Two hundred?"

"Maybe more. These planes can go as much as five hundred miles an hour."

"What do you think?" Bob was asking. "Do you think we're likely to get a rescue today?"

She squinted up at the sky, at the tiny ice crystals still pelting them. "Well, I wouldn't say I'm an expert, though I've probably had more training than anyone else here," she said, "but the weather was definitely a factor in bringing us down." She winced and clutched her hands closer to her. "If the ice stops soon, maybe. Otherwise I'd say tomorrow, if the weather clears up."

Tomorrow. No big deal in the ordinary world, but out here, in the cold and wind, a single twenty-four-hour period could be deadly.

Daniel handed his gloves to Kecia, thinking through the problem, but she shook her head—he needed his gloves, she said.

"You have to put them on," he said. "If you don't, your hands will freeze in minutes, and then you'll lose them."

"All right." She pulled them on very carefully while Daniel looked inside the rear galley and found a single glove and a single mitten. A mismatched set, but they would work at least.

They'd have to shelter in the nose section of the fuselage. They'd have to find something to build a fire, if they could. And they'd need to gather as much food and water as they could find before darkness fell.

"We'd better get back," Daniel said.

Kecia was looking up toward the top of the hill clutching her arm to her like a broken wing. "Oh God. I'll never make it to the top like this."

"I'll help you as best as I can," Daniel said. "Trust me. We should all stay together. It'll be safer if we do."

He looked over at Bob, who was looking at the cans of soda and the bags of snacks lying just inside the door of the rear galley.

"Kecia," he said, "how much food do you figure was on the plane today when we took off?"

"Enough for every passenger to have one box meal. Some fancier stuff in the first-class cabin—some poppy-seed chicken, pasta, stuff like that. The rest are pretzels, cans of soda and water. They don't weigh us down with too much food these days. Sometimes we even run out."

"But we probably have enough to get us to tomorrow, right?" Bob said.

"Depends on how many passengers are left. How many were in the nose?"

"A couple of dozen, from what I remember. We should gather all this up and take it back over the hill."

"Let's get her back first," Daniel was saying. "We can come back for the food later. Get some other people to come help us collect everything. It's too big a job for just you and me."

"I don't want to make a second trip," Bob said. "It's damn hard work climbing up this far. A second trip would be extra effort we shouldn't expend."

"I realize that, but we need to get Kecia back safely to the nose section first. Then we can gather as much as we can carry and bring it back."

"I can make a sled. I'll drag it behind me. It won't be too far."

"Fine. But you'll have to do it alone, because I need to help her." He looked at Kecia. "She can walk. It's just her arm that's hurt."

"She'll have trouble keeping her balance in all this snow unless one of us helps her."

He frowned; Daniel watched his mouth working around the problem as if he were chewing on tobacco. "All right, all right," he grumbled, sounding like an angry bear woken from hibernation a month before spring. "What we really need is one more set of hands. I should have made Phil come with me."

"Phil was hurt. A lot of people were."

"Hmm," he said, not a noise of assent as much as a delayed argument. "Let's get this over with."

After Bob had gathered as much food as he could carry, they started back up the hill slowly, Bob leading the way and Daniel following behind, holding Kecia under her good elbow and moving carefully so she could keep her balance. It was slow going up the hillside, and she kept stumbling on hidden rocks and branches under the snowpack, leaning forward in steep spots to keep from sliding backward, always with Daniel's hand there to catch her when she started to pitch forward. He was gratified to see he'd been correct in what he'd said to Bob—while Kecia could have walked steadily enough on even ground or pavement, she would have had a hell of a time making it to the top of the hill in the snow without Daniel's help.

She stumbled again and fell forward onto her knees, letting out a small startled cry. Daniel helped her back to her feet and looked up toward the summit. He said, "Almost there. When we get to the other side, we can slide all the way to the other half of the plane."

"Almost sounds like fun," she said.

"Easier, at least."

They looked at the broad form of Bob's back ahead of them up the hillside, a blue airline blanket full of food boxes slung over one shoulder.

Kecia asked, "That guy seems like a real barrel of laughs. You work for him?"

"Yeah."

"And you like it?"

Daniel grimaced a little, lowered his voice and said, "Maybe not today so much. Today I might give the job a three."

She gave a sound that was almost a laugh, and then they were silent for a minute, huffing their way up the hillside. "That high?"

Daniel said, "Can I ask you something?"

"Sure."

"You said the emergency transmitters don't always work. Do you know how often they don't work? I mean, what are the percentages, the likelihood that it wouldn't have gone off in a crash?"

"To be honest, I think it's something like seventy-five percent of the time they go off. A quarter they don't."

"And we're a long way from any landmarks, aren't we?"

"And off our planned route, too. We had to make a pretty wide turn back toward Whitehorse, and we were only halfway through it when we went down."

"How wide?"

"Could be a hundred miles, could be ten. I don't really know. Turning around in midair isn't like pivoting on a dime. The pilots would know, but . . ." She left that thought unfinished, but he could see her mind working over the idea of the pilots, dead and frozen in their cabin.

"How well did you know them?"

"Who?"

"The pilot and co-pilot."

She tilted her head to one side to look at him. "Well enough. The captain and I have worked this route together a lot. We both have family in Chicago, so we like to get back when we can."

"I suppose you get a nice discount, working for the airline."

"Discount? *Phhfpht*," she said. "After this, I better get a damn lifetime pass."

Daniel blew out a single breath, almost a laugh. "I suppose they do owe you that."

They were approaching the crest of the hill. The trees were thinning out, making it easier to see where they were but also providing fewer handholds. Daniel held his hand under Kecia's elbow once again until she stood on the summit and looked down. Far below, in one direction, they could see the smashed-up tail section, silent as a coffin, their own footprints already buried by snow. On the other side they could see the nose section, where people milled about like fleas deserting a corpse. Not for the first time Daniel wished he could fly, that it would be as simple as stretching out his arms and jumping.

"I hope they come for us soon," he said. "Going to be a long night otherwise."

He was thinking of the people down in the nose—Kerry and Phil, the rest of the walking wounded. It would be up to him and Bob, and anyone else who was still able-bodied, to keep the hurt people warm and alive until help came. He didn't want to think about the task before him if help didn't come quickly enough.

Kecia looked up at the sky. The light was changing, the dimness growing thicker, gray sinking down bit by bit into black. Pretty soon it would be night again. "You're thinking they won't be able to search for us in the dark, aren't you? That if the ELT isn't working and the black box isn't pinging, they'll never know where we are?"

"That, too. But the cold's what I'm really worried about," he said. "It's going to be pretty frigid out here soon."

"You're right. We should get downhill as soon as possible."

From up ahead, they could see Bob starting down the hill toward the nose, his way made exponentially easier with the help of gravity. Slogging through waist-deep snow became a lot easier going downhill instead of up.

"Come on. Let's get back to the others."

Daniel found a piece of metal to use for a sled and offered to let Kecia sit and rest on it for the downhill trip. She settled onto it gratefully, easing herself down with Daniel's help. She said, "I feel like I should be the one helping you. You were a passenger and I was the flight attendant."

"We're all going to need to help each other before we get out of this one," Daniel said, then turned and fixed her with a level look. She was the best resource they had to figure out what kind of help was coming, and when. If they were going to be able to wait for rescue or take matters into their own hands. If it was a matter of someone going, he knew he would be the one. And he wanted the truth from her—all the truth.

"So tell me," he said, settling behind her on the makeshift sled and getting ready to push off, "how will we know if the ELT went off the way it was supposed to? Is the cavalry really coming or not?"

She lifted her good arm so he could hold on for the long slide down, an echo of the disastrous landing they'd made just a couple of hours before. He held on tight, teetering right at the edge of the precipice, ready to push off, let go.

"I guess we wait and see," she said.

11

As *darkness closed* in around the crash site and it started to dawn on them that they might be out in the woods all night, the surviving passengers of Flight 806 started to realize they were hungry, that they hadn't eaten since breakfast. Kerry and Phil volunteered to go to the front galley to check for the food stashed there for the first-class passengers—fruit and cheese and crackers, bread and pastries and coffee, soup and pasta and grilled chicken that had long gone cold. The galley wasn't exactly overflowing—it had been only a six-hour flight, after all—but between that and what Bob had brought back from the tail, there was enough for everyone to ease their hunger until the morning, and their inevitable rescue.

Under the direction of the flight attendant Kecia, they broke open the first-class liquor supply, too, bottles of Scotch and gin, vodka and beer, good California wine. Kerry opened a small bottle of gin and had drunk half of it before she remembered her missed period, put the cap back on the bottle and the bottle in her pocket. Maybe gin wasn't such a good idea under the circumstances.

"You okay?" Phil asked.

"Yeah. Just saving the rest for later."

They passed out the alcohol, which warmed them and made them relax, and soon everyone was falling asleep, the cabin filling with the soft sound of snoring and the rustling of people settling down for the night. Lit by a single flashlight, which gave everything the look of a slumber party for the damned, the cabin had been cleared of broken seats, debris and bodies, which were now outside in the cold, already half-buried in the snow.

Kerry didn't want to think about all those bodies, the people who had been alive just this morning. She squirmed and tried to get more comfortable on her hard, cold piece of floor, but no matter which way she turned, something was poking her—a person, a piece of metal, a bit of plastic.

"Can't sleep?" Daniel said in her ear, tightening his arms around her.

"Not really," she said, drawing up her knees to her chin for extra warmth. "I know you're going to wake me in an hour or so anyway."

"No choice. Beverly says I need to wake you every couple of hours to make sure you're still conscious."

"I wonder if anyone's ever told Beverly she's a royal pain in the ass," Kerry whispered. Beverly was, in fact, asleep at her back. Either she didn't hear Kerry's insult or didn't care.

Daniel looked over Kerry's shoulder at the sleeping nurse. "I think she would consider that a compliment," he said.

Kerry reached up and touched his face, feeling the stubble beginning to pop on his chin; it had been nearly a full day since he'd last shaved. She wasn't sure she'd ever seen Daniel with so much beard—he said beards made him itchy—but she decided she liked it. It lent his appearance a bit of roughness that made him even more appealing, new almost, both familiar and strange at the same time.

He wasn't settling in to sleep. There was a wakefulness to him, a watchfulness, that she knew all too well.

"Don't stay up tonight," she said. "You need to sleep, too."

He rearranged his limbs, trying to get comfortable, and said, "I'll sleep when we're rescued."

"You can't take on everything yourself."

She was afraid—afraid for him, and for herself. Kerry was uncomfortably aware that the dizziness she'd been feeling all day was growing. At first it had been mild, nothing more than a bit of a tilt at the edge of her perception, but all afternoon the dizziness had grown, so that now every time she closed her eyes she felt as if the cabin were lurching sideways, about to tip her over, and then the sickening sense of falling from a great height. That was the real reason she didn't want to close her eyes: it was like reliving the crash over and over again.

Combined with a slight queasiness that had only grown worse since she ate her bit of cold chicken for dinner, the feeling had Kerry worried. If she were pregnant, if what she feared were true, then the baby would suffer from everything she suffered from. There were other people here more damaged than she was—people with crushed and broken bones, people with puncture wounds, people dead—but she knew what she was feeling wasn't usual or ordinary. She just didn't want to tell Daniel, didn't want him to worry, especially when he could do nothing to stop it or make it better.

She was falling again, the plane lurching to the side, and she jerked herself back to equilibrium.

"Are you cold?" Daniel asked, wrapping himself more closely around her.

"Everyone's cold," she muttered, "but thanks. It does help."

"Go to sleep," he said. "I'll wake you in a bit."

She closed her eyes, but she couldn't seem to sleep. It was like a hand just out of reach—she couldn't grab hold of it. "I'm glad you're still here," she told him. "I don't know what I'd do if . . ."

He untangled the hair from her face and brushed his lips against her ear. "I'm glad you're still here, too."

They didn't talk about who wasn't there any longer, but they were both thinking it, their thoughts outside with the bodies in the snow.

As promised, Daniel hadn't told her about Judy when he returned. He hadn't needed to—she'd seen him coming down the hill toward them with a dark-skinned woman of about forty wearing a flight attendant's uniform and cradling her broken arm in front of her. Kerry had glimpsed them out the back of the cabin and had felt the cry reach her throat before she could stop herself. Judy wasn't with him. Judy was dead. Daniel had folded her in his arms and let her cry until she was wrung out.

Afterward, exhausted and heartsick, she'd watched Daniel and Bob and Kecia taking charge of the other passengers, organizing a group of the less wounded to clear the cabin of broken seats and dead bodies, another group to go outside to look for wood for a fire, a third to gather up whatever clothes and blankets they could find. Daniel had stood out clearly in the middle of the crowd, quietly giving orders, and Kerry had been amazed at how calmly the other passengers listened to him and accepted what he was saying as the course of action they should take. Maybe it was only that they were shell-shocked, or maybe they were glad to follow anyone who gave the impression he knew what he was doing, but they did as he asked without arguing. Daniel was a natural at this, she realized—he was at his most calm and collected when everyone else was falling apart. She closed her eyes and thanked God he'd been spared. That they both had been.

By the time it was full dark, the teams of passengers had come back with stacks of firewood, though it quickly became clear the storm had made everything too damp to burn. Even the seat cushions would not catch, though the passengers made a good attempt at lighting them. Flame-retardant, Kecia said—to protect the passengers in a cabin fire. "Ironic, isn't it?" She shrugged and pulled her coat around her more tightly.

When it was clear they wouldn't have a fire that night, Daniel and Bob stacked the firewood inside the cabin to dry and organized the healthy passengers into a team again, asking them to take all the carry-on bags and stuff up the hole in the fuselage to keep the wind and snow out until morning.

When the others started grumbling about why they were preparing to spend the night at the crash site instead of signaling to the rescue planes that should be arriving any minute, Daniel explained about the ELT and the black box and said it was likely the storm would prevent anyone from reaching them until it blew itself out. "We're probably going to be spending the whole night out here," he said, with an authority in his voice that Kerry recognized was the same one he used in his job, "and if we don't have a fire, the only warmth we have is each other. We have to stay as warm as possible as long as possible, if we still want to be here in the morning for someone to find us."

So they'd huddled together on the floor of the cabin for warmth, one after another after another, like spoons in a drawer, covered with coats and sweaters and whatever blankets they could find, their collective breath making the inside of the plane a bit steamy, a bit close, like a barn stuffed with animal smells and sounds. Beverly was sleeping on the other side of her, and Phil on the other side of Daniel, back to back to back. Somewhere in one of the corners, the flight attendant, Kecia, huddled with the other flight attendant, Amber, the two of them murmuring to each other. Bob was here somewhere, too—every so often Kerry saw him get up, move aside a couple of the suitcases, and head outside to grab a smoke in the wind. Apparently he wasn't sleeping any better than Kerry was.

Every two hours, without fail, Daniel would gently shake Kerry awake and ask her how she felt, and at each wake-up call, she felt herself growing more sad and frustrated. She wanted to sleep—not just because the concussion made her sleepy (though it did), but because for those minutes she was asleep she didn't have to remember where they were and why. She didn't have to remember that Judy was dead.

Now she watched Bob stand up, stretch and step carefully over the sleeping passengers on the floor of the cabin, heading out for his fourth cigarette of the night. The minute he moved a piece of luggage, a gust of cold air and snow blew down the length of the cabin, making the rest of the passengers shiver. He always kept a spare pack on him at any time, but she'd seen him smoke at least ten so far. At this rate, he'd run out well before they were rescued, Kerry thought. Would serve him right.

Now she brushed a few snowflakes from her eyelashes, turning toward Daniel, sliding one arm underneath him and pulling him to her. The familiarity of him pressed against her made her think of their bed at home, the down comforter, the feather pillows smelling of lavender. The light from the city outside reflected on his face. She whispered, "I wish we were alone right now. I wish we were home in our own bed and you could make love to me tonight." She slid her hands up his back, running her fingers in the groove of it, and tried to imagine they were at their apartment in the city, listening to the sounds of traffic below and not the howling of the fierce northern wind.

He let out a breath as if he'd been holding it and kissed her very gently on the forehead. "I would like that, too. Soon, sweetheart. I promise."

"I hate—I hate this. Being so close to you and not able to really touch you. I need you right now. I wish all these people weren't here."

"I know. Me, too." He shifted and pulled her closer. "I can wait, though. We have the rest of our lives to be together."

She rubbed her cold nose against the middle of his chest, trying to warm it. "Do you really think they'll come for us in the morning?"

"Absolutely," he said. "Without question."

"Daniel."

"Okay, okay. I think so. I hope so."

"You know you can always tell me the truth."

He shifted with either impatience or because the floor was as uncomfortable to him as it was to her. "The ELT should lead them to us—that's what Kecia said—so they should have a decent idea about where we are. They should be able to hear our signal and come find us."

"That's a lot of *shoulds*."

Daniel tucked his hands underneath her arms to keep them warm. "The signals don't always go off the way they're supposed to. That's what she said. They work about seventy-five percent of the time."

"Comforting." Kerry closed her eyes. "You could have said so. When you came back. You could have said there was a chance no one would know where we are."

He put his chin on top of her hair, making a cave of his body, curled around her. "I didn't want everyone to panic. There was so much to get done. People act more rationally when they think things are working the way they're supposed to. When they think the people in charge are largely competent and know what to expect. Or even that there *is* someone in charge, in a situation like this."

She tilted her head up to look at him. "Why does that someone have to be you?"

He gave a little half-laugh and pulled her closer. "Don't worry, babe, tomorrow we'll get out of here and go home. Go back to our lives the best we can. I will gladly relinquish the reins the moment that happens."

"And if we aren't rescued?"

"Let's worry about that tomorrow," he said, kissing her ear. "Right now I just want to hold you while you sleep. Go ahead and close your eyes, babe."

"I can't. I'm scared to. I'm scared I won't wake up."

"Don't be. I'm here, I'll look out for you. I promise."

She tightened her grip on his shoulders, feeling the tension there, the strain he was bearing on behalf of them all—just like he had in Barrow, just like he always did. "You always take too much on yourself. Let Bob or Phil or one of the others take care of the rest of the passengers."

"It's my job."

"Not this time it isn't." She was silent for a moment, thinking. "Daniel?"

"What is it?"

"I have something to tell you. I don't know how you're going to feel about it."

He sat up on his elbow, alert. "Okay. I'm listening."

"I missed my period."

Silence. Then: "Wait, what?"

"I figured it out yesterday, before you got back. I took a test and everything. I'm definitely pregnant."

"How did this . . . ?" Daniel started to say, then she felt him sit up and shake his head. "Never mind. I don't care how it happened, I think it's great."

"You do?"

"Of course I do. We're getting married in two weeks, aren't we? So this is a little sooner than we might have planned, but we always wanted kids."

"So you're happy?" She sat up and looked at him. He was smiling, his light-brown eyes dark inside the plane.

"I'm thrilled. It's not the time or the place I would have imagined hearing this kind of news, but I couldn't be more thrilled."

"I'm so glad. I didn't know how you were going to take it. I wanted to wait to tell you until we got home."

"Go to sleep, Kerry. I know you're exhausted," he said, and kissed the top of her head with a little sigh. "It will all be okay. I promise."

She closed her eyes and tried to go to sleep once more, but the world kept on spinning and spinning, and she kept thinking of the baby growing inside her, the little shape curling itself inside her in the dark. It had surprised her, but she knew now that she wanted the baby, would do anything to keep it safe. It was hers and Daniel's and that was all that mattered—that, and surviving. If it weren't for the feel of Daniel there, so solid next to her, she would have been sure she was spinning right off the face of the earth.

12

A faint light had crept into the cabin by the time Daniel opened his eyes, and for a minute he wasn't entirely sure if he was awake or dreaming. His mind was still clouded with visions of ice, of flames, of blood and the sound of someone calling for help while he dug his way through a pile of junk that seemed to get deeper and deeper the faster he dug.

When he realized it was morning, that the light coming through the cracks in the wall of suitcases was daylight and that he'd slept through the night, he sat up quickly, accidentally whacking Beverly on the nose with his wrist. The nurse had been sleeping on the other side of Kerry, but now she sat up, rubbing her nose. "Ow. What was that for?"

"Sorry," he muttered. "It was an accident."

Beside him Kerry was still asleep. It had been hours since he'd woken her; the last time he looked at his watch it had been near midnight. Sometime after that he must have fallen asleep. *Damn it, how long was I out?*

Kerry lay in the dim inside of the cabin, her skin pale and freckled, and he brushed his lips against her ear. His pregnant fiancée. Could it really be true? It might be—she'd taken a pregnancy test already, and she said it had come back positive. Part of him was thrilled, of course, but the other part was very much afraid. They were already in a precarious position as it was, and to add a baby to the mix . . .

He shook her shoulders a little, but she didn't so much as stir. "Kerry," he said, "wake up, babe. It's morning."

"*Hmmpf,*" she murmured. So she could respond. She wasn't in a coma, at least.

How long was I asleep? He looked up again at the windows, which were buried under a thick blanket of heavy snow. He could see it pressed down and compacted against the Plexiglas; there must be several inches' accumulation above it, but at the back of the plane the light was growing steadily brighter, the first sign of the polar dawn, which might last as long as a couple of hours. They were below the Arctic Circle here, but it was still close to the winter solstice, and the daylight hours would still be very short. If the weather had broken, if the rescue planes were coming today, they might already be up in the air.

He held his breath and listened. The inside of the fuselage was quiet, the air thick and warm—much warmer than it had been the day before. He smelled the scent of unwashed human bodies, heard the occasional snore, the soft breathing of a couple of dozen half-frozen people, and the blast of the wind in the trees, buffeting the sides of the plane. And was that the low droning sound of a plane's engine overhead?

He stood, listening, but he couldn't tell if the sound he was hearing was a plane or merely the wind. *Their* plane, the crashed plane, was full, the luggage wall still intact. Everyone was asleep, everyone safe inside the fuselage—which meant no one was outside to signal to rescuers.

He flung himself toward the wall of carry-on bags, thinking only of getting outside, finding a way to signal the search teams and let them know there were people alive down here, people who needed help. He tripped over the passengers as he went, not listening to the curses of the people he was waking, the sounds of interrupted sleep. What did it matter if he woke everyone up if it meant they were found?

If the noise he heard *was* a plane, that meant the pilot must have been following the black box signal directly to the crash site, which meant he was in range. They'd be saved—sometime today, after they'd been airlifted out of the crash site, they'd be warm and fed, their injuries seen to, their families contacted to let them know they were alive. The dead would be buried, the injured healed. Kerry would get a doctor, a hospital, a real CAT scan and the best medical care in the world. Soon this whole nightmare would be over.

He pulled a couple of suitcases away from the opening in the fuselage, ready to see the rescue planes circling—and was met by a wall of snow instead.

It was light and soft, but deep, deeper even than he'd suspected from inside the cabin, nearly up to the top of the fuselage, where a bit of pale gray light filtered in. It was still snowing, hard, with no signs of stopping.

My God, Daniel thought, *even if there are rescue planes out there, could they see us? Could they even find us, in all this snow?* He stood still for a moment and listened, but the earlier sound that he'd thought was a plane's engine wasn't there any longer. If the storm was still raging, it was likely there never had been a plane. Maybe he'd imagined the whole thing. Wishful thinking. The airline wouldn't dare come after them until the storm stopped, wouldn't risk additional lives lost; they'd never be able to set down helicopters in this mess. And how much longer would the storm last until it blew itself out? Storms in Chicago rarely lasted more than a day, and twenty inches would be a lot of snowfall there, but the Yukon was not Chicago, and the storm that had been moving in from the coast the day before had been a monster by anyone's reckoning, moving up from the south and carrying a massive amount of moisture with it. Daniel tried to remember how long it had been predicted to last, but he couldn't remember now, and anyway, predictions were useless when dealing with actual conditions on the ground. It was still snowing; there was nothing he could do, whether it lasted an hour or ten.

Someone was standing behind him: it was Phil, holding his injured belly. "Great," he said, looking at the white wall that stood between the passengers and the outside world, their only exit. He looked more stricken by being trapped than he did by his own injuries. "Now what do we do?"

"We dig."

Daniel had worn his gloves all night, knowing the dangers of frostbite, and now bent to the task at hand—scooping snow out of the way so the passengers could get outside.

There was very little room to work inside the plane, so several of the less-injured passengers took turns making a hole on one side of the opening, trying to push the snow away with their hands. Daniel thought the snow might be acting as a natural insulation, keeping the inside of the plane warmer than it might have been otherwise, more protected by the wind, so they decided not to remove all the snow from the hole in the fuselage but simply make a doorway through which a single person might be able to come in and out. They stomped the loose snow underfoot and packed it down on the sides, making a kind of ramp or incline of it, until there was just enough room for one person to climb out, ducking his head to keep from bashing it on the top of the cabin.

Bob was the first out, claiming the right for himself before anyone else could speak up, and Daniel stood watching his broad back disappear up the incline and out into the weather. The snow was still falling fast, and away from the packed-down incline, the snow was deep enough that Bob sank up to his knees, sputtering and cursing. Daniel clambered out after him, standing over Bob and resisting the urge to smile or laugh while the old man struggled to pull himself out of the hole he'd fallen into.

"Need help?"

Bob looked up. "Don't be so smug, Albrecht, help me up." He held up his arms, and Daniel pulled. Together the two of them got the Petrol exec out of the deep snow.

Together they tamped down a spot around the mouth of the cabin, making a flat area that might allow the others to come outside for a minute or two when the closeness and confinement inside the fuselage got to be too much. It was a small area that was passable to them; if they needed to go much farther than a few feet around the plane, though, things would be more difficult.

Daniel kept tamping down more and more snow with his boots, trying to make the area bigger. When he was finished, Bob pulled out a cigarette and sat down on one of the suitcases to smoke, huge fat flakes of snow falling around his head and shoulders, covering him in more white. "You heard it, too?"

"What?"

"I woke up to the sound of a plane's engine. Must be one of the search-and-rescue teams looking for us."

"I don't know what I heard. I certainly didn't *see* any plane."

"You don't have to be cautious with me. It was a plane," he said, as if wanting it to be a plane made it so. "They'll be back. All we have to do is wait."

Daniel stood in the snow next to his boss, saying nothing. He wanted to believe, too, but he knew something of search-and-rescue operations, after all. He knew that the airline and the Canadian authorities wouldn't want to risk a second crash, losing more people and aircraft in this weather, especially when they probably feared that everyone aboard Denali Flight 806 was dead already, or soon would be. He knew that the bigger and more remote the area where the teams had to search, the longer and more drawn-out the process would be. It was likely the plane wouldn't even be visible from the air. The storm had dumped a prodigious amount of snow on the crash site and debris. The place where they'd put the bodies of the dead the day before was completely covered, not even visible here at ground level, and the pile of garbage from inside the cabin looked like nothing more than a small hillock of rock covered with snow. Even the long path the nose had made through the snow the day before had disappeared completely, buried in new snowfall.

No—if the ELT wasn't working properly, if it had been damaged in the crash, if they were too far off course for rescue planes to pick up the pings of the black box, the survivors would be completely invisible from the air. And that was assuming rescue crews were even in the air already, looking for them.

"You know we're not going to be able to wait forever," Bob said, stomping his cigarette out and lighting another.

Daniel raised an eyebrow at Bob, looking from the cigarette to his boss and back. "You're going to run out of those if you're not careful."

Bob shrugged and took a long puff, blowing it out like a bored dragon. "I'm not planning on being here much longer."

"Oh? You have an inside track on how long it's going to be until we're found?"

"This weather can't last much longer. And if it does, then we go find help."

"You're out of your mind. The safest place is here, with the plane. Anyone walks out of here, they'll never be seen again."

"I didn't say it had to be you, did I?"

"Who, then? Surely you're not thinking of yourself."

"I don't see why not."

Of course Bob didn't see why it shouldn't be him. He never did. He charged into situations and then made everyone else clean them up—everyone else being Daniel. Well, not this time.

Still, worry nagged at him. The passengers were cold; they had very little food or water. Most of them were hurt, some badly, especially Kerry and Phil. Daniel stood staring at the whiteness swirling overhead and knew that their best chance would be if the snow stopped in the next hour, and the rescue planes could have maybe four or five good daylight hours to find them. Find them, and airlift them to safety.

But if the rescue planes didn't find them today, people were going to die. It was that simple. Daniel thought of all the injuries he'd seen inside the plane—the broken bones, the bloody limbs, the internal injuries. At least two bad puncture wounds that he'd seen. And Kerry . . . Kerry, with her concussion and her new pregnancy, struggling to stay awake against cold and hunger and pain.

If the planes didn't come today, it was likely they wouldn't be coming at all, that they didn't know where the plane had gone down.

Someone would have to find help, Bob had said. A phone, a town. Someone would need to lead the rescuers to them.

It was insane to think about; it was suicide. Leaving the crash site and walking into the Yukon wilderness with no supplies, no food, no decent equipment? Bob was crazy even to suggest such a thing. Well, let *him* go. Daniel had people here who needed him, and he wouldn't leave them, not for anything.

He shuffled back inside, his eyes adjusting to the sudden dark. He answered the questions thrown at him by the shivering survivors as best he could: *Are we rescued? Have they found us?* He looked around at the sea of hopeful faces, the injured and sick, and shook his head, no. "Not yet," he said, trying to sound more hopeful than he felt. "But they're coming. I'm sure of it. Don't worry, everyone, it will all be over soon."

One of the younger kids said, *I want to go home!* until his mother shushed him, saying, "We all want that, so there's no use crying about it," and quieted him down again.

Daniel kept his face down, going as far forward as he could in the main cabin until he came to the place where Kerry lay on the floor. He knelt beside her and brushed the hair out of her face. She was cold, cold on her face and hands, and he picked them up and started rubbing them to warm them.

"Kerry," he said. "Open your eyes, babe. Please."

Nothing. He bent over her and brushed his hand across her cheek, across the dark circles under each eye like a dusting of soot. "Hey," he said. "Wake up. It's morning."

"Mmmm, no," she murmured, but she didn't open her eyes. She looked very young and pale, even the freckles on her nose drained of color. But they were all pale, all weak, suffering in various forms from shock and cold and lack of food. Maybe she wasn't any worse off than anyone else. Or maybe she was.

How *could* he have been so stupid, so careless, as to fall asleep when he'd promised to take care of her? He'd sworn he would keep her safe, and the moment she'd needed him the most, he'd failed. *I should have set my alarm. I should have woken myself.*

You take your eye off the ball for even just a second and someone could die.

He shook her a little more vigorously now. "Hey," he said. "Don't do this to me. Please, Kerry. I need you to look at me right now."

She stirred a little and opened her eyes, briefly fixing on him. "Something's wrong," she muttered.

"What do you mean, 'something's wrong'?" he asked, but she was out cold again—no amount of calling her name and shaking her would wake her up again this time.

"Beverly!" he exclaimed, waking half the plane with a single word.

Beverly came awake at once and crouched over Kerry. "What's wrong?"

"She opened her eyes and said, 'Something's wrong.' But then she went back to sleep, and now I can't wake her up at all."

Beverly opened each of Kerry's eyelids and flashed the emergency flashlight in them. She lowered her voice and said, "That's not good."

"What do you mean, 'not good'?"

"I'm not a doctor! Don't bark at me!" Then she took a breath and said, "I don't know all the details. She might end up with memory problems. Maybe some physical or mental impairment. If we're not careful, she could slip into a coma."

Coma. The word he'd dreaded the most. His beautiful Kerry, damaged—and pregnant. What would a coma do to the baby, out here away from anything but the most rudimentary medical care? "Would it matter if she was pregnant?"

Beverly's eyebrows lifted. "What do you mean?"

"She said she might be pregnant. A few weeks. She took a pregnancy test, and it came up positive."

Beverly shook her head as if she couldn't believe they'd been so careless; Daniel could hardly disagree with her under the circumstances.

"She needs a hospital and an EEG, maybe a CAT scan. I can't

help her like this. I don't know what else to do. I haven't worked as a nurse in eight years." Beverly put her hands out, and Daniel could see that her eyes were hard with frustration and helplessness. There was nothing any of them could do under the circumstances.

Oh, hell.

In a day, they'd gone from planning their wedding to worrying about memory loss, brain damage, coma. Death, though he knew Beverly would never say so out loud.

Come on, Kerry, wake up. Wake up and show me this is all a bad dream, that it's not as bad as I'm imagining it.

He lifted her eyelids one by one, but she still didn't stir.

"Is it a coma?" he asked.

"Not yet, I don't think. She did speak, you said. She opened her eyes. But if we don't get her help soon . . . I don't know . . ."

"Isn't there something I can do?" he begged.

"I hate this waiting around. She needs a hospital." Bev held out her hands as if to encompass the plane, the passengers, the whole sorry and sordid situation in which they all found themselves. "I don't even have decent bandages to work with here. And there are some people a lot more hurt than she is. I've treated two serious puncture wounds, and there's at least one compound fracture that I'm worried about. Not to mention your friend Phil. He might have internal bleeding and possibly bladder damage. He's very pale, and there's a hard spot in his abdomen where the leg of the chair hit him. That's usually a bad sign."

"And you haven't told him yet." Daniel looked over at the place where Phil sat with his eyes closed, leaning against the wall of the fuselage.

She glanced at him, too, as if afraid of giving away her concern. "I don't want him to worry more than he has to."

"We're all worried. He deserves to know the truth."

The former nurse shook her head and changed the subject. "Kerry needs to be airlifted out of here as soon as possible. If we can get any kind of wireless signal . . ."

"We can't. I tried, believe me. I climbed up to the top of the ridge and checked. Nothing."

"What about a fire?"

"It wouldn't do any good until the storm lifts. No one would see it."

Daniel looked over at the place where Phil sat against the wall of the cabin, his hands pressed against his abdomen as though he were trying to stem the invisible tide of blood inside his body. Daniel thought of the sound he thought he'd heard outside, the low drone of a rescue plane, or had it only been the wind?

"They'll come back soon," he said, mostly to himself.

Bob had talked about leaving, about going for help, walking toward—what? They didn't know which direction to go. Daniel had told him it was suicide, and it was.

He looked down at Kerry, all the color drained from her face, and thought, *Bob can go if he wants to, but I won't. I'm not leaving her to do his damn bidding, not this time.*

13

Phil wandered out of the fuselage into the dim midday light, shielding his eyes to watch the sky for signs of human life other than their own. He felt tired, achy and listless; the spot where the chair leg had hit him felt swollen and a little too firm, as if the flesh beneath were slowly turning to stone. Worst of all, he felt useless, one more of the walking wounded, not well enough to help gather the last of the food or wood for a signal fire, not well enough to dig or, like Beverly, treat the injured, but not sick enough to lie down or sleep, either. All he could do was sit and worry about Kerry, worry about the rescue teams that weren't coming, worry that he wasn't doing enough to help anyone or anything.

He could see Kerry asleep on the floor near the front of the cabin, deep inside where it was warmest, Daniel sitting with her head in his lap and stroking her hair, his eyes dark and haunted. Phil knew that look only too well; he'd seen it in the mirror not so very long ago.

So when the inside of the cabin started to feel like a grave, Phil had done the only sensible thing and climbed outside. The cold air on his face should have felt good after a night inside the plane with the collective breath of fifty other people, but it was too cold to be pleasant, only bitter. Yet it was the only place he wouldn't have to sit and watch Kerry and Daniel suffer, so it would have to do for the moment.

He found a couple of suitcases and piled them one on top of the other to make a seat, pulling the hood up on his coat and tucking his hands inside his pockets. Near a spot next to the fuselage, protected from the wind, a few passengers and the flight attendant from the tail section, Kecia, were trying to get a fire going, but the wood Daniel and Bob had stashed inside the cabin the night before was still damp, and the passengers were only able to get a little bit of paper to burn, a quick puff of light and smoke that flared up and went out almost in the same moment. Phil thought of offering to help, then thought better of it—there were already four people huddled around the makeshift fire pit. Everyone, it seemed, was trying to find ways to fill the hours, trying to find something useful to do with themselves while they waited for the storm to blow itself out.

After a little while Daniel came outside and sat down next to Phil on a couple of carry-on bags, watching the others at their fire-making, his face twisted with annoyance. "You might as well try to get the snow to burn," he told them. "Look how damp that spot is. You need to scrape all that snow away from the ground or you'll have nothing but a soggy mess. And you can't use that wet stuff for firewood, it won't burn."

"It might," answered the flight attendant, whose injured arm Beverly had strapped to her side. "If we can get it to catch."

"I tried it last night. No good. It might be dry enough in another day."

"We have to have a fire," said a figure in a navy-blue coat and black balaclava; Phil thought it was a man until it spoke and revealed itself as a woman. Phil didn't know why he was surprised; none of the passengers were wearing their own clothes. Everything had become communal property.

Daniel said, "Better take the wood inside and let it dry out. Tomorrow we can try again."

"We can't wait until tomorrow," the woman said, her voice rising to the edge of panic. It was the mother of the little boy with the broken teeth—Zach, Phil thought his name was. He'd never found out the mother's name. "We're going to freeze to death out here if we have to wait until tomorrow with no fire."

"Listen, the storm doesn't seem to be letting up," Daniel said. "Our best bet is to stay inside out of the wind."

"Couldn't you lie and let me hope?"

Daniel frowned. "What good would that do?"

"Another whole day." Her voice cracked and her arm went around the boy, who'd come outside looking for his mother. "What will we do?"

Her face began to crumple, and Daniel said, "I tell you what. I could use your help. I might try making some snowshoes. If we had some snowshoes, we could get around a little easier. Maybe find a cell-phone signal or something."

"Snowshoes?"

"Find some green branches, anything with leaves or needles, anything relatively thin and bendable. The lower branches would work fine." He turned to the boy, huddled close to his mother. "You look for string, or twine. Anything like that. Bring it to me when you find it."

"You know how to make snowshoes?" the boy asked.

"I do. It's easy."

"You promise?"

Daniel drew his fingers slowly across his chest. "Cross my heart and hope to die," he said.

The mother and son jumped up and scurried off to do the things Daniel had asked of them, relief on their faces.

"You really know how to make snowshoes?" Phil asked when they'd gone.

"No, but I've worn snowshoes before."

"Not really the same thing."

"I might be able to figure it out. It's kind of like a tennis racket for your foot."

"Sounds like wishful thinking to me."

"You have any better ideas?" Daniel asked. They were both silent for a minute, then Daniel said, more gently, "They needed something to do. It'll keep their minds off how scared they are."

As the woman and her son were bustling around looking for the things they'd been asked for, judging the worthiness of this or that piece of wood or bit of string, Phil started to see the purpose of it, "purpose" being the apt word. Daniel had given them something to occupy their thoughts and make them feel useful, at least for a little while. In a group of people on the edge of hysteria, a little purpose, a little direction, went a long way. It was no wonder Bob trusted Daniel so much: he understood how to deal with people in terrible circumstances.

Phil watched Daniel stand up, ducking his head to go back inside. Probably checking up on Kerry. *She needs a hospital,* Beverly had said when Phil asked the nurse about her. A doctor, an EEG scan. She needs an IV and a warm bed and something to eat.

Don't we all, Phil had said, and went outside to wait.

The snow continued all that day and into the dark hours after the sun set and the temperatures dropped, the wind picking up even more. The passengers who'd been sitting outside went back in, driven by hunger and cold, and Phil followed them. They'd eaten what little food they had the night before and early this morning, not bothering to ration, assuming they would be found by the end of the second day. Now there was nothing left. They were facing another night in the cold, this time with nothing to eat or drink.

This was when things would start to get bad. He'd seen it so often at accident sites, after natural disasters, whenever he had to deal with the grieving family members of dead employees. The first day of bad news was always one of shock and slow, desperate acceptance. It was the second day when the anger started, when people who'd received bad news started to ask themselves the hard questions: *Why my family, why now, why this?* The second day was always the loudest day, the one in which the china got broken, the cars got totaled. The second day was when Phil's real work began.

The third day, on the other hand . . . Well, with a little luck they wouldn't be out here for the third day.

It was late, and Phil was resting against the bulkhead when the flight attendant he'd spoken to immediately after the crash— Amber, her name was—went outside with a pan to scoop up a few handfuls of snow and bring it inside for the thirsty passengers. She'd already handed out several handfuls of the stuff when Daniel started shouting, "Don't do that!" startling Amber into dropping the snow, and the entire plane full of passengers turned to look at him. "It will drop your body temperature! You'll give everyone hypothermia."

The flight attendant stopped and gave him an irritated look. "What do you suggest we drink? Urine? People are dehydrated."

"Look, we can live a couple of days without water, but not if we all freeze to death first."

"I don't remember you being in charge here."

"I'm telling you, if you give them snow to drink, you will kill them."

The passengers were looking up at this exchange, fear and horror on their faces, not sure which of the two of them to believe. On the one hand, they were thirsty. On the other hand, were they willing to risk dying for a drink of water?

Amber shoved the pan of snow at Daniel and said, "Fine, then *you* be the one to tell them they can't have anything to drink."

"Fine."

Phil watched this blowup in alarm. Just minutes ago Daniel had managed the situation outside with care, taking into consideration the fragile emotional state of the survivors, but now he was causing just as many problems as he was solving, starting to crack under the strain of *why me, why now?* "Hey," Phil said to Daniel in a hoarse voice. "Don't scare them. They're already scared enough."

"Someone has to keep everyone alive," Daniel said. "You going to do it?"

Phil ignored that dig and said, "You're taking too much on yourself. Why don't you check on Kerry again? Maybe get a little rest?"

"Don't tell me how to do my job, and I won't tell you how to do yours."

Phil didn't answer. All day Daniel had been bearing the weight of Kerry's illness, of the frustration and fear of the rest of the passengers. His emotions were stretched to the breaking point, and his co-worker was nothing more than an easy target. Phil knew that. He wasn't taking it personally.

Phil only said, "This isn't a Petrol accident. None of this is your job."

Daniel stopped what he was doing and fixed Phil with a long, level gaze, long enough that Phil could see the things he was fighting with contending in his expression: fear for Kerry, for all of them; anger at the situation in which they found themselves; exhaustion; the desire to keep busy, to be useful.

Finally his shoulders slumped, and he said, "That's how it's feeling right now. That it's my job to keep everyone alive."

"It's not, though. Your job doesn't have you looking after Kerry. It doesn't have you working without food or water or electricity in the middle of the wilderness."

He leaned forward to put his head on his knees. "I can't help feeling like it's all up to me. If even the flight attendants don't know enough not to give people snow to drink . . . I mean, *how* are we going to keep everyone alive long enough to be rescued?"

Phil didn't say anything for fear he'd betray himself. He was in love with Daniel's fiancée, and that fact had long kept him from making friends with this man, had made Phil dislike and resent everything about him, but the truth was that he admired Daniel, admired the way he didn't sit around feeling sorry for himself, he *did* things, took charge. No wonder Kerry loved him, had chosen him. Daniel was the kind of person other people looked up to, the kind of person other people followed. Just then Phil wanted, for once in his life, to be that kind of man himself.

Phil pressed a hand against the sore spot near his bladder as if he could contain his pain. He said, "I don't blame you for being worried. I'm worried, too. But don't take it out on them."

Daniel gave Phil a look that changed from anger to surprise to something that looked like grudging respect, all within the space of a few seconds. "You're right," he said. "I'm sorry. I was out of line."

"I'm not really the one you should be apologizing to."

Daniel nodded, then approached the flight attendant and knelt down. He was sorry, he said—he didn't mean to scare her, but he *did* need to ask that no one eat snow in place of water. It would make them too cold, as cold on the inside as they were on the outside, and right now they needed to be warm, to horde their warmth like misers with gold. Amber had nodded grudgingly and asked, "Okay, then. What do we do?"

Daniel grinned, his expression reversing back to its usual cheerfulness. "I'll teach you the trick of it. You melt the water in your armpit."

She wrinkled her nose. "That's disgusting," she said.

"Not really. Watch."

Daniel knelt and scooped up the snow in Amber's tray into an empty plastic bottle, showing her how to tuck it into her coat, inside her armpit, to melt the snow into drinkable water. After a few minutes went by, the flight attendant pulled out the plastic bottle to reveal several swigs of drinkable water inside. "See?" Daniel said, watching her open up the bottle and take a drink. "*Voilà*! Water for everyone."

"Won't it take a long time to make everyone enough to drink it this way?" Amber asked.

"It may interfere with our big plans to sit around freezing to death, sure, but I think we can manage," Daniel said, but the flight attendant gave him a tentative smile, the tension finally broken. Phil was gratified to see that Daniel's defensiveness and sarcasm were completely gone now, replaced by his usual easygoing manner. He'd be all right for a little while longer. Until tomorrow, anyway.

When the passengers had all been given plastic water bottles for their own drinking water, Daniel came back and sat down beside Phil. "So," he said.

"So."

"You were right, I was acting like it was a job site and I was in charge."

"Only natural. That's what you do all the time—you clean up disasters."

Daniel looked up at Phil, his face going gray as the light faded. "And you're a human-resources director. You manage people."

"I try."

"I'm sorry about before," Daniel said, his expression full of something new that Phil had never seen before—respect, maybe. "I was out of line."

"It's fine. You're worried about Kerry. Anyone could see that."

He'd almost said *scared* but knew that would be going too far. They were not really friends, after all.

"But anyone wasn't paying attention," Daniel said. "You were."

"I've seen it before." Phil looked carefully down at his hands. He didn't want Daniel to know just how closely he'd been paying attention. "Plenty of times."

Now Daniel was the one paying attention. "Plenty of times, but one time in particular." He narrowed his eyes at Phil. "One time when it was you, in my situation."

Phil said nothing. Saying it out loud had always been difficult for him.

"Who was it?" Daniel asked quietly. "Girlfriend? Wife?"

"Wife," he said.

"What happened?"

"Ovarian cancer."

"Sounds bad."

"It was." To Phil's relief, the other man didn't cluck or make sympathetic noises or give him any hollow words of condolence. He sat for a while listening, watching the passengers huddling down for the night, curling around each other, while Phil told him about how fast everything had happened: the diagnosis, the treatments that didn't work, the way the disease had robbed Emily of everything by the end, even her humor, even her beautiful mind. Every once in a while Daniel rubbed his hands on his jeans, both men's thoughts on the sick woman in the corner. *If she died* . . . But Phil wouldn't think about it. Not yet.

"That wasn't the worst of it, though."

"No?"

The sound of Daniel's voice startled him. He'd almost forgotten the other man was there. It was like being in a confessional, he thought, like telling all his sins to a priest. Daniel never interrupted, didn't judge or cringe or turn away as Phil told all his darkest, most appalling secrets.

"I ran away. Near the end. She'd been so vicious to me all day, telling me I was killing her, that I wanted her dead. She slapped me and kicked me. I mean, I knew it was the medicine making her act that way. The hospice nurses had warned me she'd have mood swings, that I wouldn't even recognize her sometimes, but I never thought she would *hate* me so much." He was still, the noises of the wind outside and the soft snoring of people the only sounds besides his voice. "One night I just had enough. I'd worked a ten-hour day and then went straight home to let the nurse go, but nothing I did was right. The look in Emily's eyes—it was like she wasn't even the same person. I got up and walked out of the house and left my dying wife alone in our living room. I was gone for three hours."

This piece of information, possibly the most painful thing Phil had ever said out loud, still didn't seem to faze Daniel. He only asked, "Where did you go?"

"I hardly remember. I went to the lake for a little while. Parked my car and just sat there, watching the moon come up over the water. I couldn't believe this was my life. Then after a little while, I turned the car around."

Daniel was sitting and listening, nothing more. "Then what happened?"

"Then nothing. I came home."

Daniel said, "But there's more to it than that, isn't there? Something you've been blaming yourself for all this time."

"I—"

How much could he trust Daniel, really? How much could he live with the man knowing, with anyone knowing what he'd done? What he'd nearly allowed to happen?

They were probably going to die out here anyway. What did it matter if he confessed his most grievous sins?

He said, "I didn't even know how long I was gone until I got back and found the home-health nurse there, and the fire department. Emily was passed out on the kitchen floor. She'd been trying to make herself soup and accidentally left a kitchen towel on the stove. It caught on fire."

"Jesus."

He screwed his eyes shut and rushed onward. "If a neighbor hadn't seen the smoke coming out of the house and called the fire department, Emily would have burned the house down. She would have burned to death there in the house, because I left my dying, delirious, hallucinating wife alone for more than three hours.

"She was right where I'd left her, but she was crying and calling for me. When I went to her, she said, 'I thought you weren't coming back.' I mean, who does that? How could I have abandoned her?"

"You didn't do anything wrong."

"Didn't I?"

"You didn't. But I understand why you'd blame yourself."

It was nearly full dark, but Daniel didn't say anything more. Phil looked around the fuselage, at the passengers huddling together once more against the cold. Maybe it was the fact that they weren't looking at each other that was making it possible, for the first time, for Phil to talk about Emily with someone. Or maybe it was because he knew Daniel couldn't see his face. Or maybe it was simply that Daniel was the first person he'd known who didn't pity him, who knew exactly what it was Phil had suffered all those days by Emily's bedside. He'd seen it in the man's face, hovering over Kerry: the look of utter and complete helplessness in the face of someone else's suffering.

Phil stood and went to move back to his own piece of floor, but he couldn't let the moment go: Daniel was still there, still listening. "If I could do it all again, I'd never let go, not for a second. Those three hours were a gift, and I threw them away."

He lay back down in the dark and curled around himself, his memories making sleep impossible. If only he could go back and do it all over, he thought. How different things would be then.

14

That afternoon, the boy Zach and his mother had brought Daniel a number of green branches and enough shoelaces to reach from one end of the cabin to the other. Daniel had praised the boy's ingenuity in coming up with a good substitute for string. "Shoelaces!" he'd said. "What a clever idea. I would never have thought of that on my own." And the boy had beamed.

Now, unable to sleep, Daniel asked Kecia for one of the working flashlights, and he and Zach sat down to make snowshoes while Zach's mother—Alice, her name was—watched nearby, wrapped in several coats and smiling a little at her son's boyish enthusiasm. It must be hard for her, being out here with him on her own, Daniel thought, and then he wondered about the boy's father, if he was at home waiting by the phone for word of his wife and son. He pictured the man—a solitary figure in khakis and a sweater, his damp-combed hair done in a neat part—arriving in Whitehorse with the rest of the families, pale and nervous, drinking bad hospitality-suite coffee and chatting halfheartedly with the other mothers and fathers and sons and daughters, tense and unhappy, waiting for news, dreading it, halfway convinced that the worst had already happened and hoping wholeheartedly it had not. He thought about all the mothers and fathers on board the plane, the living ones and the dead, and their families waiting for word of them, anything but waiting around, not knowing. It was not only Kerry who needed saving.

Daniel put his head down, talking to the boy quietly over their work, afraid to disturb the others, though it was only near six o'clock, long before bedtime, and inside the plane no one was really asleep. But it felt wrong to raise their voices inside the cabin somehow, like disturbing people praying in church. So Daniel and Zach sat with their heads together and whispered to each other—instructions from Daniel, questions from Zach—while they worked on the task of making snowshoes out of shoelaces and branches.

At one point Zach stopped and looked at Daniel. "Have you done this before?" he asked.

"Made snowshoes? No."

"Then how do you know it will work?" the boy asked.

Daniel thought a minute about how he should answer that. "Well, I don't exactly *know*," he said. "I think it will work. I've worn snowshoes before. Not ones like these—metal ones, bought at the store—but these aren't so different from the ones that people have been making for thousands of years in these parts of the world."

"Really?" the kid asked. "Thousands of years?"

"Yep. The native people learned how to do it. Mostly you want to distribute your weight outward so you don't sink straight down in the snow. With some good strong shoelaces and branches, we should be able to make a decent pair of snowshoes."

"What are you going to do with them?"

"Well," Daniel said, weighing his words carefully, "I might be able to gather more firewood, or look for more food. Maybe I could make it to the top of the hill and see a town or a road, something like that. The snowshoes will make it easier for me to walk now that the snow is so deep."

Zach was getting excited now. "You're going to help the rescuers find us?"

"Zach," his mother warned. The kid's face fell.

Daniel said, "I can't go far. Here we have a place to sleep that's warm and dry, and we have each other to help if we need it. If I left, I'd have to go by myself. It would be very dangerous."

"What about our phones? My mom has a phone. Isn't there a way we can call?"

"The phones don't work if there are no signal towers nearby, and out here there are no towers, because there are no towns and no people. Besides, we haven't been able to charge our phones in two days. The phone batteries are all dead."

The boy looked over at the place where Kerry lay unconscious, her head cradled for the moment in Beverly's lap. The nurse was stroking her hair and touching the spot near her temple where she'd hit it in the crash. "The red-haired lady. She's your girlfriend?"

"That's right."

"Doesn't she need a doctor?"

"Yes, she needs a doctor. She's very sick."

The boy was quiet, holding the ends of the branch together to make the frame of the snowshoe while Daniel tied it tight with the shoelaces. "I hope they find us in time," the boy said.

"Me, too," said Daniel.

He tied the ends of the snowshoe together and then began weaving the shoelaces across the frame, diagonally at first and then in and out, but as it turned out he didn't tie it tightly enough, and as soon as he pressed down in the center of it with his hand, the shoelaces gave, pulling the frame apart with them, so that Zach ended up holding the long green stick and a lap full of multicolored shoelaces.

"Well," Daniel said, "*that* wasn't the right way to go about it. Let's try again."

On his second attempt Daniel wrapped the branch with a shoelace first and used the wrapping to anchor the diagonal lines in place. He anchored two short branches in the center of the snowshoe for cross-pieces and wrapped them with laces as well, tying everything so firmly that even when he pressed down in the center of it, it barely gave. Better. It might actually hold his weight. The only question was for how long?

The second snowshoe was even more difficult than the first one. The branch he'd chosen was too dry, too brittle to bend, and snapped in half when he went to close the loop. He had to send Zach's mother to the woodpile with a flashlight for another branch. Luckily, the one she brought back this time was green, long as Daniel's leg, and with a little manipulating, Daniel was able to get a second snowshoe ready to go.

He was brushing pine needles off his lap when Bob came over. "What are you doing?"

"Making snowshoes."

"Bullshit."

"Watch the language around the kid," Daniel said, but Bob didn't apologize.

"About time we took matters into our own hands. This mean we're going to take off in the morning?" he said.

"No. It means we're making snowshoes, and that's all."

"We should walk out of here. Get some help."

Daniel didn't think Bob knew the slightest thing about what he was saying. Walk into the Yukon wilderness in December in homemade snowshoes, with no fire and no equipment? The guy was insane. "We need to stay with the wreck."

"Listen, you think Kerry's going to last much longer? You said yourself she's barely conscious. We have no food, no water. God only knows how long this storm is going to last. You and me, Daniel, we have the chance to do something here, really do something."

Like get ourselves killed? Daniel thought. "I'm not going any farther than the top of that next hill, the one to the west. If I don't see anything, I'm coming straight back down to wait. That's all," Daniel said, but he knew better than to disabuse his boss of an idea once he got it into his head. The old man was right about Kerry, even if he was wrong about the two of them being able to do anything to help. Still, Daniel was genuinely surprised when Bob asked, "You got enough for a second pair of those?"

"Not really." There were maybe three or four shoelaces left, hardly enough for a full pair of snowshoes.

"I'll have to see if I can find something else to work with, then."

"What for?" Daniel asked, already dreading the answer.

"I'm coming with you."

Daniel shook his head. "Bob, no, don't even think about it. We need to stay near the shelter. Going out into this weather without the proper equipment is insane."

"We can't sit around and wait. Some of these people are seriously hurt. You said yourself that the ELT was probably damaged. If we can find a road or a house and let people know where we're at, why wouldn't we do it?"

Daniel didn't want to say what he was really thinking: that Bob was in no kind of shape for the trek to come, nor did he have the slightest idea of how quickly exposure to the elements could shut down a human body. Daniel didn't want to be saddled with him out in the wilderness, just the two of them, miles from help or even the limited comfort of the plane's fuselage. If he got sick, if he collapsed . . .

"I can't sit around here all day waiting," Bob said. "It's driving me nuts. All these people with nothing to do."

"We need to stay here to look after them. We can help them plan and organize, get ready for when the rescue planes come."

"Phil can do it."

"You're not thinking clearly. What happens if the weather clears up and the rescue planes find the crash site? We would be caught away from the wreck. They'd never find us. Not to mention it will be hard going. *Very* hard going. Walking in snowshoes isn't like taking a stroll in the city."

Bob narrowed his eyes at Daniel and said, "You telling me you think I'm too old and out of shape to go with you?"

Daniel looked at Bob's well-fed physique, but he only said, "I wouldn't dream of saying so."

"Hmph. You know me well enough to know I'm doing this whether you want me to or not. Now, show me how to make a pair of these things."

Daniel shook his head. There was no reasoning with the man. He could make all the snowshoes he wanted, but one trip up to the top of the ridge huffing and puffing the whole way would show him how wrong he was. If he even *made* it to the top. Daniel said, "Have it your way. I can't stop you."

Bob turned to the boy. "You think you could find more branches for me? You found all the best ones last time."

The boy beamed and ran back to the woodpile, but Daniel said, "I don't know what we're going to use for laces. The kid scrounged everything he could find, even off the bodies outside."

"There's no more string?"

"You know where to find some, I'm all ears. Planes don't carry much except basic necessities."

Bob thought a minute, then leaned over to ask Kecia if there had been any duct tape aboard. She gave him a small smile. "Yes," she said. "We keep it on board in case we ever need to secure an unruly passenger."

Bob looked surprised. "And have you?"

She was still grinning. "Once or twice, maybe."

"Do you know where it is?"

"I'll give it a look," she said, and disappeared toward the first-class galley.

"What else are we going to need for this little expedition?" Bob asked.

Daniel sighed, thinking. "Extra clothes, as many as we can put on. There's no food left."

"I stashed some. Some bags of pretzels, some water, a couple of sandwiches I brought back from the tail."

Daniel was silent. Bob had hidden away food that could have been feeding the passengers, thinking only of himself as usual. It didn't matter. Bob was Bob no matter where he went. He was always thinking of himself first. "Fine," Daniel said.

"What else?"

"A map of the area would be nice."

"Can't help you there."

"Didn't think you could, but since I was wishing . . ." He thought a minute. "A couple of empty water bottles instead. Um. Snow goggles."

"You think they have any on board?" Bob asked.

"We can make some. A strip of dark cloth will do the trick. We can tie it around our eyes and cut slits in it to see through. If the sun comes out, it's going to get awfully bright out there. Our eyes won't last half a day."

"How would you know that?"

"Ever gone for a walk in the snow? It doesn't take a genius to figure out."

"Okay, Grizzly Adams. Anything else?"

"A compass, though I doubt we have much chance of finding one."

"There's a compass on my watch."

He held up his heavy titanium military watch for Daniel to see, showing off the compass dial on the face. Daniel had often noticed the watch and wondered why his boss had spent ten grand on such a thing. He couldn't really have known there would be a time when such a thing would be helpful, even necessary.

Daniel shook his head at the senior VP and said, "All right. We have a compass."

"So what's the plan, then?"

"If we're lucky, the snow will have stopped in the morning and we won't need a plan."

"If we were lucky, we wouldn't have crashed in the first place. Now, seriously, which way should we go?"

"Don't think we're going farther than up that hill," Daniel said, "because that's it. We go to the top to see if we can spot any manmade landmarks. Roads, bridges, that kind of thing. If not, then we come back down."

"And if we do see any landmarks?"

"We try to use my phone to signal. If that doesn't work, we build a fire. The bigger the better."

"With all this wet crap?"

"We bring some dry kindling to get it going. Anyway, the wet stuff smokes more."

Bob nodded along to all of this. Daniel could see him thinking it over, could see his jaw working the problem like a mule chomping at the bit. He wasn't going to give up on the idea of walking out of here to find help; once he seized upon an idea, he'd never let it go. But he only said, "Good as any plan we're likely to come up with."

Bob sat in his spot on the floor nearest the first-class cabin, pulling one of the thin airline blankets around himself and settling down to wait for the boy to return with branches to make himself a pair of snowshoes. In the dim light, Bob's white hair looked like a crown, like something out of an old legend or fairy tale. *There's no way,* his face said, *that a man like me is going to die out here.* "Bet you never thought you'd be managing a disaster from the inside, did you?" he said to Daniel, who shook his head. The old man was *enjoying* this. He wasn't thinking about the hardships they were going to face away from the plane, he was only thinking about being a hero. And Daniel had let himself be goaded into it, once again: letting Bob bully him into taking a risk he knew was foolish.

"You're right, Bob," said Daniel. "I never did see myself like this."

If the old man thought he would goad Daniel into walking all the way into Whitehorse, though, he was sadly mistaken. Daniel was going to the top of the hill, and that was that. He wasn't going to abandon Kerry here in the wilderness. He wasn't going to let her go.

That night Daniel lay curled around Kerry in the dark, willing not only his body heat but his health, his strength, into the frail form beside him. Her and the baby both.

He was tired but not tired enough to keep his mind off the tasks he still had to do, the decisions he still had to make, hoping beyond hope that when he woke in the morning the sun would be shining and the question of whether to stay or to go would have been taken out of his hands.

When he wasn't worrying over the trip to come, he was reliving the entire plane ride, starting first at the airport in Anchorage, when he'd watched the news and been relieved the flight was being allowed to leave. When the flight attendant came on the intercom and said they would begin boarding, he should have turned to Kerry and suggested they get a hotel for a couple of nights, wait out the storm. He should have known then. But she'd been so glad to be on her way home, where they'd start planning for their wedding just a couple of weeks away, and he had to admit he'd been relieved, too. He'd wanted to go home. They all had.

Then he was blaming himself for taking the aisle seat and leaving Kerry the bulkhead. If he'd taken the window seat, it was possible Kerry wouldn't have received such a vicious blow to the head. Daniel hated the window seat, said looking out the window made him feel ill, and Kerry had always given the aisle to him, no matter where they were flying, or for how long. Just that once, couldn't he have been more generous?

Two days they'd been out here, hurt and freezing, with no sign of rescue. He kept one ear tuned to the sky, but there was nothing but the soft silence of falling snow outside, the occasional snore of his fellow passengers, the butterfly flicker of Kerry's pulse against his cheek. *She's only asleep,* he told himself. *It isn't a coma. Beverly said so.*

Tomorrow, if everything stayed the same, he was going to have to make a difficult decision. *You need to sleep, too, and all this worrying isn't helping.* But he didn't. He lay beside her, half-awake, half-dreaming.

Sometime in the night, Kerry's whole body went rigid, her legs trembling as if she were in pain. Daniel sat up immediately. Something was terribly wrong: Kerry was stiff, her hands clenched, but no matter how he shook her she wouldn't wake.

"Beverly!" he called.

Half the passengers sat up and rubbed their eyes, wondering what was wrong. Beverly leaned over Kerry with one of the still-working flashlights, shining it into her eyes and away again, in and away.

"What is it?" Daniel asked. "What's happening?"

The nurse said, "Her pupils are not fixed and dilated, which is a hopeful sign, but . . ."

"But what?"

"She seized for a moment there. The shaking legs—that's a bad sign."

"Help her. Please help her. I'll get you anything you need."

"She needs fluids; she's dehydrated."

"Can't we get her to drink something?"

"She'd choke. She should be hooked up to an IV."

"There might be an IV in the emergency kit."

"Sure, but it's a block of ice. I already checked."

"Then what?" he begged, his patience wearing thin. "What can I do? Tell me anything and I'll do it. What would you do if she came into the emergency room?"

"If she came into my ER unconscious and seizing, I'd intubate her and sedate her."

"That sounds bad."

"It *is* bad. All of this is very bad." The tiny woman was shaking her head, and Daniel could see tears in her eyes: tears of helplessness, of rage, of resignation. This was where they were now: not alive or dead but somewhere in between.

Daniel knelt near the bulkhead and pressed his forehead against the cold plastic, feeling his own knees tremble, feeling the breath in his lungs threatening to choke him. The decision he'd been dreading the past two days was on him now.

"What are you going to do?" she asked.

He looked up at the gray sky, the low clouds, the first changes in the light that preceded dawn. All night he'd hoped and prayed for the snow to stop, for the sun to rise, for the survivors to be rescued. He'd wanted the decision taken out of his hands, the decision of whether to go or to stay.

"The only thing I can do," he said. "I'm going to try to get us all some help."

15

"*We're almost to Edmonton,*" I say. "Twenty miles. We should probably stop there for the night."

For the last hour, Jackson's been quiet in the back of the car, listening. This part of the story is another thing we've never really explained in detail—just how hurt Kerry was in the accident, how badly her life was threatened. I go quiet for a while, listening to the sound of the road under the tires, the *swish-swish* of the wipers clearing the windshield of a light, sleety snow. There are more buildings here, the towns closer together, signs for hotels and restaurants springing up along the highway. It seems a good time for a breather, to let our son take in everything we've told him so far, absorb it.

"Where do we want to stop?" Kerry asks, reading the signs one by one. "Look, this one has a pool, honey. What do you think?"

But Jackson isn't thinking about pools or even dinner, which is how I know the story is really getting to him: he's not the kind of kid who ignores his stomach. He says, "Is that why you sometimes have nightmares, Mom? Because you were hurt in the accident?"

Next to me I feel my wife stiffen. She says, "Sometimes. I don't remember this part really well. Your dad knows more about it than I do and a lot of this story was told to us by other people who were there, after it was all over. I was pretty sick. It was scary, for a while. We didn't know how it was going to turn out."

"I didn't know you could have died. I mean, I've heard you talking about the time you hurt your head, but I didn't know it was so bad."

"In some ways I was really lucky. Other people were hurt worse than I was." She touches the black journal in her lap. I know very well what's in there, what it says. Jackson will, too, soon. And what will happen then? Will it change him? I wonder. Will it change all of us, the life we've built?

He's quiet again for another minute. The radio is playing some oldies, David Bowie singing "Modern Love." "It must have been scary for you, too, Dad," he says.

"It was," I say. "We were all scared. But I suppose if we were never scared, we'd never need to be brave, would we?"

In the rearview mirror, I see him working his jaw, see him come to a decision. He says, "Yeah. That makes sense."

In the car the three of us go quiet. "Okay," I say, coming up on a hotel that looks clean, just off the highway. "Let's stop here. Should we get pancakes?"

"Sounds good to me," Jackson says. The moment's over. Tomorrow we'll have more to tell him, but for now it's time to rest.

16

When the sun rose, the snow was still falling, the sky was still low and gray, and after another long and nearly sleepless night, Phil opened his eyes to the sight of Daniel, grim-faced, shaking him awake.

"Hey," he said, looking around. "Can I talk to you about something? I need your help."

"Can't it wait?" Phil rolled over and felt a throb at the tender spot in his belly, felt the numbness at the tips of his fingers and his nose. He felt sluggish, unable to think clearly. He was aware of pain, and that something was wrong with him, but he couldn't remember just at that moment what it was or how it had happened. His head was still full of half-remembered dreams: endless ice, endless cold, and something lost in the whiteness that he was looking for but could not find.

Daniel shook him again. "It can't, I'm sorry."

Phil sat up a little too quickly, the reality of their situation coming back to him all at once. "What happened? Is Kerry all right?"

Daniel was looking away, not at Phil but at the place where Kerry lay on the floor nearby, covered with the winter coats of the dead or missing passengers. There was a stillness about her that morning that Phil didn't like one bit. He had to resist the urge to hurry over to her and shake her awake, beg her to open her eyes.

Daniel shook his head like he was answering a question no one had asked. He said, "I need you to take care of Kerry for me for a little while. Keep her warm, keep her safe. Beverly has more than she can handle already. You'll look after her, won't you?"

It was starting to dawn on Phil just what Daniel was saying. "You're leaving?"

"I have to."

"She needs you. I won't do her any good." Phil felt his anger rising. What did Daniel mean by deserting her when she was so ill? What could be so important?

"If there were anyone else to go, I'd gladly let them."

"Anyone else *could* go. It doesn't have to be you."

"I know a little bit about surviving outdoors."

"A *little bit*? Why, because you have a house by Lake Superior? That doesn't make you qualified to lead an Arctic expedition." Phil couldn't think of anything more stupid and reckless. Hadn't Daniel told Bob, just the day before, that leaving would be suicide?

"I know that!" he said. Then: "I've spent time in the woods. Not in this kind of cold, it's true, but . . ." He looked grim. "I can't ask anyone else to go instead of me. I'm not hurt, not sick. Believe me, I've thought of all the excuses."

Phil frowned but only said, "So what are you going to do?"

"I'm going up that hill, to start with." He nodded at the heavily wooded rise to the west of the crash site, pristine under a blanket of new snow. At the top the trees thinned, showing a dark rocky out-cropping that was higher than any of the others. It would make a good vantage point. "That was the direction we were heading in when we crashed. If we're lucky, if we're close enough, I might be able to spot a town or a road from that rise. Power lines. Anything that looks man-made would do."

"And if you don't?"

"If I don't, and the rescue planes haven't come by then, then I'm going to keep going."

Phil couldn't believe what he was hearing. "Kecia said we might have been as much as three hundred miles away from Whitehorse when we went down. You going to walk the whole way?"

"I'm hoping it won't come to that. I'm hoping I'll be able to spot a road or a town. Something."

"And if not?"

"If not, we'll keep going until we do."

"Wait a minute. Who's 'we'?"

Daniel's mouth pressed into a grim line. "Bob's coming with."

"'Bob's coming'?" Phil gave a laugh of derision. "That's just great. Bob's in no kind of shape to be running up hills. He'll only slow you down. Leave him here, put him in charge of watching over Kerry and the others."

"I tried, but you know how he is. Wouldn't hear of it."

Phil got to his feet. "This is a stupid idea."

"I agree."

"I'm sure they'll find us today. They'll find us, and you and Bob won't be here. We won't even know where to look for you."

"You're probably right. They probably will come today." Daniel shook his head slowly, like a man on death row who'd lost his last appeal. Phil was struck at how exhausted he looked: eyes sunken, three days of stubble on his cheeks, his mouth drawn with marionette lines of worry. He looked too worn out to make it to the top of the first hill, much less all the way to Whitehorse. "If they come today, fantastic. Bob and I will see them from the top of that ridge, and we can hurry back." He looked over at Kerry again. "But if they don't, if the ELT is broken, if the storm doesn't let up soon, if they can't find us . . ."

Phil didn't say anything. He was angry; what Daniel was talking about was insane. He was going to leave his fiancée to play the hero, taking stupid risks when his place was here with Kerry. And here Phil had just started to like him.

"I can't believe you'd do this to her." He glanced over at Kerry. "You know what it will do to her if you die out there. You don't even care—"

"That's not it at all," Daniel said, standing up inside the cramped space, towering over Phil.

"You're going to freeze to death, you're going to kill yourself this time, and all because you're constantly trying to prove yourself to Bob—"

"I told you, *that's not it*." He spoke through clenched teeth.

Phil went silent. *If he thinks I'm going to go along with this, him and Bob getting themselves killed to prove what men they are . . . Stupid macho posturing . . .*

But Daniel was looking over at the two pairs of snowshoes he and Bob had made the night before, one pair made of colorful shoelaces, the other of silver-gray duct tape. For a minute he seemed much older than thirty-seven, like he'd aged ten years overnight.

"Look. Kerry took a bad turn last night. She had a couple of seizures. Beverly says she needs IV fluids, maybe oxygen, too. She's dehydrated because she's been unconscious too long." Daniel was shaking, actually shaking, and not from the cold. "Phil, she's pregnant. I just found out. I can't let her and the baby die like this. I can't, I can't sit here and watch it happen."

Phil felt the world slow down around him, everything gone heavy and slack, as if he'd fallen into a deep pool wearing a heavy woolen cloak. She was pregnant. And what would Phil have done, if he and Emily had been able to have kids? If he could have saved even a part of her?

He knew the answer: anything. He would have done anything at all.

"Don't we have IV bags in the first-aid kit?" Phil asked. "I could have sworn I saw some yesterday. We could get her hooked up, it could be fine—"

"Bev is trying to thaw them out right now." He gave Phil a mirthless smile. "The problem is that even if she gets them working, they won't last very long. Not more than a few hours at most. They're really not meant as a long-term solution."

Immediately Phil saw the problem: if she didn't wake up soon, she'd die from dehydration before they could ever get her treated for the concussion.

"It's already been at least twenty-four hours since she's had any water," Daniel said. "We can't afford to wait any more." He dropped his voice to a conspiratorial whisper. "You see what I mean, don't you? Someone has to go try to get help. I'll never be able to live with myself if I don't do everything I can."

Phil could see the need on the other man's face, his desperation. He was going to do this. He had to.

"All right," Phil said, taking a deep breath and blowing it out again, slowly. "I'll do whatever I can to help her until you get back. You can count on me."

"Thanks. I know—I know it's not easy for you, either. But I know you'll look after her. You won't let her die, will you?"

Phil looked at the still form of Kerry on the floor of the cabin. He couldn't bear to look at Daniel, for the other man to see the pain on his face, the fear. They both loved her. They would both try to save her life, if they could, but only one of them was the father of her child.

"No, I won't let her die."

"I swear I'll be back as soon as I can."

Phil felt his jaw clench. It was all wrong. Daniel should be staying here with Kerry, not Phil. Phil didn't have anyone waiting for him, no one to rely on him. Maybe he could make it. Maybe he could put on the snowshoes and make it up the hill . . .

He was kidding himself. Phil was no kind of outdoorsman, even in the best of health, and he knew it. He'd never make it five feet, much less to the top of that hill or to a town or a road, not when every step caused him so much pain he saw stars, when the hard spot in his abdomen grew hour by hour. No—if anyone was equipped to walk out into the wilderness, if anyone had a chance, Daniel was right: he had to be the one to go.

Already Daniel was layering himself up in two pairs of socks, two pairs of gloves and a knit hat in addition to his own down parka. "If we get to the top and don't see anything, and if the rescue crews don't come today, we're going to have to keep going. You'll need to tell the rescue crews where we've gone. We'll be walking over the hill and straight west. That's the direction the plane was headed. If we come to a road or a creek, we'll follow it."

"How will you know which direction to go?"

"If it's a creek, we'll head downstream. More chance of running into a town. If we find a road instead, we'll keep heading west and south and hope we can get picked up by someone on their way to town. Can you remember that?"

"Downstream. South and west. I'll remember." Then Phil said, "What happens if she wakes up? Then you wouldn't have to go."

Daniel looked thoughtful for a moment. "If she wakes up today and I can still see the camp, you can signal me. Light some of those green branches. They'll send up a bunch of smoke, and we'll come straight back down. If I get to the top and there's nothing, and if I don't see your signal, though, we're going to keep going. Got it?"

"Yeah. I still think you're crazy, but I'll do it."

Daniel stuffed a few supplies into a backpack he'd found among the luggage: a few candy bars, a couple of bags of peanuts, an extra coat and blanket. He hesitated, then packed a black book from his suitcase, the one Phil had seen him scribbling in from time to time.

When he was done he tied it all up in a small bundle. It wasn't enough. It would run out fast, and they'd be working hard, climbing up those hills on nothing but a little sugar and a few nuts.

When he was done, Daniel stood and fixed him with a sympathetic look. "I know you'll do everything you can for her. I trust you."

Phil shook his head. "I don't know why you would."

Daniel put a hand on his shoulder. "You didn't do anything wrong, you know," he said. "Emily, I mean. You left for a few hours. You needed a break."

"She nearly died."

"But she didn't die. You didn't abandon her. You came back, and the fire department got there in time. Listen, I understand why you're being so hard on yourself. It must have been hell, trying to take care of her under those circumstances. Anyone could understand that."

Would they? Would his wife forgive him, if she were here in front of him now? He'd left when Emily had been near the end. When she'd needed him the most, he'd run away. He'd never be able to make it up to her, never. He could never take it back.

You idiot, said the voice of Emily, the one that lived still in his head. *You know I never blamed you for any of it. You're the one who won't forgive yourself.*

Daniel had turned and knelt down beside Kerry, stroking her hair and kissing her. Her eyelids never fluttered as Daniel whispered in her ear. When he stood up, he looked back at Phil and said, "You'll take care of them for me?"

Them. Kerry and the baby, that little spark of life, barely more than a promise. "I'll stay by her the whole time. I swear."

He'd said the same thing to Emily once. He'd meant it just as much then, too.

He watched Daniel make his way out of the plane to join Bob outside, a little snow swirling in behind him. *Maybe this time I can do something right. I can't make it up to Emily, but I can be here for Kerry and Daniel now. I can do that much.*

He looked down at Kerry's face, still unconscious. Phil didn't want to say *asleep*, knowing there was nothing restful in the way she lay on the floor inside the dark cabin of the crashed jetliner. She looked even more pale than she had the day before, her skin utterly devoid of any of its normally healthy pink color, her eyes sunk in hollows like the shadows between hills. She hadn't moved a millimeter, not even when Daniel kissed her, not even when Daniel said he loved her.

"You'll be okay," he'd said. "Both of you. I'll make sure of it."

Phil watched him go and felt a wave of despair wash over him, large enough to bury them all. *Hurry up, Daniel. Hurry up, or you might be breaking that promise whether you want to or not.*

17

They were just about at the midpoint of the rise, halfway between the top of the hill and the floor of the valley below, when Daniel heard Bob's labored breathing coming up the hill behind him like the sound of a steam engine about to break down—they would need to stop soon to let the old man rest. Bob would never admit he was out of shape, that it was taking everything he had to keep up with Daniel, though Daniel was thirty years younger and a hundred pounds lighter, not to mention that Bob had been a two-pack-a-day smoker for years. He had his pride, and though Daniel was irritated that he had to slow down for the other man's sake, he still stopped, announced that he wanted to take a break, and stood back to look down the hill at the crash site far below them. With a little luck, he might be able to talk Bob into turning back now, before the going got any harder than it was already.

Daniel sat down on a fallen trunk, pulling the bottle of melted snow out from inside his coat and drinking it down in a few swigs. It was warm from his body heat—which was a good thing, cold water being a hazard in these temperatures—and tasted wonderfully clear and clean. Then he filled the bottle again with new snow, capped it and replaced it in its spot next to his skin, which was hot with exertion. In a little while, when the snow melted down, he'd drink again, preferably at the top of the ridge with a view of the city of Whitehorse below his feet.

The snowfall had picked up once more while they'd been climbing, filling the air with whiteness and obscuring the far distances, but Daniel hoped that by the time they got to the top of the ridge it would fall off again. How many days in a row could it snow here? Even during the famously bad Chicago winters, a snowstorm would only last a day or two and then clear out, which made him think that today, the third day since the crash, the storm would surely begin to blow itself out, and then the airline would be able to get rescue vehicles into the backcountry to pick up the survivors.

Finally Bob huffed his way over to the spot where Daniel was sitting and plopped down heavily on the trunk. "Why are we stopping?" he asked, between breaths.

"Just taking a break," Daniel said, not looking at the other man. He didn't need Bob collapsing on him here, so far from help.

Bob took out his water, swigged it, filled it back up with snow and replaced the bottle in the waistband at the back of his pants, then took a pack of cigarettes out of his pocket and lit one, taking a long draw and blowing the smoke out into the air.

"Is that a good idea?"

"I don't want to hear it."

Daniel didn't say anything else on the subject of Bob's smoking. If Bob had ever planned on quitting, it probably wasn't going to be now. Still, he hated the smell of cigarette smoke and turned away a bit so he wouldn't have to breathe it in. "A bit harder than it looks, isn't it?" he asked.

"A bit. I thought it would be more like walking. The tape is holding, at least."

"That's good," Daniel said. "Your legs tired?"

Daniel's own thighs burned with the effort of climbing the ridge in deep snow, but Bob said, "Not at all. I'm doing fine." Bob was too proud to admit he was hurting.

Daniel looked back down the hill at the crash site. Even from this close, maybe less than two miles away, the body of the downed jetliner was nearly invisible, buried almost completely by the snow that had been falling incessantly for the past three days. The groove that the jet's body had worn in the snowpack as it slid down the hillside had been erased, and all the other small traces that might have given them away—the broken wings, the debris field, even the broken trunks of the trees that the plane had hit on its violent descent— were completely covered with a heavy blanket of new snow. Utterly invisible.

No smoke rose from the crash site, which meant Kerry was still unconscious. Daniel felt his hopes sinking further and further.

He said, "The rescue planes aren't going to be able to see them from the air like this. They should start a signal fire. Make themselves visible. Something."

Daniel could feel Bob looking at him. "There are smart people down there. Phil. Those two stewardesses. I'm sure they'll know what to do when the weather clears."

He shook his head. "It's not just a matter of knowing. They don't have anything to make a fire with." He glanced at Bob. "You should have left them your cigarette lighter."

"I'm sure I wasn't the only smoker on the plane."

Daniel put his hands on his thighs and stood up. "Maybe you should go back down, Bob."

"You'll need a fire tonight, too."

"I'm not just talking about the lighter," he said. "I don't even want to think about what we're going to have to do if there's nothing over this hill."

"We stick to the plan," Bob said, stubbing out his cigarette. "Just like you told Phil. Follow a road or a river. Find a town. Bring help."

"It's just a lot of risk." He looked over at his boss. Bob's face was red from exertion or cold, or both. "I'm not trying to embarrass you. It's just—I might be able to go faster on my own."

Bob stopped, fixed Daniel with a cold, still look and said, "Don't bother trying to get rid of me, Albrecht. I'm still your boss. I can do this by myself if I have to."

Daniel sighed. It was no use trying to reason with Bob—he followed his gut. This time, his gut might be getting them both killed.

A blast of cold air shook the trees, and Daniel shivered. He could still feel Kerry's mouth under his, how still it had been, how she hadn't even stirred when he said her name. He was feeling it as he sat looking down at the crash site, the dark shapes of the passengers coming outside in twos and threes to check the sky. The brush of her lips on his. The metallic smell of her breath, sickly. The pale skin over her closed eyes. He had tried to memorize her face, to absorb every bit of her before the task that lay ahead of him. He'd gathered her hair into his hands and breathed in her scent: soft, faintly floral, a little smoky. She hadn't opened her eyes, hadn't said she loved him, too. The stillness of her only served to remind him of all the reasons why he was determined to go, determined not to wait. It had to be now.

Still, he watched the sky, hoping beyond hope that even now, he'd hear the sound of a plane's engine, a helicopter's rotor. But there was nothing but the sound of the snow falling, softly falling through the branches of the trees, burying the wreck a little more every hour.

He bent down to check the laces on his snowshoes. They were holding well enough at the moment, though it was less than a day that he'd been walking on them. Daniel worried what would happen if he *did* have to walk all the way to Whitehorse.

When he was sure his feet were still tied securely to the snowshoes, he turned to Bob and said, "All right. Let's keep moving."

He looked up at the ridge, trying to gauge how long it would take them to get to the top, whether they'd make it before the daylight ran out. The ridge wasn't particularly impressive, not anything close to a real mountain, but it was probably at least a thousand feet high from the valley floor, if not more, and it had taken them nearly two hours to get this far. Reaching the top before dark would be no easy feat, especially with a sixty-seven-year-old man trying to stroke his own ego by tagging along. With any luck there would be a road or a town or a cabin on the other side where he could call for help. Something.

And if there wasn't, he'd deal with that problem, too. But one thing at a time.

Daniel pushed the two of them hard to make it to the top of the ridge—he wanted to get there before darkness fell again, before it would be impossible to see what was below—but Bob seemed to go more slowly minute by minute, his breath labored. With each step, Daniel became more and more determined to send him back down the hill to the wreck to stay with the others. It would be the right thing to do for Bob's own sake. It was clear now he'd never make it ten miles out here on foot, much less a hundred or more.

The snow was tapering off when they cleared the trees near the top of the ridge, the snowpack lighter here, scoured away in places by the fierceness of the wind. The ground as well grew more rocky, the footsteps of the two men less certain, until Daniel stripped off his snowshoes at last, going the rest of the way to the summit in only his leather boots. He couldn't wait for Bob any longer—he reached the top about twenty paces ahead and pushed the last few steps until he saw the slope fall away below him.

The line of hills was unbroken as far as he could see, one after another after another like waves on the ocean, some nearly bare, some covered with trees, all burdened with a heavy cover of snow. Down below, glinting faintly, he could see the dark line that marked a creek or small river meandering between the hills. Flowing north, as far as he could tell, but there was no town, no city, not even a road, nothing that hinted that human beings had ever been here.

Even though he knew it was futile, he pulled out his cell phone and turned it on. No signal, just as he'd feared.

When he turned and looked back toward the crash site, hoping to see the black smoke of a signal telling him that Kerry was awake, there was nothing but swirling white. The snow was obscuring the crash site. Even if Phil had built a signal fire, Daniel wouldn't be able to see it from here.

They could go back. They could return to the crash site and wait with the others. For a moment that's exactly what he thought he would do. Then he remembered Kerry and the baby, and sat down hard on a rocky outcrop.

He wanted to weep. He wanted to fall on his knees and scream into the wind, but there was no point. It would be a useless waste of precious energy, and he needed all he could manage.

He had only two choices: go on, or go back.

Next to him, Bob struggled to stand up in the wind and took in the scene below, dim in the fading light. "Well," he said, taking in the scene, "looks like we're fucked."

Daniel didn't answer. As usual the old man had a way with words.

There was no use feeling sorry for himself; he had to get about the business of survival. He started gathering wood for a fire, looking for a good place to bed down until dawn and fighting off his own sense of desperation. Darkness would be coming soon.

He spotted a conifer a little way down the slope. Underneath it, the snow was less deep and the branches of the tree, weighed down with heavy snowfall, would help protect them against the wind and the threat of exposure. He could dig down into the snow and use it to build up a wall against the wind, then maybe line the pit with branches to keep them off the cold ground. If he was lucky, he might even be able to manage a small fire pit to warm their cold hands and feet and faces. With a shelter and a fire, and wrapped in the extra coats and blankets they'd brought, they might make it until morning.

The last of the light was fading. In the morning, he'd have to go down to the creek and follow it, and there was no way to know where it led. It wasn't a great plan, but the alternative—waiting at the wreck until they were found—wasn't a solution, either.

"Come on, Bob," he said. "If we're going to last the night, we'd better get a fire started."

18

For a long time after they'd left, Phil stood outside the fuselage and watched the small, dark figures of Daniel and Bob making their way up the side of the ridge, going quickly at first, as if anxious to get to the top, then more slowly as the way became steeper and more difficult. When they were finally obliterated by distance and snow, Phil shuffled inside to the place where Beverly was tending to the sick and injured and sat down next to Kerry, who lay still, her lashes dark against her cheeks, tucked under a layer of coats and blankets. He didn't want to think about who those coats had belonged to originally, which of the dead passengers had brought this red parka, that black wool overcoat. It felt wrong to be glad of the extra coats, but he was, if only for Kerry's sake.

He picked up her hand and peeled back her gloves, then his own, to check for frostbite—her skin was icy cold and pale. Phil rubbed her hands vigorously between his own for a minute or so each, hoping the friction and the movement would increase her circulation. Then he tucked her hands back under the blankets and touched her forehead, her cheek. Her skin was softer than he'd anticipated, her forehead unlined with worry or age. He envied her that—her youth, her beauty. Her hopes, her future. And she was carrying Daniel's baby.

Phil felt a surge of jealousy so big and ugly it nearly threatened to overwhelm him. A baby was a permanent thing, a connection between Kerry and Daniel that could never be severed. They were bound to each other forever, and even if Phil had thought he could manage it, he couldn't get in the way.

"Kerry, can you hear me?"

Just for a moment it looked to him like her eyelids fluttered, the pale bluish skin moving just millimeters. His breath caught—but then nothing happened. She was as still as before, like a wax statue of herself. Even the fact that he could sit so close to her, be close to her, didn't offer him any relief. He couldn't help her.

He felt the anxiety of the past few days turning to despair, like gravity pulling him down. There was no way Daniel and Bob were going to find help, no way they'd make it to a road, a town. They'd probably freeze to death on their first night, away from even the flimsy shelter offered by the wreckage of the plane and the body heat of fifty other people. No—the survivors were lost in the woods, invisible to the searchers, who must be beginning to doubt if there were any survivors, who might even now be starting to think about how long they could afford to look before giving up the search.

For the first time since the crash, he thought, *Maybe it would be all right if we were to die out here. Maybe there are worse things that could happen than closing your eyes and slipping away peacefully in your sleep.*

As soon as he thought it, he looked down into Kerry's face and knew it was wrong to give in. She deserved to live; her baby deserved to live. Phil was only feeling sorry for himself again. The search parties would not give up after only three days—sooner or later the snow would stop, the skies would clear, and they'd be found. Of course they would; no one would give up the search for a commercial jetliner with a hundred people on board. The only question was whether the rescue would be soon enough.

He knelt down beside her and pulled a piece of her hair out of the corner of her mouth. Just looking at her, he could hardly tell that she'd been injured; only a bruise just under her hairline, over her ear, gave any indication of what had happened to her. Then again, Phil himself had barely more than a bruise to mark his own injury, and he knew it was more serious than it appeared. It was the third day since the crash, and he was more tired than ever: he felt the pressure growing in his belly and knew something in him was broken, something slow to manifest but definitely painful and possibly dangerous. Even standing to go outside to piss was getting more and more difficult; by tomorrow morning he might not be able to stand at all, period.

God only knew what the doctors would find when he got back to civilization. *If* he got back to civilization.

"What's the matter with you?" Bev said. She was sitting near Kerry's head, rubbing an IV bag back and forth between her hands like she was trying to will it back to life. They'd found two intravenous bags in the medical kit, both frozen solid since the crash, and a single tube and a couple of needles. The cold had made even the simple act of running an intravenous line nearly impossible, but Bev swore she could get the line started if they could get the liquid sufficiently warmed up.

Beverly tucked the icy IV bag into her armpit like Daniel had shown her and said, "You look like someone walked over your grave."

"Maybe someone did."

"Oh?"

"I was just wondering if it would make any difference."

"If what would?"

"Staying alive."

"Well," she said, her mouth twisting up at the corners, "I think most of these people would like to see their families again. I know I would. My husband and kids must be out of their minds worrying about me. I don't even want to *think* about the rest of my family."

Phil shook his head gloomily. "That's just it, though. I don't have a wife or kids. If I didn't come back, would anyone really care?"

Beverly gave him a significant side-eye, and Phil could almost feel her weighing her words. "Has anyone ever told you you're a bit of a pessimist?"

"People mention it from time to time, yes."

She grinned. "There's nothing that says just because your wife died that you couldn't remarry. You could have a family still. You're what, forty?"

"Forty-two."

"Plenty of time."

As if he could just snap his fingers and make it happen. "It's not that easy for me. I don't bounce back that fast."

Beverly gave a small half-laugh that reminded him so much of Emily that it startled him. "You really enjoy feeling sorry for yourself, don't you?" She switched the IV bag to her other armpit. "I thought it was just the crash talking, but now I'm thinking this is really who you are. A real Eeyore."

"Who?"

"The donkey from Winnie-the-Pooh. The one who's always walking around feeling sorry for himself."

"I do not *enjoy* feeling sorry for myself!" He felt a surge of anger so fierce that it actually made him warm, the first real heat he could remember feeling since the crash. Who the hell did Beverly think she was? He didn't need a shrink, didn't need her psychoanalyzing his worst traits, his ugliest fears. His wife had died. He'd survived a *plane crash*. If he didn't have the right to a little self-pity after that, who did?

"Sure you do."

"Jesus. Who do you think you are?"

"You think that because you've lost people, that gives you the right to be ugly, to be selfish, when the truth is that you can't live in this world and not lose someone you love. It's not possible."

"How do you know about that?"

"I heard you and Daniel talking. This plane isn't private, you know."

"Great." His face burned, as he considered how many people might have heard him talking to Daniel, saying out loud his most shameful secrets.

"You think your losses are special," Beverly went on. "Different from everyone else's. That you've suffered more."

"I never said that!"

"Not in so many words, no, but you wallow in self-pity like a pig in shit. You lost your wife. All right, that's unfair, it's horrible, but everyone loses their spouse sooner or later, don't they?"

"Emily was only thirty-five!"

"Who gets to choose where and when? Nobody." Beverly was talking loudly now, half the eyes of the plane on her. "Your plane crashed. That sucks. But look around you: everyone you see was in that crash, too. Not just you. You're just acting like you were the only one. You *survived*. You didn't die. A lot of people died, but not you."

"I know that. Thank you, Oprah."

"Do you? Do you really think your wife would have wanted you to sit around moping for the rest of your life, making yourself miserable, making the people around you miserable?"

"I am not making other people miserable."

"I wouldn't be so sure." She looked from him to Kerry and back, her expression full of the weight of judgment.

Phil exploded. "Fine! I make people miserable! Maybe I even think you're right, on some level, but what good is it going to do me right now? I could die any minute out here."

"Before you die, would you consider thinking about other people's feelings for a change and give me a hand warming up these bags? Some of us *do* have things to go back to."

He took one of the bags from her. "Thanks for the sympathy."

"I've had it with pity parties just now. Sorry. Maybe when we get rescued I'll be in a more tolerant mood."

She gave Phil that same significant look and kept rubbing her IV bag. He was surprised to see her hands were shaking, only a little, but noticeable enough: Beverly was afraid, too, though she was trying very hard to hide it. She was as scared as the rest of them, but she was still doing what needed to be done.

Then Phil was ashamed, deeply ashamed of himself. Here was a woman who had a husband and children back home, a sick mother whose deathbed vigil she was missing. A woman who'd put aside all her own worries and strains and had taken on the burden of caring for the sick and wounded single-handedly, and *he* was moaning to *her* about his own loss, about lacking purpose? For a moment he looked at himself as she must see him, thought about himself as she must think about him, and he didn't like what he saw and thought.

He was afraid—but he was supposed to be afraid. Being afraid, in this situation, was just good sense.

You never did understand what it meant to be one of the lucky ones. It was Emily's voice, teasing, never letting him feel too sorry for himself for too long, never letting his misery get the best of him for more than a moment. She'd always balanced out his worst qualities, kept him on an even keel. Without her, he'd let himself sink so far down he barely even recognized himself anymore. She'd be ashamed of him, if she could see him now, wallowing in self-pity "like a pig in shit," Beverly had said. She'd tell him to grow up, get a grip.

You still have plenty of living left to do. If you're still breathing, then you've got something to go back to. You know that, don't you?

Do I? Phil thought. *What would that be?*

The small voice said, *Yourself.*

The light outside was changing, growing dimmer, and Phil thought maybe it wasn't only Daniel who was able to do something, who could do something to help them all survive.

His hand crept forward for the clear IV bag Beverly was holding and took it out of her hand. He looked at it for a moment, the clear liquid frozen into a block near the bottom of the bag. *It's something at least. It isn't despair.*

He put the IV bag in his armpit, the warmest place he could think of. The bag was freezing cold, a little jolt to his senses. Immediately Phil began to shiver, a little at first and then more and more. "This is just great," he said. "You and I will probably end up with hypothermia before we get the IVs thawed."

"Probably," she said, her mouth turning up at the corners.

"And we're out of food."

"Yep."

He took the bag out of his armpit and glared at it. "We need a fire for this job," he said. "With a fire we could get the bags thawed in no time."

She gave him another look and said, "We tried the fire yesterday. There wasn't anything dry enough except some pieces of paper, and we burned most of it."

"Not all of it. There are still the seatback magazines. The wood we brought in might be dry enough by now."

To his surprise, Beverly actually smiled at him, a genuine smile that broke over her face like the sun coming up. "If you really manage to get a fire going, the folks around here will elect you king. Just be careful, okay? I have too many patients as it is."

"Hey," he said, "a little confidence, please?" She looked up at him and rolled her eyes, but she was still smiling.

He stuck the IV bag in the waistband at the back of his pants and approached the back of the plane for the firewood they'd stacked against the fuselage the day before in the hopes the wood would dry enough overnight to use. There was a good-sized pile of it, deadfall branches and a few larger pieces, some as long as Phil's leg. They might burn a good long while.

He started picking up pieces and dragging them outside. A few of the passengers came out to see if they could help, first Kecia and Amber, the flight attendants, then Alice and her little boy, Zach. Kecia stood hugging her oversized coat around herself with her one good arm, giving Phil a skeptical look. Beverly had splinted and wrapped her broken arm when Daniel had brought her back from the tail section, and though she had to be careful of her injury, she still knew a lot of things that had been helpful the past few days. Phil was glad she'd lived.

Now she asked, "You really think that wood's dry enough?"

"We can't wait anymore. The temperature's dropped since yesterday, and we need to get the IV bags thawed out or my friend in there is going to die of dehydration."

"All right," said the flight attendant, thrusting out her chin in a determined way that made Phil like her more already. "What do you need?"

Phil thought for a second. He wasn't used to people looking to him for answers, and he'd grown accustomed to letting Daniel make all the decisions about survival matters since the crash, but Daniel wasn't here now. Phil would have to rely on his own judgment. He only hoped it would be enough.

"First things first. We need a lighter, if that's possible," he said. "Can you ask around to see if one of the other passengers has one? If there's one in one of the bags?"

"There shouldn't be any lighters in the bags," said the other flight attendant, the one named Amber, "because the TSA doesn't allow them. But let us see if any of the passengers has one on them."

"What about me?" asked the boy, Zach. He'd been bored all morning, driving his mother crazy because he didn't like being cooped up inside the fuselage. She kept telling him it was too cold outside, but the kid didn't care—he hated sitting around in the dark with a bunch of mopey adults, and Phil didn't blame him. The prospect of activity, even something as simple as starting a fire, interested him greatly. "What can I do?"

Phil put a hand on the kid's shoulder and said, "Bring me as much paper as you can find. Books, newspapers, the magazines from the seat pockets. Bits of cardboard. Anything you can find, I want it."

The boy grinned and dashed off. His mother stopped for a moment, opening her mouth as if to ask something of Phil. Then she followed her son into the plane. "We'll be back," she called over her shoulder.

Phil walked around the open end of the fuselage, looking for the best possible place in which to build the fire. It should be sheltered from the wind, and close by—Daniel and Bob had made two crude pairs of snowshoes, but they'd taken the rest of the shoelaces and the duct tape with them in case they needed to make repairs, so there was no way to make another pair, and that fact limited the remaining passengers to the area around the crash site. *Just as well, really,* Phil thought—they should all stay close. When the rescue came, they would need to be ready, and that meant they needed to stay together.

At last Phil picked a spot near the side of the plane. It was on the northeast side, the most sheltered place possible. Next he'd need to get rid of all this snow; a fire would turn it into a wet, soggy mess. He used the side of his foot to dig a spot in the snow, going down and down until he'd removed all traces of snow and reached the dirt beneath, and though it was painful and his injury bothered him, he didn't complain, for once. He scraped at the ground until he had a good bare patch going, raw icy earth the gray-brown color of mouse fur. He broke off the smallest branches of the dry wood and made a little tent of it in the bare patch.

He looked up at the sky. The snow was lightening a little, but the clouds were still thick and heavy, and he worried that even if they were able to get a fire going, it wouldn't last in this weather, that the snow and the wind would smother it. But it didn't matter, they were going to have to try. Phil was determined not to think the worst, not anymore.

The first people back were Zach, carrying an armful of magazines, and his mother, handing Phil a few paperboard boxes that once had held food. He thanked them and piled everything carefully on top of one of the suitcases to keep it dry, tearing out a few pages from the magazines and twisting them into strips, setting them beneath the tent of twigs.

Now they only needed a lighter. Kecia and Amber were going from passenger to passenger, hoping someone had a lighter or some matches. Something. Amber came outside and gave Phil a look: nothing yet.

"You wouldn't have had one stored in the galley?" he asked. "Nothing tucked away somewhere?"

"No, I already checked. Lighters aren't usual equipment. They don't really want to encourage us to start fires on board."

"I suppose not."

Then something seemed to come over her face. "Wait a minute," she said. "One of the pilots was a smoker. He must have a lighter on him. If we could get in there . . ."

Amber grew quiet. If there was a lighter on one of the pilots, someone would have to get into the cockpit to retrieve it.

"I'll go," Phil said, before she could volunteer.

She laughed. "Why, because you're a guy?" She gave him an appraising look, up and down. "You're hurt, though you're trying your damnedest to hide it."

"I'm not so bad."

"Don't be brave," she said. "You've been clutching your side all day long. Even bending over makes you wince. You're not in any shape to climb up into the cockpit window."

Phil thought about arguing with her, but in fact she was right: the dull throbbing in his pelvis was growing alarmingly in size and seemed to get worse whenever he bent over or tried to sit down. Even scraping the snow away from the fire pit had made him a bit light-headed. And he'd started pissing blood, the snow tinged pink whenever he went outside to relieve himself. He'd started covering it up with snow after, so no one would see, *no one* being Beverly. There was nothing she could do about it.

But he wouldn't think about that now. He could afford to be scared when they were all safely rescued, safely home. Until then, he'd do whatever he could to keep them all alive.

"All right," said Phil to the flight attendant. "Lead the way."

All that day the snow fell, and though Phil could have sworn he heard a plane's engine overhead once or twice, no sign came from above that they'd been found. Over and over the passengers ran outside, hoping against hope, but by the time darkness started falling in the early afternoon and it had been several hours since they'd heard an engine, Phil was starting to realize they would have to resign themselves to spending another night in the plane. The last one, if they were lucky.

They had to be lucky this time. They simply had to be.

It was the third day since the crash, the one when the survivors would start to turn on each other. They had enough water, barely, but hunger and fatigue had left passengers snapping at each other over a piece of floor or a blanket, over the warmest spots in the cabin or an unclaimed coat, and anyone suspected of hoarding food was threatened with spending the night outside. Everyone was tired of peeing in the snow, of sharing a cabin with fifty other snoring, farting people during nights too long to sleep. They were tired of being in pain, of being simultaneously bored to death by waiting and terrified that the waiting would never end.

So it had been no little bit of relief when, with the lighter Kecia found in the co-pilot's pocket, Phil finally got a fire going outside the fuselage, in the snow, just before dark—a little flicker of orange in the growing blackness. Catching his breath a little, he had knelt in the bare spot, lit a twist of magazine paper, then tucked it beneath a tented pile of dry twigs. When the flames grew, he arranged a few larger twigs on top. The wind whipped up for a second and the flames withered, threatening the whole enterprise, but after two or three seconds the wind died back down and the flames rose up again, crackling cheerfully in the dim and the snow. After about ten minutes, the fire was hot enough that Phil put the larger branch on top, watching the fire grow, a small but significant victory in the battle for survival.

Word had gotten out quickly among the passengers that the fire was going at last, and they trickled out in groups of two and three to come see it, their faces reflecting the warm bit of light and their expressions easing little by little. They nodded to him in gratitude and crowded around close: if they could have a fire, they seemed to be thinking, then everything would be all right. They'd make it. The storm would die out and the sun would rise and the smoke from their fire would lead the rescue teams to them. With a fire, they didn't need the ELT; they only needed to wait.

Phil went inside to get the second IV bag from Beverly, stopping for a minute to check on Kerry. She was so still that for a moment he was afraid, until he saw the slight rise and fall of her breath, the tiny flutter of a pulse at her throat. She was alive, but barely. The IVs couldn't wait any longer.

When he'd come back outside with the bag, there were so many passengers crowded around the small fire that Phil could barely see the pit he'd dug, much less catch any warmth from the small blaze. He tried ducking through, but the crowd wouldn't part for him, and as he tried to push his way toward the fire, he started to notice movement within the mass of the fifty survivors, here and there an arm or a leg pushing out, a head jutting forward. The survivors were jostling each other for position, the strong pushing away the weak, everyone muttering about the cold, the impossibility of cold and fear. Each one insisted he needed to get close to the fire first, and Phil watched them with horror until one of the men, a big guy with the face of a punching bag, pushed young Zach out of the way, picking the kid up by the hood of his coat and tossing him aside into the snow.

Phil picked the kid up and brushed the snow out of his eyes. "You okay?" he asked.

Zach nodded, but Phil was still incensed. He and Amber and Kecia, and Alice and Zach, hadn't worked all morning to get the fire going for only the handful of passengers who were big enough and strong enough to push the others out of the way. He needed to get Kerry's IV bags warmed, for one thing—not to mention that Zach had helped build the fire and now found himself outside the circle of warmth. He stood looking at the man's back, thinking, *How dare he? I mean really—how dare he treat us this way?*

He stepped forward and tapped the man on the shoulder. "Excuse me," he said. "We need to get through."

The big man kept his head down and pretended not to hear him.

"You pushed this boy," Phil said. "He has more right to be here than you do."

Still nothing. Zach said, "Don't worry about it."

"I will. It's not right. You helped me build this fire, and now it's being taken over by people who were too scared or lazy to come out here and help us."

The man stopped pretending he didn't hear Phil. He turned around and said, "What did you say to me?"

At home Phil would never have confronted the other man; confrontation wasn't his style. He was a negotiator, a mediator, the person who prevented disputes, not caused them. But it was possible he'd never been so angry in his life, finding himself and the boy pushed away from the fire they'd worked so hard to build in the few minutes he'd taken to go inside the plane.

"You heard me," Phil said. "I built that fire. Now, move your ass."

The bigger man turned away again. "It's a nice fire. Thanks so much."

"I didn't build it for you to push this boy away. He helped me gather the materials for the fire. You didn't."

"Oh?"

"That's right. He made the fire, he gets to stand in front of it first. That's the fairest way to do this."

Phil felt his hands shaking, but he wouldn't back down now. He needed to get to that fire, and he needed it now. Kerry needed it.

"That's right," he said, raising his voice so all the survivors in the clearing could hear him. "That's the rule. If you tend the fire, you can warm yourself over it. We'll take turns, twenty minutes each. But if you don't help gather wood to keep it going, or if you let the fire go out, you won't get to sit by it anymore."

The big man shifted so that he was staring straight at Phil. "You think you're going to stand around and give the rest of us orders? You aren't in charge here. No one's in charge here. We have to do what we have to do to survive, and that's all."

Phil caught Kecia's glance. The flight attendant's eyes were wide as she wondered what Phil was going to do. Imperceptibly, she gave him a little shake of her head, *no*. She didn't want him to start trouble. And he didn't want trouble, either, but there were only so many times a person could stand by and let things happen to him instead of the other way around.

The fire was too small to give them all much warmth, but big enough to warm Kerry's IV bags and the frozen hands and feet of the passengers, but not if a few bullies decided to take it all for themselves.

"What are you gonna do if we don't move?" said another passenger, with the wiry look of the oil-riggers who worked for Petrol. "Nothing, that's what. You'll go back inside and freeze your balls off like everyone else. I don't care what you do."

Phil kept his hands in his pockets and said, "I can put out that fire."

The huddled passengers lifted their heads to look at him. "What?" said the first man, the red-faced one.

"You heard me," Phil said quietly.

"You're full of shit," said the second man, folding his hands under his armpits again. "You wouldn't."

"I would, and I will," he said. "You get twenty minutes, then you move away and let someone else have a turn."

"And what gives you the right?"

"I built that fire. I scraped the ground for a spot to build it, and

I gathered a lot of that wood. This boy and his mother gathered the paper to help get it going." Phil didn't raise his voice, just said quickly and quietly what he would do. "I'm the only one who knows where the lighter is. You don't move away after twenty minutes, then I let the fire go back out, and you won't have another one."

He stood back with his arms folded, keeping his expression completely still at all times, betraying no passion. If they were going to survive out here, they were *all* going to survive, or else they would all perish together.

The bigger men stood back and seemed to consider Phil anew. Would he really go through with it? He could see the doubt on their faces, the uncertainty—but he was absolutely serious. He didn't move, didn't twitch. They would know he was serious, or they would pay the consequences.

"What do you say we kill you and take the lighter?" said one of them in a low voice.

Phil felt the tremor start in his belly and work its way up his body. They *could* kill him and take the lighter—but they didn't know that. "If you kill me, you'll never find the lighter. I've hidden it someplace completely safe, and I'm the only one who knows where. So you *will* listen to me, and you *will* be fair about the fire, or I *will* let you freeze to death."

He felt Zach start to say something and put a hand on the boy's arm to keep him silent. In the quiet outside the plane, they all waited. The fire flickered and started to die; the logs settled into coals. Phil couldn't quite believe he'd found the strength to stand up to these men, but it was too late to do any differently. Besides, he'd been angry. It wasn't fair of them to hog the fire, and they knew it.

Finally the first big man stepped aside and said, "I was getting too hot anyway," and let them pass.

Phil and Zach moved through the hole in the crowd toward the fire, which Phil built back up with a smallish log and a little breathing on the coals. In a minute, the fire was crackling again.

"Wow," murmured the boy so only Phil could hear. "That was amazing. You weren't scared of those guys at all."

That wasn't precisely true—his hands were still shaking, the adrenaline coursing through him. "I *was* scared," Phil whispered to the kid. "But I was more pissed off than anything. You deserve to get warm, too."

Phil gave Zach one of the frozen IV bags and the two of them sat holding the bags up to the warmth of the fire, close enough to melt the ice but not the plastic itself. In just a few minutes, the IV liquid was thawed, ready to use at last. Phil tucked the spare one in his shirt to keep it warm and went inside to give the other one to Beverly, the crowd parting without a word of protest or anger to let him pass.

He sat next to Kerry while Beverly worked to hook up the IV. He picked up her hand and held it wordlessly, Beverly watching him the whole time, waiting to see what he would do. "I can feel you watching me," he said.

"I'm not." The nurse was barely visible by the light of the emergency flashlight, which was flickering, starting to die—the batteries were wearing out.

"You are. Might as well say what's on your mind."

"I was just thinking how wrong I was about you."

The sarcasm level in Phil's voice went up two or three notches.

"You were *wrong* about something? Got to be the first time that's happened."

She made a little huffing noise, almost a laugh, and said, "You were kind of amazing, really. I saw the whole thing. They could have killed you, but you didn't back down."

"Didn't feel like it just then."

"I was proud of you."

"Gee, thanks."

"I know that sounds condescending, and I don't mean it that way. I mean it was kind of thrilling to watch. To see another person stand up for someone else like that."

"I was just angry, that's all."

"It took courage. Something not everyone around here has." She nodded to the sleeping form of Kerry on the floor. "She would have appreciated it, I think. "

Phil could feel his face burning. "Why should that matter?"

Beverly gave him a strange, knowing look, the corners of her mouth turning up just a little. "I'm just saying."

"Okay. You're just saying."

He clicked off the flashlight and sat in the dark so Beverly could not catch a glimpse of the wetness on his cheeks. It was the only privacy he would find out here, in this place, and he welcomed the darkness, where no one could see him weep.

19

When Daniel woke in the morning in the hollow underneath the fir tree he'd chosen for their shelter, he caught a patch of blue sky through the boughs and felt the first ray of hope he remembered for days, a lifting of his spirits that made it seem almost possible that they would all get out of this situation alive. The storm had blown itself out at last, and instead of pushing on into the bush, he and Bob could return to the plane and the rest of the passengers to wait for rescue. Now that the skies were clear, they could build a signal fire to catch the eye of rescue flights. Even if the ELT had been damaged in the crash—by now he had to think absolutely it was, it had to be—it wouldn't matter, the clouds had lifted and they could finally be seen by human eyes. *Thank God,* he thought, unwrapping himself from the extra coat and airline blanket and pine boughs he'd used to trap his body heat during the night, shaking from hunger and thirst and adrenaline. *Thank God. It's almost over.*

He clambered onto his knees and parted the branches, eager for the sight of the sun, but outside the shelter he saw a low gray sky still, the snow falling steadily. The blue he'd seen was nothing but a small break in the midst of the ongoing storm, gone in a few more seconds as if it had never happened. A temporary reprieve, nothing more.

He let the branch fall back into place, shaking off the gloom that threatened to overtake him. Of all the things that continued to work against their survival, the weather was easily the most daunting, the storm so large, so persistent, so blinding. The cloud cover continued to hide them from sight of any rescue teams; the snow was slowly burying the wreckage and making travel by foot difficult, if not impossible; the incessant wind and bitter temperatures threatened them all with exposure. They'd all be lucky if they didn't freeze to death by the end of the day, Daniel thought, letting his hands fall limply to his sides. He looked over and saw Bob bundled up against the cold, his face completely covered and his body curled into itself, hands tucked inside his armpits like Daniel had shown him, his chest rising and falling with each breath. It was a wonder the man had survived the night. It was a wonder either of them had.

Daniel gave a great sigh and started packing up his gear, fighting the urge to curl back up into a ball on the floor of the shelter and go back to sleep himself, but he couldn't. He had to keep going while there was even the smallest chance.

He picked up the blanket and tried to fold it, only then noticing that his own hands felt numb, the tips of his fingers strangely absent, as if they'd been amputated. He pulled the first layer of gloves off with his teeth, then the second layer, and there it was, just as he'd feared—a frosty whiteness at the tips of his first and middle fingers. A border of redness surrounded the edge of the damaged spot, creeping down across the nail, though the skin below was still relatively healthy-looking, if a little pale. A few blisters had popped up on the back of the hand and along the side, pale pink and filled with fluid, like bubble-gum bubbles someone had glued to his flesh.

Frostbite. Damn.

The patches and blisters weren't too painful, at least not yet—but they would be, especially after they warmed up. *If* they warmed up—and how on earth would he warm them properly out here?

He sat back in the shelter and held his hands out in front of him, not caring in that moment that with the gloves off he was only exposing them more. All his careful precautions, and here his hands were frostbitten. A well-built shelter and two layers of gloves and blankets and even a fire hadn't been enough to prevent it, not out here, where the temperature was still well below freezing. He made a small, sharp sound that was something close to a laugh, but not quite, tinged as it was by anger and self-loathing. He'd been an idiot, thinking he could walk out into the wilderness to find help. An absolute goddamn idiot.

He counted to twenty, letting himself have that much time for self-pity and no more. Then he knelt on the pine boughs and put his gloves back on. He might be stupid, but he wasn't suicidal—nor was he going to forget what was at stake here. If the weather wasn't going to cooperate, then it was up to Daniel and Bob to find help for the passengers, and there was no time for self-pity in that.

When Daniel's hands were properly covered again, he tried to think what would be the best way to treat them. Soaking them in warm water would be best, but they didn't have a basin in which to put it, just a couple of flimsy plastic water bottles they carried in their armpits to keep enough snow melted for drinking. The dry heat of the fire wouldn't work as well—first-aid advice for frostbite was always warm water—but it would be better than nothing. Daniel knelt over the ashes of the fire, hoping to get the coals to blaze, but as he stirred it with the tip of his glove and blew on it, he could see that it had gone cold in the night. Dead and cold as the frostbite on his fingers.

Bob had been the last awake, had promised to bank the fire the way Daniel had shown him, had sworn to wake Daniel up the moment he'd started to feel sleepy, but none of that had happened. He'd let it go out. Goddamn it all, *Bob had let the fire burn out.* The one thing they really needed out here, their one bit of good luck and essential tool against the cold, and he'd neglected it when they needed it the most.

Daniel tried to choke back his anger once more, but he couldn't, not this time. What was the point of having two of them traveling together in the first place if they couldn't even take turns tending something as fundamental as their fire? Why hadn't Bob stayed back with the others instead of burdening Daniel with his slow, useless old ass all the way up the ridge?

Daniel kicked his foot to wake him. "Get up," he said, barely able to keep the anger out of his voice. "Bob, wake up. *Now.*"

He should have come alone. He should have left Bob back at the crash site with the others, but he'd allowed himself to be swayed by sentimentality: he knew the old man's pride had been wounded when Daniel suggested he wasn't up to the trip. He'd figured that Bob would have realized he wasn't up for it and turned back. He thought Bob might find a way to make himself useful. He'd counted on it, in fact: Daniel had gone to sleep in the middle of the night believing Bob when he said he'd stay up and tend the fire, and now look where that trust had gotten him.

The other man sat up straight, pulling the scarf away from his eyes and rubbing his face with both gloved hands. "What happened?" he asked. "Did they find us?"

"No," Daniel said, clipping off the word like a bit of dead skin. "You let the fire go out."

The tip of Bob's nose and both cheeks were bright red, as if he, too, might be suffering the beginnings of frostbite, but Daniel wasn't ready to let go of his anger just yet.

"Wait, what? What happened to the fire now?" Bob asked.

"It went out," said Daniel. "You must have fallen asleep without waking me. Now my hands are frostbitten and we don't have a fire to warm up to."

"No, no," Bob said. "I woke you up. I distinctly remember you saying you had the fire under control."

"You never woke me, Bob."

"I did, I know it."

Daniel gritted his teeth and said, "There's no point arguing about it now. The fire's out, and I'll be lucky if I don't lose the tips of these fingers. We needed that fire. You're going to have to remake it now, because I can't."

"Shit," said the old man. "All right, hold on." He rummaged

around in his coat and came up with the cigarette lighter and a twist of dry paper. Daniel reached into his breast pocket and took out a portion of the bit of kindling he'd stashed there to keep it dry. While Bob lit the corner of the paper and put it on the cold ashes of yesterday's fire, Daniel added his bit of kindling, then a few more twigs from the pile he'd gathered the night before, not entirely dry but better than nothing. In a minute they had the fire going again, small and smoky but significant, and Daniel put his hands out in front of it, feeling the skin on his fingers tingle and ache as they came back to life. He only hoped they weren't too damaged.

He stole a glance or two at Bob, who had leaned back to put his booted feet up to the fire and was now engaged in eating half of the last bag of pretzels, chewing each one so slowly and thoroughly they must have been turning to pulp. Daniel's boss didn't look too healthy—pale and puckered, naked almost, like a turkey that's been plucked and prepared for the pot. There were heavy shadows underneath each eye, and his lips were so chapped they were cracked and peeling. Daniel felt a moment's regret—the old man didn't want to be out here any more than Daniel did, of course—but it was followed quickly by anger. This whole cockamamie adventure was Bob's idea, his brilliant plan, and here he was jeopardizing it on the very first night. He didn't know how to do anything, be useful to anyone. He'd spent his life behind desks or on camera, not in the field.

"So what's the plan?" Bob asked, swallowing the last bite of pretzel and handing the rest of the bag to Daniel.

Daniel looked back over his shoulder, out across the valley toward the crash site. They should go back—that would be the smart thing, the cautious thing. Go back and wait for the weather to clear and the rescue teams to find them. The fuselage of the downed plane, crowded with passengers, was a far better shelter than the hollow under a fir tree.

But then he thought of Kerry, the bruise on her temple, the pale flutter of her eyelashes as her body struggled against its injuries. Of the baby growing inside her. She was in real trouble. She might not survive this situation, whether or not he risked his neck to save her, but the truth was that he'd never be able to live with himself if he didn't do everything in his power. He had to try. As long as the downed plane was invisible to the rescue teams that were out searching for them, Daniel had to keep pushing forward, toward something. Toward life.

I can't go back yet. If this is the only way I can help her, then I have to do it.

"I'm going to send you back to the others," he said. "Go on back down the ridge and tell them I'm going on. If the weather breaks, I'll head back in your direction, but until then I'm going to keep looking."

"You shouldn't be out here by yourself. You need a backup."

Daniel wanted to answer that Bob was more of a noose around his neck than a helping hand, but he didn't want to argue with his boss. "I'm going to keep looking for a road or a house. Sooner or later I'll have to come within range of a cellular tower, or else the rescue teams will pick up my signal. Something. Either they'll find me first and I'll send them after you, or they find you first and you send them after me."

"I'm not going back," Bob said, almost to himself. "So you can forget it."

"I need you back there," Daniel said. "Someone needs to be ready to light a signal fire if the weather clears up. They need someone to take charge."

"There's Phil."

"Phil can't handle himself, much less all those people."

"Phil can handle a lot more than you give him credit for. I'm not going back. I'm coming with you."

Daniel sighed. He'd known the minute the old man opened his mouth what he would say.

"All right, then," he said. "I need you to do something for me, then." He reached into his pack and took out a small gray plastic device.

"What's that thing?"

"My cell charger. If we take turns cranking it, it will charge my phone faster." The battery to his cell was depleting quickly, probably exacerbated by his turning the phone on and off and using it in the bitter cold. Still, Daniel had no choice; the phone would give him a far greater range in looking for help than two men alone on a mountaintop. It was both his lifeline to the world and the world's lifeline to him.

The charger was meant as emergency backup only, designed to give the user maybe a few hours' worth of temporary power to get him through life-or-death situations and back to a real power grid, nothing more. It certainly wasn't designed to be used over and over for days on end. Still, it was better than nothing under the circumstances.

Daniel set the charger on his lap and connected the phone to it, then cranked the handle for several minutes as hard as he could.

When his arm tired out, he let Bob take a turn. Between the two of them, they were able to get the phone to about half power—not bad for two exhausted, underfed cube jockeys.

He stopped and turned the phone on. "All right," he said. "Let's see if we can pick up a signal."

Daniel held it up in the wind to see if there was even the barest hint of a signal. Nothing—the bars remained dark. He left the shelter and walked around the hilltop for a few minutes in the blowing wind, his eyes never leaving the face of that phone, waiting to see if the bars would give even the slightest jump.

Bob poked his head out of the shelter, feeling the temperature change in the wind. "Anything?" he asked.

Daniel shook his head. He stood on the top of the hill and surveyed what he could see of the world in the first light of morning. Down the ridge, the crash site wasn't even visible any longer—the snow and the clouds obscured everything, turning the world white, as if he'd suddenly gone blind. He passed a hand over his eyes, but the world was still there, a hazy gray that shifted and whirled like smoke.

He wondered if Kerry was all right. He wondered if Phil and Beverly had been able to warm up the IV bags enough to give them to her. He hoped that she would simply open her eyes and sit up, and for a moment it was all he could do not to turn around and go back to her.

The best thing he could do for Kerry, and for all of them, was to find them some real help. He'd have to press on. He'd survived one night in the cold; he could survive another, and another, and another. He had to.

What he wasn't sure about was whether Bob could. Daniel's boss was looking a little pale and haggard this morning, four days' worth of gray stubble on his chin, deep gray bags under each eye. He'd had some pills, Daniel recalled vaguely, something he used to take every morning at breakfast; Daniel had seen him shake something out of one of the distinctive orange bottles once or twice in Barrow, but he didn't do so now. Had Bob run out of his heart medication? Would Daniel end up with a dead man on his hands because Bob was too stubborn to go back to the plane and wait with the others? If something happened to Bob out here, there would be no help, nothing Daniel could do.

He nudged the other man with the heel of his hand. "Hey," he said. "You don't look so good this morning."

"I'm fine. Let's get moving."

"No, I mean it. Are you sure about this, Bob?" he asked. "Once we head over the other side of this ridge, it will be pretty hard to get back."

"I told you, I'm coming with you."

Daniel looked over at the coals, still glowing, and crouched down beside them, warming his hands and feet against the last of the fire. "All right, then," he said. "You can get warm for a few minutes, but we need to get as much distance in as we can while it's still daylight."

The two of them sat in the last warmth of the fire until the heat died down, then Daniel buried it in snow. Bob hoisted his pack onto his back and left the shelter. Daniel saw his eyes flick briefly to the crash site down the hill, then away. "So what's the plan?"

"We're going down the hillside to that creek," he said, pointing to the valley opposite the crash site. "We should head downstream.

Sooner or later we should find a road or a house or at least a bigger creek leading somewhere. Walking on the ice will be easier than trudging over the hills, too."

"I promise to take it easy on you today, then," Bob grunted, taking out the duct tape and taping the snowshoes to his feet, his face already red with exertion.

Daniel knelt and fastened his own snowshoes on as tightly as he could, checking to make sure he still had the extra laces. When he stood up, he looked down at Bob, struggling to wrap the jerry-rigged snowshoes to his feet, and said, "Your pills. Did you run out?"

Bob ignored that question. Instead he stood, facing Daniel, and said, "Can we go now? I'm tired of all this standing around."

"Bob—"

But he was already starting down the hill, his feet sinking into the snow, leaving the valley and the rest of the survivors behind. From now on they were on their own.

Still, Daniel kept watching the sky, hoping the weather would clear, that it wasn't too late for them to turn back. But the snow kept coming, the clouds still thick, and so he shouldered his pack and went on.

20

Phil stayed up with Kerry that whole night, refusing to take his turn sleeping when Beverly came to relieve him. "Go back to sleep," he said when she tapped him on the shoulder. "You need your rest, too."

"It's only fair that we take turns," she said. "You can't do it all by yourself."

"I don't mind. I'm not going to sleep anyway, so you might as well."

"Your belly still bothering you?"

It had been growing so painful that he was having trouble sleeping, even though he felt so exhausted he could barely move. And he was still pissing blood—but he wouldn't tell Beverly that, wouldn't trouble her with it.

"A bit. Enough to keep me awake, not enough to worry about."

"You let me decide if it's something to worry about," she said, but for once she didn't demand he lift his shirt and let her examine him; instead, she watched him from her spot on the floor, looking over the setup he'd created, the line running from the IV in the warmth of Phil's armpit downward into Kerry's veins, her face impassive with sleep. Phil ran his hands back and forth over the line, slowly, to keep the liquid from cooling too much after it left the bag and sending Kerry into hypothermia. It would be better to be outside by the fire, which one of the other passengers had promised to tend through the night, but that would expose them all to the wind, and Kerry would be difficult to lift without a stretcher. Better to be inside, where the warmth of fifty human bodies made the space bearable, if not livable, and the wind couldn't get in.

Beverly's eyes were heavily shadowed; he knew how tired she was, and he knew even more how badly they all needed her to stay well. She was their best asset in getting through this ordeal.

"Really, Bev. Go ahead and close your eyes. I promise I'll wake you if I need you."

She leaned back against the fuselage and closed her eyes. Then she said, "It's no wonder you're in love with her."

"What?"

Beverly gave him a look that said, *Don't play coy with me*.

"I'm just doing what I can," Phil said. "What anyone would do under the circumstances."

"Sure. Anyone."

Phil felt the plastic of the line moving slowly under his hands. It unnerved him, how Beverly was able to lay open the things he wanted so desperately to keep secret. Like everything he felt or thought was just there for anyone to see.

He said, "It doesn't matter. It's nothing."

"It's not nothing. Believe me."

"Well," he said, the line smooth as Kerry's skin under his hands, not sure how to finish the thought without saying something he'd regret. Back and forth he moved them, keeping the liquid flowing, as if it were her blood he was warming.

Beverly yawned. "You promise you'll wake me if you start feeling too tired?"

"I promise," he said. "I'm too restless to sleep. You go on. You've been doing so much by yourself, you need to rest, too."

"Thanks," she said, the last part of the word obscured by another enormous yawn, and then she was asleep again.

Phil rubbed the plastic tubing back and forth, back and forth, the friction and the warmth from his hand keeping the liquid at something close to body temperature, the rhythmic movement and heat keeping him calm and letting his mind wander.

For the first time since he could remember, he felt a momentary happiness, sitting here next to the woman he loved, doing something tangible and real, something that was helpful. Even if she never knew about it, never understood how Phil had cared for her when she needed it most, he wouldn't mind. He felt like a useful person, a good person even, and that was something he hadn't known in a long time.

He felt for a moment like he had in the early days of Emily's illness, when he'd always assumed that the treatments would be successful, that she would recover. It was the twenty-first century;

people survived cancer all the time, didn't they? Phil had busied himself with the minutiae of her treatment, the dosages and the weights and the white-blood-cell counts, the appointments and the specialists. He hadn't realized at the time that he was happy, because it had all been covered with the haze of worry over the seriousness of Emily's illness, but he could remember it now and recognize it for what it was. He had been determined to be her savior then, and when he hadn't been able to save her, it was himself that he blamed.

He looked down at Kerry's sleeping face, a white moon in the dark inside the cabin. And would he blame himself again if another woman he loved slipped away despite his efforts? Probably. But Kerry was not his—even if she lived, she loved someone else, she was marrying someone else. There was never going to be a place in her heart for him. Strangely, the thought made him feel a little bit better. He was helping her not to keep her for himself but for her own sake. He would never tell her his feelings, he would never confess his love for her, but he could do this much for her. He would be the one who kept her alive.

He felt the IV line slide through his fingers, smooth and slightly warm, and imagined it was her arm he was touching. If he closed his eyes, he could almost believe it was real.

The light outside was starting to go gray when Kerry's eyes fluttered open. Dawn. Phil had been watching the last of the IV fluid going into her arm, the drip slowing as the bag finally emptied. For fifteen minutes or so he had been wondering if he should wake Beverly and ask her for the second bag, which she had tucked into her shirt to keep warm, when he saw the change coming over Kerry's expression, not exactly wakefulness but consciousness at least—he could feel her thinking, almost. Could feel her listening.

"Kerry?" he whispered, not wanting to wake the others.

Her eyes flickered—he definitely saw it that time.

"Kerry, are you awake?"

"Hmmm," she murmured, and her hand in its fleece glove reached out and found his own. Then she rolled on her side and wrapped the other around his legs, pulling him toward her.

It was instinct, automatic she wasn't really awake yet—but Phil froze, feeling her fingers moving against his side, up under the edge of his coat, holding on. She had just mistaken him for Daniel in her confused, half-asleep state. Still, there was another, deeper part of him that wanted to think she knew exactly whom she was embracing.

Don't move. Don't breathe.

She blinked and looked up, saying, "I'm so cold."

Phil kept his voice steady and said, "I'm sorry." He held himself rigid. He was afraid. He wanted very badly to take her in his arms, to kiss her, but he knew he couldn't. She might still be sick, confused, but *he* was not: he was acutely aware of the boundary wall going back up between them. He couldn't let himself cross that divide.

"Please," she said, pulling him toward her.

Phil felt the wall crumbling, felt it turn into a landslide. He slid downward, stretching himself out along the floor next to her, until her head was even with his shoulder and their feet entwined. She pressed her nose into his chest and said, "Mmm, better, thanks."

He could smell her hair, faintly smoky and floral, the smell of her skin and the last remnants of her perfume, could feel their temperatures equalize as she pressed into him. It was much warmer this way, he had to admit, almost as comfortable as being home in his own bed. His eyelids were growing heavy, pulled down as if by gravity. How long had it been since he'd slept? He was in pain, he'd been hurting all day, pushing aside thoughts of taking care of himself because there were so many others who were worse off than he was. Maybe it would be all right if he closed his eyes just for a little bit.

The woman he loved was in his arms, asleep. How strange life was, that here in the middle of nowhere, far from any safety or comfort, in fear for his life, he could find some happiness at last. Emily would have laughed, if she could have seen him.

He felt himself drifting off, and the thought came to him: *If this is the most we will ever be to each other, if this is the only time in my life I ever get to hold her, then that's enough. It's still enough.*

21

It was much easier going downhill than up, so when Daniel and Bob reached the creek at the bottom of the ridge sometime around noon, they still had a good bit of energy and barely stopped to take a drink and refill their water bottles. The snow had tapered off, but the wind was picking up—coming from the west, still blowing off the Bering Sea. Daniel took a compass reading from Bob's watch and noted that the creek flowed north and west, not south like he'd hoped. The wind would be in their faces the whole time, but downstream was still likely their best bet. Wasn't it true that all over the world, humans had built their communities at the places where creeks became streams, and streams turned into rivers? He was sure he'd read that somewhere. Surely he and Bob would come to a cabin or a town before nightfall, a road or a wireless signal. Even this far out in the bush, the trappings of civilization would still reach, sooner or later. If they had even a little bit of luck.

What would he do if they didn't have any luck? He was making an educated guess about the right direction, but what if it was the wrong direction, and they never found a cabin or a road or a town, much less a wireless signal? What if they never came across help? What if he'd let Bob goad him into taking another dangerous risk, and this time it would cost them their lives?

Then it would be the end of them. The end of Daniel, the end of Bob—and maybe the end of Kerry and the others.

He couldn't afford to think that way. This would work. It had to. Anything that went wrong—and okay, yes, something surely would go wrong, something always did—they'd deal with it when the time came.

"All right," Bob said when he'd refilled his water bottle with snow and replaced it under his jacket. "We have maybe three hours of daylight left at best. We have to cover as much ground as we can in that time."

Daniel looked up at the sky. The snow had started to taper off, but heavy clouds still covered everything. "We're going to need to go fast if we're going to cover much ground. Are you sure you can keep up?"

The old man's face was red from the wind or from anger—Daniel couldn't tell the difference. "If you ask me that question again," he growled, "I will personally rip off your head and shove it up your ass."

Daniel thought of several things he'd like to say, but finally he settled on, "All right, then. Let's get going."

The creek they'd seen from the top of the ridge turned out to be little more than a trickle, a narrow patch of ice snaking along the valley floor between a series of low, barren hills. Small bushes and fir trees grew along its banks, and the snow was deep, deeper than they would have thought from above, the newness of it broken occasionally by animal tracks; but in places, the wind had scoured the snow away, leaving much of it smooth passage, almost like a path left just for them. *A first bit of luck,* Daniel thought, and his spirits lifted a little.

For a while Daniel kept behind Bob, watching as the older man's movements, which had started out so vigorous, began to slow more and more as the afternoon wore on. Each step in snowshoes required lifting the foot a bit higher than was comfortable, and the shoes were often heavy with clinging snow. It was tiring work under the best of conditions, but they were exhausted and hungry and going in a direction that was still mostly a hunch. The burn in Daniel's own thighs was significant, and he started to feel more and more impatient that he'd allowed Bob to talk him into making the trek. There were more important things at stake here than one man's pride, Daniel thought. There was Kerry, back at the crash site. Kerry with her brain swollen against her skull, the pressure building second by second, Kerry with their baby clinging to life inside her. There was Phil growing weaker and sicker from blood loss. *Internal bleeding,* Beverly had suggested, though she didn't know for sure. Not to mention the countless others—the broken legs, the broken noses, the puncture wounds, the smashed-up hands. As long as the storm lasted and the clouds covered the sky, the crash site was invisible to search-and-rescue teams. Daniel didn't like to admit Bob was right, but there it was. Going back was no solution at all.

By midafternoon Daniel pushed ahead of Bob at a pace that felt to him vigorous but still manageable. His feet and hands and face grew very cold as the day wore on, the tingle moving up his fingers in a way that he knew was dangerous. He should put them under his armpits to warm them, but that would leave him all but unable to keep his balance, and the need to press on was outweighing the dangers of frostbite. He could tend to his hands once they'd found help—or stopped for the night.

Daniel looked over his shoulder: Bob was red-faced with exertion and his breath came fast, but he was keeping up, at least so far.

Periodically they stopped to drink more water and to refill the bottles, sitting together in silence—Daniel filled with urgency, Bob with a kind of coiled determination—as if talking would be one more form of exertion, a waste of precious calories.

Whenever they stopped, Daniel would take out the phone to check for a cellular signal, walking around a little to try to catch something, but there was nothing, not even a flicker of a bar on the cell phone's flat, digital face. Afterward, he and Bob would take turns cranking the handle of the emergency charger, getting the phone up to at least half power and hoping it would be enough. Then they'd get up and get moving again, never fast enough, never sure of the way.

He kept looking up at the sky, at the low clouds, and imagining the people who even now must be up there looking for them. The phone was his SOS into the gloom. *Find us*, it said. *We're still out here. We're still alive.*

All the rest of that day, they followed the ice downstream, north and west with the wind in their teeth until the sky started to darken little by little, first a deeper gray, then slowly fading to black. Occasionally they came across animal tracks, caribou or moose, and once Daniel and Bob caught each other's eyes at the sight of a series of wolf tracks and scat, at the red blood of some small animal dead in the snow—rabbit, maybe. "Should we be worried?" Bob asked.

"There are almost no fatal wolf attacks in North America. Wolves don't like to be near people."

"*Almost* none. Which means some."

"We'll worry about it if we have to worry about it, Bob. It's far more likely we'll freeze to death."

"That's comforting."

They didn't stop to make camp until well after nightfall, pushing hard even when the light began to change, hoping to get closer, just a little closer to some form of civilization. Around one bend he was sure they'd find a road or a town, something, but when he turned the corner and the way opened up, there was nothing but snow and rocks and trees, the incessant wind, and the great gray lowering sky.

Finally Daniel picked a spot on the bank where the trees were taller and thicker and the wind lessened. The sound of Bob's breath behind him was like the sound of some agonized animal struggling for life, and when he'd pointed out the campsite he'd chosen, Bob fell into a snowbank like it was a featherbed, his face nearly purple with exertion. For a moment Daniel thought he might be dead, except he could just make out the rise and fall of the old man's chest under his coat.

But they didn't have time to rest. "Get up," Daniel said. "I need you to clear us a spot for the fire. Break off any low-hanging branches that look dry and save them for kindling. Scrape the snow clean down to the dirt. Don't leave any snow on the ground or the fire won't burn."

"Why can't you do it?" Bob asked between breaths. "You're better at that kind of thing."

"I'm building the shelter, so you need to do the fire," Daniel said, hunger and exhaustion making him lose his patience. "Come on, this isn't a board meeting and I'm not letting you delegate. It's dig or freeze."

For a minute, Daniel nearly expected an argument, but then Bob heaved himself to his feet and started scraping snow from the spot Daniel had pointed out. It was dark under the tree, and Daniel had to use his hands to dig a spot for them to sleep, packing the snow against the windward side of the pine to protect them against exposure. He had no choice about using his frostbitten hands—he had no shovel, and frostbite wasn't fatal, usually. He hollowed out the spot and lined it with branches he broke off from the pine. He would be able to warm up at the fire afterward.

When Bob had a bare spot scraped with his boots and Daniel had at least a rudimentary shelter built, they repeated the careful procedure to start the fire, Bob with the lighter and paper, Daniel with the dry kindling he'd carried in his pocket all the way from the crash site. After a few minutes they had a decent small fire, warm enough in their small space, if a little smoky—the wood he was using was too green and too damp, but it was all they could find—so Daniel alternated putting his frozen hands in front of the flames and tucking them under his armpits until they tingled and started to come back to life, a little at first, and then more and more. In a few minutes they hurt like hell, and he worried about the tips refreezing and gangrene setting in, but he didn't want to take a chance on peeling off his gloves to look at them, either. There was nothing he could do, and anyway, if he didn't see his fingers he wouldn't have to think about them. Instead, he squinted at Bob through a red haze of pain and remembered why he'd agreed to go on this suicide mission in the first place: for Kerry. Always for Kerry.

He lay down and tried to sleep, but the pain in his hands kept him up. Instead, he shifted position inside the shelter, rolling over and over to try to find a warm spot, bumping into Bob so many times the old man threatened to tie him up.

It was no good—he couldn't get comfortable, couldn't relax enough to sleep. He was hungry and in pain and past normal exhaustion; he'd moved into a kind of restless wakefulness, as if he were afraid to sleep, though his body and his mind were in desperate need of rest. He rolled over one more time and with a grunt flung the airline blanket off himself, disgusted.

He stood and pulled out his phone, turned it on, watching it blink to life, and then walked about the campsite and down the frozen creek a little bit, hoping for a signal. He was fully aware of what a strange thing the phone was out here, the screen illuminating everything in pale green, an incongruously modern piece of equipment lighting up the primitive darkness. But without a signal, it wasn't much more than a block of glass and metal—it wouldn't speak to him, wouldn't answer. The one time in his life he wished for the phone to ring, and it wouldn't.

He walked back toward the campsite and past it in the other direction, all the while holding the phone aloft, looking for a signal. "Damn," he muttered.

Behind him, Bob stirred. "Can't sleep?"

"Not really."

"You should get some rest. We can try again in the morning."

"I'm always afraid there's going to be a signal somewhere, and I'll miss it."

"You won't help her by wearing yourself out," Bob said. "Come on, give me the phone." He came out of the shelter and held out his hand to take it.

Daniel couldn't quite believe what he was hearing. "What?"

"You need to quit thinking that thing is going to save us. The only thing that's going to save us is finding *people*."

"The phone increases the chances we'll be found. You know it does, Bob."

"It's a distraction, nothing more. Give it here. I'll keep it until morning. That way you won't be tempted to look at it."

"The hell you will," Daniel said. "I'm not a kid who's been sent to his room. It's my phone, and I'll be damned if you'll take it away."

"Put the phone away, Albrecht."

Bob took another step, then another. Did he really think to take the phone away from Daniel by force? Just who, exactly, did Bob Packer think he was?

"Hold on—"

Bob was marching toward Daniel. "I said put that goddamn phone away."

Daniel was holding the phone away, out of Bob's reach. If the old man actually thought he was going to take it away, he had another think coming. "No."

Bob grabbed at it. The phone flew through the air, the green glow of the screen illuminated momentarily against the snow and the trees and the darkness. It spun, then fell with a resounding crack onto the ice of the creek.

Both men froze. The crack could have been the ice breaking, but it wasn't. Daniel went on his hands and knees along the creek ice until he found his phone at last. It had gone dark and he could feel a long rough crack running down the face from top to bottom like a jag of lightning. He tried turning it on again, but it stayed dark.

"You sonofabitch," Daniel hissed.

"If you'd put it away like I'd asked, it would still be intact."

"If you weren't intent on always having the last say, it would still be intact," Daniel said. "Now what will we do?"

"Same thing as we were doing before," Bob said. "We go downstream. We find help. We bring it back to the others."

"Goddamn you!" Daniel exclaimed. He was angrier than he'd ever been in his life. "I should have left you back at the wreck. You've been nothing but a problem for me since the minute we crashed."

"*I'm* the problem," said Bob, "when you've been kidding yourself about the phone this whole time? Walking around like a tiger in a cage? That thing's nothing but a useless hunk of junk."

Daniel couldn't hear, his whole body was buzzing so with anger.

He could see nothing but the sight of Bob's red face in the snow, his cheeks and nose white with frostbite and his eyes small and black in his round face, and he'd never wanted to hit another person so much in his life.

He could do it, too—he imagined launching himself at Bob's knees, taking the old man down, the two of them falling together in the snow, Daniel sitting on Bob's chest and hitting him hard two, three times, the satisfying crunch of his knuckles hitting Bob's nose until it bled.

But that wouldn't help. It would just expend energy he didn't have on a lost cause. So he did the next best thing instead.

"I quit, Bob."

"Don't get emotional. You know you don't mean it."

"No, really. I mean it. When we get home, I'm submitting my resignation. I won't come back."

"Fine, you quit," Bob said. "Now I'm freezing. Get in here and get to sleep."

I should keep walking. Just keep walking downstream and let him freeze to death out here. For a moment he was tempted to do just that—pick up his pack and keep going. It certainly seemed saner than spending the night under a fir tree with the world's most selfish old bastard.

Instead, feeling a profound weariness settle into his bones, he crawled back inside the shelter and lay down with his back against Bob's. The two men curled up against each other in the small space of the shelter, using their body heat and the small fire to chase off the cold. *Don't think I'll forget this. Not for a second.*

He still couldn't sleep, his anger a towering thing, burning so brightly that he could hardly keep his eyes closed. He should turn back now, he thought—just go back to the crash site and wait with the others. By the time he made it back, the weather would surely have cleared up, and they could build a signal fire so big it wouldn't be missed by rescue teams. That was the only sane thing to do. *Get up and leave right now, Albrecht. Get up and let this old fool take responsibility for his actions himself, for once in his life.*

So why couldn't he do it? Why couldn't he just stand up and leave Bob sleeping there, alone in the bush?

Because Bob wouldn't last the night without him. He'd be leaving an old, sick man to certain death in the cold and snow. And Daniel couldn't do that to another human being, no matter what the miserable sonofabitch had done to him.

He curled into himself, not really awake but not sleeping, either. There were noises around them, small scurryings that kept him wakeful.

As the hour grew later, Daniel felt the wind shift and change, the temperature drop once more. At one point he crept out of the shelter to look and saw that the night sky was clear, at once darker and brighter than he had ever seen. Clear! The storm had lifted at last.

Within that window, the black sky was completely lit by stars, more stars than Daniel had ever seen before, with the bright yellow-white cloud of the Milky Way at the center of the sky. His breath caught. It was beautiful. He hadn't been expecting beauty, not out here.

The stars were all dead now, their light reaching him long after they were gone. Growing up in the northwest Indiana side of Chicago, surrounded by steel mills and factories, he'd never realized the sky was so full of stars. Even in the places he'd camped as a child—Wisconsin, Michigan—there had almost always been a town within a few minutes' distance of the campsite. The light had never been able to reach him.

The night sky of the Yukon was something else indeed. It went on and on, sublime—almost like being in church. How many of his ancestors had stared at this sight? How many poems had it inspired, how many lovers, how many dreamers? Daniel felt a part of something greater than himself, a link in a chain of survival that reached back and back into the past, into the darkness.

He wished Kerry were here, so he could show her the stars.

He felt his eyes drooping, but he knew he couldn't sleep away from the shelter; it would be the end of him. Only the shelter, the fire, the bit of human warmth that lay there would keep him alive until morning, so he crawled back inside, his back to Bob's, and he dreamed he was back home in his own bed in Chicago, where it was warm, and Kerry was rolling over in the darkness to kiss him good night. *Sleep well, sweetheart*, she said to him, her mouth touching his eyes, his nose, his mouth, her breath sweet, turning to sugar, spilling over something warm and dark, spilling in countless grains as numberless as the stars. He tried to tell her about the stars, but she stopped him again with a kiss and said, *Go to sleep, Daniel. I'll wake you in the morning, I promise.*

22

Kerry woke with the sound of snoring in her ears and the feel of Daniel's arms around her. Her back—where Daniel lay with one arm pillowed under her head and the other resting lightly on her hip—was warm enough, but the rest of her was freezing, her hands and feet and face especially, and she turned and buried her face in Daniel's chest to warm herself. She had the feeling that she had fallen asleep someplace she shouldn't have, like she'd drunk too much at a party and had needed to spend the night on a friend's couch, but she was glad Daniel was there, glad of his closeness. The smell of him was strange, smoky, as if he'd been standing by someone's fireplace, and there were strange sounds around her, the breathing of many people at once. She stirred and came back to herself. Where was she? She had a sense of lost time but not how much. A few hours? A few days?

"Daniel?"

She opened her eyes to a pale blue-gray light and the sense she was in a crowded place with many people. She could smell and hear rather than see them—people covered with soot and pine sap, people breathing and whispering to one another, crowded close together on the floor. The space in which she found herself seemed to be the inside of an airplane, but all the seats were gone. Also, it was terribly cold, much more so than she'd realized at first, because the part of her that had been pressed against Daniel was so warm.

Was it Daniel, though? The man lying next to her was darker than Daniel, with short-cropped black hair and long, dark eyelashes against sallow cheeks, several days' worth of stubble obscuring his jaw. Not Daniel, then—but who was he, why was she lying next to him? He didn't look healthy; he gave the impression of someone who'd just gone through surgery, some kind of ordeal that had sapped his physical strength. She squinted, and the man's features rearranged themselves into something she recognized. Someone.

"Phil?"

He sat up, still holding her around the waist with one hand. "Sorry," he murmured, taking his hand away. He blinked several times and seemed to come back to himself. "You're awake. Are you feeling all right?" His voice betrayed a combination of relief and concern both.

"Sort of." She looked around her, trying to put together the things she remembered with the things she saw around her. She remembered being in Alaska, the airport in Anchorage. She remembered talking to Daniel about something important. The wedding, she thought it was—and something else, something that nagged at her but that she couldn't remember. She remembered terror and falling, and walking around the bodies of the dead, trying not to look at them. "How long was I out?" she asked.

"Two days, give or take."

Two days—no wonder she felt so strange. Light-headed. Thick-headed. "Where's Daniel?"

Phil kept watching her with that same intense look, but he didn't answer her question. "What's the last thing you remember?" he asked.

"I don't know. The airport in Anchorage I remember, and then I remember waking up on the ground. Daniel was here, and I remember talking to him." She sifted through the images that came to her, unsure which were dreams and which were real. "Daniel left for a little bit, but then he came back. I'm sure of that. He came back with another passenger from the tail, didn't he? I think I saw him sliding downhill toward us."

The talking was helping, the sound of her own voice bringing her back to herself despite a strange mixture of terror and slowness, as if her body would not let her get the words out quickly enough. She felt drugged, almost, but with a core of pain nestled in the middle of her like a bullet in a wound. She only knew that Daniel was supposed to be here, and he wasn't. She'd been so sure. The last thing she remembered, he had been *right here*.

Phil was looking over at someone else—a tiny dark-haired woman in the corner, who was sitting up and watching the whole exchange. She looked familiar, too, but Kerry couldn't put a name with her face. Some kind of look passed between them.

"What's going on?" Kerry asked.

Phil said, "Daniel left to go find help."

"Why? Shouldn't he have stayed here with the rest of us? Wouldn't that be safer?"

Phil's face pinched itself into a look Kerry knew well—the frown, the eyes hooded with discomfort. He didn't want to be the one telling her this. "He was worried the rescue teams were having trouble finding us, because of the weather. He was sure the emergency transmitter was damaged in the crash, and then, things started to get bad . . ."

"What things?"

"You were hurt—" Phil started. Then he must have seen something in her face, because he stopped, pulled back and started again. "A lot of the passengers are hurt. Not just you. I'm hurt, Kecia's hurt, a lot of people. He thought he might be able to find a road or a cell-phone signal."

A panicky, fluttery feeling clutched at her, clawed at her throat. "But there's no shelter, no food. He'll freeze to death!"

"He was scared. We all were. You wouldn't wake up, and then Beverly said you might lose the baby . . ."

She stiffened. The baby—that was the thing she hadn't remembered right away. Now it came flooding back to her, the missed period, telling Daniel. But the pregnancy was so unexpected, so new, she'd barely had time to think how she felt about it, much less decide how she wanted other people to feel about it. "How do you know about that?"

Phil blinked several times and looked away as if in apology for bringing it up. "Daniel told me. He thought I should know. He asked me to look after you until he got back."

Rising panic again, her breath coming fast and heavy, her heart shattering her ribs. "That's why he left, wasn't it? He thought we were in danger. The—the baby and me."

She could barely speak. Daniel was out there alone in the cold and the snow. He'd taken on a suicide rescue mission all because of her.

"It wasn't just you. It's been too long—no one's found us. If the storm stops, he said he'd come right back. But someone had to go, and Daniel was the best chance we had. He knew that."

She pulled herself up into a standing position. "If I wasn't pregnant right now, he might not have gone at all, would he?"

Phil looked over at the woman in the corner again, quickly, then back at Kerry. The woman's eyes were pleading with Phil, *Don't upset her, keep her calm, don't get her riled up* . . .

Kerry felt her emotions all snap into place. "Tell me the truth, Phil! I'm not a child! Daniel risked his life for me and the baby, didn't he?"

Phil didn't answer. The force of her anger was a power she couldn't contend with; it would sweep her up, sweep her away. Suddenly the inside of the plane was stuffed with too many people, it was too close, too crowded, and Kerry needed to get out of there, get out, get out . . .

She staggered woozily to the back of the plane, pushed aside some suitcases and lurched outside into the snow. The sky was clear—the storm had broken during the night—and coming over the horizon was the clear yellow globe of the sun.

Dawn.

A few passengers were huddled around a small fire built in a bare spot next to the plane's fuselage, protected from the wind. Kerry shouldered her way to the front until she felt the warmth and heat of the fire on her face, the most warmth she'd felt in days, probably. She couldn't get rid of the picture of Daniel trudging through deep snow, only his eyes showing, head bowed against the wind. Because of her. Because of the baby. He always took responsibility for everyone else, he never thought of himself, and now if he died out there, if he didn't come back, she'd never forgive herself, never.

If she'd been awake, she would have told him not to go. Begged him. No matter what Phil said, she knew he'd gone because of her. He would not have been able to sit still and wait for help when Kerry was hurt; it wasn't in his nature. He was a man used to taking matters into his own hands, and he had a little experience in backcountry situations; he might have been able to convince himself that he could manage. But this wasn't the Upper Peninsula of Michigan in the middle of July, this was the Yukon in midwinter, one of the remotest spots on earth. The chances that he would find help were almost nothing, but the chance that he'd freeze to death out there, away from the shelter of the plane, was very great indeed. She might not have much experience in the woods on her own, but she knew that much, at least.

One of the other passengers was watching her from across the fire, a slender, dark-skinned woman around forty or forty-five who was wearing a coat so large it dragged on the ground. One arm was bandaged and splinted, and she held it in front of her like a wounded bird. She was the flight attendant Daniel had brought back from the tail section.

"You're awake," said the woman.

"Much good it's doing me."

The woman came around to stand next to her. "You look better. Bev and Phil were so worried about you."

Kerry couldn't think of the woman's name, but it was obvious they'd spoken before. "And Daniel," she said.

"That's right, Daniel, the one who left to find help. He's your fiancé, isn't he? You two are getting married when you get back to Chicago."

Kerry felt her eyes starting to blur with tears. "That was the plan."

"Aww, honey," said the woman, putting her arm around Kerry. "Don't worry. Worrying only invites trouble. Imagine him finding a nice warm cabin with a phone. He might already be on his way back."

Was she serious? Everything that could have gone wrong in this situation *had* gone wrong. Why should their luck change now? "I'll try."

"He said he spent a lot of time camping, hiking in the woods, that kind of thing. Surely he knows what he's doing, right?"

Kerry smiled. "Camping" made it sound more rustic than it really was. They'd always had the best equipment whenever they'd gone out in the woods. Fleece jackets, waterproof tents, magnesium fire starters, enough food and water for a small army. But he had spent time in the woods, more than most. Maybe the flight attendant was right, and Daniel would come back to her, whole and safe and alive. It was possible, wasn't it?

She leaned close to the fire and felt the orange heat on her face and wondered if anything had ever felt so good. Her hands and feet tingled, coming back to life, and she could see the way the other passengers leaned toward it—greedy, as though they would like to swallow it.

"Who built this fire?" she asked the flight attendant.

"Phil did it, the day before yesterday," said the other woman. Kecia—that was her name. "You should have seen him. He was trying to warm up that IV bag for you—it was a block of ice before he made the fire. But he was determined. He and Amber and that kid, Zach, gathered all the wood and paper and found a lighter and everything. He was like a man on a mission, trying to warm up those IV bags."

"Phil did it?" Phil Velez, her dour, pessimistic co-worker?

"And then when some of the other passengers tried to take over the fire," Kecia said, lowering her voice in case anyone was listening, "he chased them off. Said he'd put the fire out and let everyone freeze to death if they couldn't learn to take turns with it."

Now, *that* she couldn't picture at all. The Phil she knew was an avoider; he'd go twice around the globe if it meant he wouldn't have to talk to Kerry, sit near her, deal with her at all. How could he *possibly* have worked up enough moxie to take on a bunch of starving, freezing, greedy passengers? "Unbelievable."

"That's what I said. Anyway, he got your IV warmed up and Bev hooked you up. It must have done you some good."

Kerry didn't know what to think. Phil had done all of that for her sake?

She couldn't think straight. Daniel was gone, and Phil had stayed behind to take care of her. Clearly the world had changed while she was asleep. Up was down, black was white, and Kerry Egan was no longer certain she knew anything of the world, or the people in it.

When her twenty minutes were over—apparently the passengers had taken Phil's fire rules very seriously—Kerry went back inside to sit against the bulkhead, pulling her coat around her to hold on to the warmth. It was strange to be there without Daniel. Her thoughts kept turning to him, to the vision she had of him falling to his knees in the snow, his eyebrows full of ice, ice in his mouth and his eyes. *Why did you go?* she kept imagining herself asking him. *Why would you leave, when the thing I need most is to have you here?*

Across from her she could see Phil sitting in his own spot against the bulkhead, Beverly hovering over him. She was pulling up the tail of his coat and then his shirt, asking questions too soft to hear and then telling him he needed rest. "Stop running around after the fire and everyone else," Bev admonished him. "You're whiter than all this damn snow. Sit your ass down and stay there."

From across the plane, Kerry said, "You're still in a lot of pain?"

Phil looked up as if he hadn't realized she was there. He pulled his shirt back down quickly, though Kerry had seen nothing more than an expanse of pale stomach marked by a purple bruise. "It's been getting worse. I can feel it."

"Is it bad?"

"Bad enough," Beverly said, turning around to fix Phil with a steely glare. "And I know you're peeing blood, so don't bother trying to hide it anymore." Then she stomped toward someone coughing near the rear of the plane.

"What's her problem?" Kerry asked.

"She's working without a net." He followed Beverly's movements, watching her thrash around the plane like a caged elephant. "She's worried she won't be able to keep us all alive until we're found."

This struck Kerry as more insightful than she would have given Phil credit for, and again she found herself shifting her perceptions of him, her long-held assumptions. He wasn't anything like she'd thought—arrogant, proud. Instead here he was, caring for her, for all of them, as a real friend would.

Maybe Phil wasn't the problem after all. Maybe *she* was the one who'd been too proud, and she'd never been able to see it.

"I want to thank you," she said.

He looked up at her, the surprise on his face too evident, and she watched as he fought it back and settled his expression into something close to neutral once more. "For . . . ?"

"Everything you've done for me the past couple of days. It was above and beyond the call of duty."

He smiled, but it was tinged with sadness. "I didn't do it for duty," he said. "I'm glad you're doing better. We were really afraid for you for a while there. We thought you might end up in a coma."

She touched the bruise on her head and said, "I don't know that I'm all better yet, but I suppose being awake is a good start."

"When we get rescued, they'll give you an MRI and make sure everything's okay. I'm sure you'll be fine," he said.

She sat and watched him carefully. There was a tension around

Phil's mouth and eyes that gave him away: he knew more about this situation than he was telling. What was he not saying?

"You had this happen before, didn't you?"

He smiled, grimly. "I know a little something about it, yes."

"So tell me," she said.

"You don't want to hear about my life."

She waved her arms around, encompassing the plane, the passengers, the boredom and cold. "You have a better time to talk to me than now? Come on, let's hear it."

And so he told her about Emily, her diagnosis, her treatment. How the cancer moved from her ovaries throughout her whole body, eventually metastasizing in her brain. How it changed her moods, her personality, made her angry, made her hateful. How he'd cared for her evenings and weekends for months on end, working all day to keep their health insurance and then tending his dying wife all night to keep her comfortable, keep her alive. It was the most beautiful picture of devotion she'd ever encountered, and it made her desperate, thinking of Daniel freezing in the snow and herself unable to help him in any way, unable to do anything but sit and wait. As helpless as Phil had been, watching Emily die little by little. At least Phil had gotten to be *with* Emily when she died. Kerry might never see Daniel again.

When he was done, she said, "It's possible he'll never come back, isn't it? Daniel, I mean. We might get rescued, and if he doesn't come back, I may never know what happened to him."

Phil said, very quietly, "It's possible, yes."

She shook her head to get rid of the image of Daniel half-buried in snow, his face blue. "Would you have gone? If it had been your wife, your Emily, would you have left her?"

Phil was silent for a little while. He said, "I did leave her."

"What?"

There was a grave hesitation on his face, emotions crossing one over the other so quickly Kerry could hardly keep up with them. "I left her once. At the end."

"Why?"

"I—" She could see him fighting with himself, trying to decide how much to trust her, trying to decide if he wanted her to know so much. If he could live with her knowing. Then he said, "There was a day, a terrible day, when I'd had enough. She was so sick, and I was exhausted and wrung out. She'd been throwing up all day, and her medicine was making her hallucinate. She thought I was her father one minute, and then the next minute she said I was trying to kill her, that I was poisoning her food. She hit me, and I . . . I lost it. I walked out the door and got in the car and drove around."

"Where did you go?"

He told her about driving to the lake. The towel, the stove, the fire—everything. She could hear his voice cracking, breaking.

"My God," Kerry said.

She was thinking how lucky they were, how much worse it could have been, but Phil's face crumpled in horror and self-recrimination. He was punishing himself for what he saw as an unforgivable act. How long had he been beating himself up for this so-called crime? For a moment of entirely human weakness in the face of devastation?

"The home-health nurse covered for me, said she'd sent me to the store to get Emily's medication, but she knew, she knew I'd left. It was only because of the nurse that I didn't go to jail, only because of a neighbor I didn't kill my own wife through negligence."

"Phil, I'm so sorry—"

"I'm a horrible person, Kerry. I don't deserve to be happy, I don't deserve your pity or your friendship." His voice was so choked with emotion he could hardly breathe; the sight of him gasping for air brought her to tears. No wonder he'd been so reserved, so cold all this time. No wonder he never talked about himself. He'd been shouldering the most terrible self-hatred she'd ever seen. Here it was, naked and human, and beautiful, in its way.

She stood up and went to him immediately, putting her arms around his shoulders and letting him sob into her neck as she said, "You didn't kill her. You didn't cause her cancer or give her hallucinations. You had a moment of self-preservation, Phil. That's all."

"I didn't, I left—"

"The nurse didn't turn you in because she knew what you were dealing with. She'd probably seen it a hundred times before. Everyone has his breaking point."

"She was my wife. I should have been there to take care of her every minute."

"And if you hadn't left, she still would have died," Kerry said. "You have to forgive yourself. That's what she would want, I'm sure of it."

"You think so?"

"Of course," Kerry said. "She loved you."

23

Daniel woke with the first light of the morning on his face and the feeling that he was alone.

He sat up. It was dawn, the light growing blue around the edges of the world, but the snow had stopped. For the first time in days, the wreck would be visible from the air. The lost passengers could be found. He and Bob could start back immediately, he thought, and started gathering his things, the first real hope he'd had in days making him move faster than he'd thought possible.

He rolled over to tell Bob the good news and only then realized why he'd thought he was alone: the old man wasn't in the shelter. He'd taken his roll of coats and blankets and gone. His footsteps— the big fish-shaped print of the snowshoes Daniel had helped him make with duct tape—led down toward the frozen creek, then went downstream, farther away from the wreck.

Damn. He knew exactly what had happened: Bob had woken early, seen that the skies were clear, and known that Daniel would want to go back. *Damn him!* Bob was so sure this was the way to help, that there'd be a town just around every hill. He must have thought he could keep walking and find help, find a road on his own. He hated waiting around for someone else to rescue them, and he always had to be right—it had to be his way.

He'd left because he'd been sure, he'd known, that Daniel would come after him.

Not this time, Daniel thought. *Let him freeze his stupid ass out here. You don't have to go after him. You don't have to. The old man's lost his mind. The only smart thing to do is turn around and go back and wait with the others.*

That wasn't such an easy decision, though. They'd been walking for two days. It would take two to get back, at least. But if there was a town nearby, if they were close . . .

Jesus. He was doing the same math Bob had, apparently. Whichever direction he chose might be fatal. There was no way to know.

The wind was so powerful that it felt like it was pushing him backward with all its might. He was weak from hunger and lack of sleep. His cheeks and the tip of his nose were completely numb. His hands, too, were literal blocks of ice, an icy blue-white that ran nearly the length of each finger. Frozen solid. He could no longer feel his fingers well enough to tie on his snowshoes or unzip his pants without Bob's help. And he needed to piss, badly.

Using the edges of his gloves, he rolled the pants down over his hips, gasping from the feel of the cold on his genitals. *Oh God, hurry up.*

He looked down and saw a dark-brown stream staining the snow. That was a bad sign.

His most urgent need taken care of, he wrangled his pants back up and tried to think. Near the creek lay a small bloody bundle of fur that had been a rabbit, its fur matted with blood. Most likely a fox had gotten it the night before. The fox needed to eat; it was a fox, after all. Daniel couldn't spare any pity for the rabbit, not under the circumstances. Then again, he was thinking that the rabbit, given a choice, would probably have preferred to live.

Keep your eye on the ball. You take your eye off the ball for even just a second and someone could die.

There were so many variables Daniel couldn't control. If the black box was working properly. If the rescue planes were near enough to hear it. If Phil managed to live long enough to tell the search crews the direction Daniel and Bob had gone.

If Kerry was still alive. Too many ifs.

At last he gathered his bundle of coats and blankets quickly and set out after Bob, though he didn't see any sign of the old man on the horizon. He must have left much earlier than Daniel had thought. So he walked. Without snowshoes, it was extremely difficult going, so he stuck to the creek, where the snow was thinner over the ice. The wind, which had moved in from the north now that the storm had blown itself out, roared down the valley floor between the hills and right into Daniel's face like an angry bear. More than likely the rescue planes would find the wreck today. More than likely Phil would tell them the direction Daniel and Bob had gone. More than likely they would reach a road or a town sometime today. It was still possible, wasn't it?

It was also possible that the rescue planes, sent in their direction, would find nothing but two men from Chicago frozen to death in the snow.

He didn't want to admit to himself that half the problem was stubbornness, his own as much as Bob's. He'd set out to do this thing, to find help. He'd promised Kerry that he would see it through to the end. He couldn't go back.

By noon he'd made little progress—only about two miles by Daniel's reckoning—so he stopped to catch his breath and drink his little ration of water and refill his bottles. His face was so stiff he could hardly move it. Probably it was white with frostbite; he'd seen photos of mountain climbers with the planes of their cheeks and forehead blackened with it, the tips of their noses damaged beyond repair. Daniel hardly needed a mirror to know that his own face must look similarly wind-blasted, though it was much too late to worry about disfigurement, about scarring. Staying alive was the only thing that mattered.

The only thing in the world was snow, and the frozen dark line of the creek. The wind, the sun. He pulled his coat against him. His eyes hurt from staring at all that white in the blinding sun, but nowhere did he see a speck of a plane or hear the *thwack-thwack* of helicopter rotors. The only sound was the rattle of his own breathing. His heart still pumping. Moving him closer to—what? He didn't even remember anymore. He picked up his feet and put them down without even remembering why.

Not long after noon, his breath so loud in his ears it drowned out the wind, Daniel found Bob sitting with his back against a tree trunk to one side of the creek bed. It was a bad spot to stop, not sheltered enough; the wind was shaking every stray fiber on Bob's clothes. He'd taken off his snowshoes and sat with them in his lap, loose in his hands, but he wasn't looking at them, wasn't trying to put them back on. He was breathing heavily—as Daniel walked up, he could see the puffs of white coming out of his mouth one after the other so quickly they were virtually indistinguishable—and his face was purple with strain underneath its coating of frostbite.

For a minute neither man spoke. The wind was louder than words, and anyway, it felt like too much effort when simply breathing hurt. To acknowledge the truth would have been to acknowledge that it had been a mistake to make the effort, and Bob never admitted to his mistakes.

Instead he made a noise of pain, a gasp.

"What's wrong?"

"Damn."

"Pain? Where?"

"My chest. Like a locomotive is sitting on me."

Daniel opened his mouth to say something, then changed his mind. What he wanted to say was, *I can't say I'm surprised, the way you smoke. It's a wonder it didn't happen years ago.* Instead he only said, "Here, lie down. Breathe slowly. I'll get you some water."

"No point." Bob's face twisted with pain again. "Sorry. About this. I'm sorry. You wanted to turn around and go back this morning. To wait with the others. Right?"

Daniel looked up at the blue sky. Surely by now the rescue planes would be circling, they'd be headed for the wreck. Back at the crash site, they were probably already building a signal fire. If Phil and

Bev had managed to keep Kerry alive long enough, she might be in the hands of medical professionals by the end of the day.

"They're probably being found as we speak."

"Yes?"

He shaded his eyes against the glare of the snow. "If they make a fire, they'll be visible from miles away. It's just a matter of hours now."

"I'm sorry," Bob said. "You should have. Turned back this morning. Left me out here. Would have served me right."

"I wouldn't have made it. It was too far. We're better off sticking together."

Daniel closed his eyes and tipped his face to the sky. Snow was falling onto his wind-blasted face. He could feel the urge to lie down powerful inside him, but he wouldn't. He couldn't.

"You still have your lighter?" Daniel asked.

Bob gave him a look that was full of questions, but then he nodded and indicated the inside pocket of his parka. Daniel took it out, then set about clearing a spot of its snow, scraping and scraping until he got to the bare dirt beneath. He gathered the lowest branches, the driest and deadest ones, along with some pine boughs. Then he took the bit of paper and dry kindling and, using Bob's lighter, set the whole thing aflame.

The little orange glow was like the first ray of hope in that white place. He added a larger branch to the fire, and when it was going enough, he set the green branches on top, watching the smoke rise and rise into the clear blue sky.

When he'd built up a good column of smoke, he sat next to Bob in the snow, feeling exhaustion overtake him, and closed his eyes.

24

They heard the first plane around noon. It was the boy, the kid with the broken teeth, who noticed it first—Zach, Kerry thought his name was. He'd stood up and pointed at the sky, insisting the plane was there, and the hopeful adults had shaded their eyes against the bright sunlight and waited with their breath in their mouths. They waited, but the blue sky showed nothing but a few wisps of cloud, and after a few moments the mother turned to the boy and said, "It's nothing, you heard nothing." But the boy insisted he was right, it was there, he was right, he was right.

The adults waited, and in a minute they, too, saw the white shape of the plane moving between the hills, and as one they jumped up and waved and shouted, "It *is* a plane! We've been found, we've been found!"

Except that the plane was too far away to see them, too far away for them to be sure. Outside in that bright air, Kerry could see that the sun was nearly overhead, the shadows shortening. The minute her face hit the air outside, she felt how much colder it was, how bitter—the storm had blown itself out and left a frigid dome of icy air in its wake. She shielded her eyes and looked. The plane was here. It had to be here, somewhere.

In the far distance, she spotted a small white turboprop making its way slowly across the blue sky a few miles to the north. But something was wrong—it wasn't moving like a rescue plane. It wasn't coming toward them. It was off in the distance, like a ship's sail seen against the horizon. Kerry stood and watched it cross between the crests of two low hills.

A voice spoke at her elbow: "Someone found us?" It was Amber, the first flight attendant, standing outside in her foraged coat and boots, watching the plane cross the distant sky.

It was too far away to see them, Kerry was realizing, barely more than a white dot on the horizon. What's more, it was going in a relatively straight line, not circling, not turning in the air like a search plane might. *Was* it a search plane? Or merely traveling from one place to another, oblivious to the fact that there was a missing transcontinental jetliner somewhere below? Either way, it was too far away to spot the wreckage where they stood.

"They must have," Kerry said. Though she felt a profound sense of unease, she thought it would be best to sound certain.

Amber watched with her for a minute. Then she said, "They don't see us. We need something to signal with. Look for as many green branches as you can find."

"What are you going to do?"

"Trying to make smoke," she said, and ran off to find Phil.

Kerry and the others broke off branch after branch, dozens of people working furiously, working with the most hope they'd felt all week.

By the time Amber came back with the lighter, the plane had moved so far off to the north Kerry was afraid there was no way their little bit of smoke would be visible. Still, they were going to try, Amber said, putting the greenest branches on the fire to smoke. In a few minutes, they had a towering black cloud billowing up hundreds of feet into the sky. If it was visible over the treetops, if anyone was still looking for them, surely they'd find it.

When the fire was going strong, the flight attendant took Kerry by the elbow and said, "You should go inside. Phil's not doing so well. He was asking for you."

Kerry picked her way through the dark inside the plane to the place where Phil lay. "They coming?" he asked, his breath coming in little gasps. Beverly was hovering over him, touching his belly, feeling the hard spot there, the place where she said the blood was pooling into his abdominal cavity. He was ghastly pale now, a green tinge around his mouth and eyes. Bleeding to death, Beverly had said. The former nurse gave Kerry a grim look. *He'll die today*, her look said. It said, *There's nothing more I can do.*

"Soon," Kerry told Phil, and was pleased when he gave her a little smile. "I promise. They'll be here any minute."

It has to work. It has to.

He closed his eyes. She knew he was hanging on by a very thin thread. She said, "In a few hours we'll be sitting in a warm building drinking hot coffee and soup. We'll have real blankets and the good painkillers. We'll have TV and Internet."

Phil smiled weakly. "Sounds good," he said. "You won't leave without me?"

"No way," she said, and took his hand. "You didn't leave me. I won't leave without you."

The sound of the airplane's rotors was growing louder, and outside the survivors were all cheering. *Daniel*, she thought. *Daniel, they've found us at last.*

25

"So they saw the smoke?"

Kerry goes silent while I turn around in my seat to get a better look at my son, to see his face. We're coming to the end of the story now. Jackson's been quiet for much of the ride, listening to his mom and me tell him what we remember, then what we only heard about afterward, when all the facts were known. Some of it, quite frankly, we've had to imagine for him, filling in the parts we didn't see or don't remember with the parts we heard about in the hospital, while we were recovering, and parts from the journal, that we couldn't have known or imagined. It isn't that hard. In the years since the accident, how many times have I thought about the one who isn't here to tell his part of the story? Hundreds of times. Thousands, maybe. I've walked those paths with him through the snow and darkness, through the wind. I have thought about the way he felt, the things he feared, the decisions he made. I've thought of him nearly every day, wondering why I'm here and he's not.

"Well, what do you think?" I ask him.

He scrunches up one side of his face and says, "They must have seen it. You wouldn't be sitting here talking to me otherwise, right?"

"You've always been a smart kid," I say.

Outside, the flat plains of Alberta have given way to the green hills and winding highways of the northern edge of British Columbia; soon we'll be crossing over into Yukon Territory again. It will not be the same as the place we remember. We'll be staying in the city, in a hotel with heat and food, with beds and blankets. The place will be brown and gold, the end of autumn, not the cold, dark, wintry landscape we lived in those five days, somewhere between hope and despair. In some ways I feel as if we've never quite left the place behind. It's always there, lurking at the back of my thoughts, just out of reach.

"They did see us," I say. "Your mom and the others made sure to put lots of green branches on the fire that morning, to make plenty of smoke. They made sure it was something the rescue planes wouldn't miss, once the skies were clear enough. They saw us, all right. They circled the campsite a few times and dipped their wings. That's what they do to let you know."

"So Mom was a hero?" asks my son.

"All I did was help build the smoke signal," says Kerry. "Other people were heroes then, honey, not me."

"What about you, Dad? Where were you?"

I look over at my wife, remembering the day we were rescued.

The moment the plane dipped its wings, as it circled the camp to the sounds of cheers, she came inside to sit next to me, let me know we were found. She picked up my hand and held it. The inside of the plane was dim; my thoughts were fuzzy, but I remember feeling, for a moment, that I might be able to fly myself, sitting so close to her, feeling her concern for me. I knew I wasn't imagining it. I'd waited so long for her feelings for me to change, and they had. It was only friendship then, but it was enough.

I'd said, "If I die, I want you to know something."

"You're not going to die now, so don't talk like that," Kerry said.

"It's still a long way back," I said. "I need to tell you . . ."

"Shh." She pulled the blanket up to keep me warm. "You don't need to say it. I know."

I coughed, painfully. "And here I thought I'd been so clever."

Now there's a sound from the backseat, and Jackson asks, "So how were you rescued?"

"We went outside, and over the hill we could see the helicopters coming toward us," Kerry says. "I don't think I ever heard such a wonderful sound in my life."

"You got to ride in a helicopter?"

"I did. I was one of the first passengers on. Your dad insisted. He was the sickest one there, so he got to go first. He said he wouldn't leave without me."

"You wanted to make sure she was okay, too, didn't you, Dad?"

I smile over at my wife. Kerry looks as beautiful as ever, but there's a sadness around her mouth, a tightening that I know all too well. "Your mom was hurt, too. I couldn't leave her behind."

"And what about Daniel? What happened to him?"

Kerry's face pales again. There are several things I would like to forget from those days in the Yukon—unlike Kerry, my memory of those days doesn't have any holes—but foremost is that look, the expression on Kerry's face when she first heard that Daniel was dead.

We were on the helicopter by then, me on a gurney, Kerry at my side. The rotors were so loud we couldn't speak until one of the men gave us each a headset. He introduced himself as Bill Abernathy, the director of crisis operations for Denali Airlines. "We're going to get you folks seen by a doctor in less than two hours," Bill had said into his headset. "I give you my word."

The relief I felt was short-lived. The next moment Kerry was asking for news of the two men who'd gone out into the wilderness to look for help. We still had hope then—surely Daniel's plan had worked, because here were the rescue helicopters. They'd found us. Had they found Daniel? Was he the one who'd led the rescue planes to us?

"In a way," Bill said, then told us how twenty kilometers west of the crash site they'd found two men in the snow, an older man who was already dead of a heart attack and a younger man, wrapped in blankets, suffering from severe exposure, his hands and feet and face covered with frostbite. By the time they'd gotten to him, Daniel was delirious, barely conscious, but Bill said when they loaded him onto the chopper he'd roused himself enough to tell them his name and that he was a survivor of Denali Flight 806. It was Daniel's signal fire that had drawn the rescue teams back in this direction, Bill said. After searching above the storm for four days with no sign of our ELT signal, the airline had started widening the search grid, wondering if the pilots had put us down farther away from Whitehorse than the airline had originally estimated. But then just that morning a small twin-engine had spotted Daniel's signal fire and sent word back to Whitehorse. They'd dispatched the rescue plane right away, which found the crash site three hundred kilometers southeast of the city of Whitehorse, about fifty kilometers east of the town of Teslin. The search had come back in our direction at last.

Daniel saved us, Bill said, but he had not been able to save himself. He'd died on the flight back to Whitehorse, his body half-frozen, his organs shutting down one by one. They'd found him a few hours too late.

Bill had brought Daniel's journal. It had been wrapped in his pack, wet around the edges but mostly legible still. Kerry took it with trembling hands, and I held her hand as Bill told us what Daniel had done, how brave he'd been, how much he'd given up for us. I remember Kerry clutching that journal and sobbing all the way back to Whitehorse, sobbing Daniel's name, for her own sake and the sake of the child she carried.

I'd never felt so helpless. I wanted to comfort her, be there for her, but it was she who was there for me. When the emergency crews were helping me into a waiting ambulance at the airport, Kerry stood above me pale and damp, her face washed with something that seemed like desperation. Probably she'd had too much death, too much loss—Daniel, and Judy, and Bob, and all the others. Or maybe she was just being brave. She grabbed my hand and said, "Don't you die on me, too."

I gave her a weak smile and said, "I may not have much say in the matter."

"I mean it, Phil. Don't you *dare*. If you die, I will kill you."

"I won't," I said, and meant it. I would find a way to live, if I could. So Kerry and I went into the hospital together, warm for the first time in days, to have our wounds treated.

It turned out she had a fairly serious concussion; I had internal bleeding from a puncture in my small intestine, a slow loss of blood that would likely have been fatal within the next twelve to twenty-four hours. The doctor told me this later, when the danger had passed. If it hadn't been for Beverly's care, or if the planes hadn't found us in time, I would likely have died, too.

Afterward, in the hospital, Kerry and I learned to lean on each other, Kerry sitting by my bedside or I hers, even while she mourned Daniel, even when she said she was sure the sadness would eat her until she disappeared. I knew that grief, I told her—I'd lived through it, too.

And then the strangest thing happened. I *had* lived through my grief, I realized. I had grieved Emily for years when I thought I couldn't go on, but I had, and came out the other side still whole, still human, even when I thought every decent and good part of me was gone.

"I want it to stop. The pain, it's too much," she said to me once, only a couple of days before Christmas. The ward at the hospital was decorated red and green; my room was strung with colored lights. I loved those lights, the electric colors, gold and blue and red. I begged the nurses never to turn them off. In the reflection of the lights, Kerry's face changed colors over and over. "When does it stop? When do you ever start to feel normal again?"

"You don't," I said. "The button never resets, not really. But you can still find reasons to go on."

"Have you?" she asked, her face streaked with tears. "I mean, really?"

I took her hand. "For what it's worth, I have."

"I don't know if I can ever be happy again."

"You don't have to think about that now. Right now it's okay to be sad. Just don't let it eat you alive," I told her. "You have lots of reasons to go on. The baby most of all."

I held her when she cried then, the same way that I held her up later at Daniel's funeral, then at Judy's. Eventually I helped her sell her condo, sorting through Daniel's things, deciding what to keep and what to let go. I stood next to her the day she gave her notice at Petrol because by then it was clear that her injuries had made it impossible for her to work with computer screens and telephones any longer. I went with her to doctors' appointments and made her dinner and helped her move. In turn she found me a new apartment near hers, took me to the movies, even went with me to pick out new furniture. She kissed me for the first time that day, more than a year after the crash. We'd found a soft leather sofa that Kerry said I *had* to get, and before I could turn to the salesman and say I'd take it, she caught me on the mouth, a look of surprise registering on her face as much as it must have on mine.

"I'm sorry," she said. "I don't know why I did that."

"Don't apologize," I said, nearly breathless. "Believe me, that was nothing to apologize for."

Kerry and I were friends, and then we were more than that.

Together we started to reassemble the pieces of our lives, little by little.

Now we're passing a sign that reads "Whitehorse 10 km." I'm still thinking of that kiss, that moment when we crossed that invisible line, when Jackson says, "So that means Dad is not my real father? Right? If Daniel was the one Mom was dating before the crash, then he's my father."

I feel my breath catch. It's one thing to know it; it's another to hear him say it out loud. *You're not my real father.* I've always thought, or at least hoped, that there's more than one way to be a father.

"Your dad is your *real* father," Kerry says. "He's been there for every important moment in your life. But he's not your biological father."

"So what you're telling me is that Daniel Albrecht was my biological father."

"Is," I say. I won't deny the man his place in my son's life. Not now. Not ever.

Kerry is clutching the journal to her chest and talking fast now, the way she does when she gets emotional, or maybe it's just that, like me, she's worried about what Jackson will say next. "Your dad has loved you, been with you, since the day you were born. You couldn't ask for a better one."

"It's okay, Kerry, let him have a minute," I tell her. "It's a lot to take in."

We're quiet again. The only sound is the buzz of the road under the tires.

Then Jackson says, "But it all could have ended differently, couldn't it? If the plane hadn't gone down, you would have married Daniel instead, right?"

Kerry glances at me, then says, "That's true. I would have married Daniel and not your dad. But it did happen. Everything changed."

I look over at her in the passenger's seat, this woman I loved for so long without being able to say so. She takes my hand and says, "We had to accept what happened and move on. That's all we have control over."

When we came back to Chicago, I did my best to step into Daniel's shoes. I was there for all of it—the ultrasound appointments, the Lamaze classes, the false labor. And when Jackson was born and placed in Kerry's arms, the next person who'd held him was me. I've been his father that day and every day since.

"So it was all an accident," Jackson says. "Everything."

"Not everything," I say.

I remember our wedding day, Kerry in her white dress, barefoot on the Lake Michigan sand, Jackson chubby in her arms, cradled between us, whining to get down and play in the sand. He was about a year old, just learning to walk. When I made my vows, I made them to him as much as to her. To love, honor and cherish. In sickness and in health.

I love them both, would do anything for them both. And yet there is always the ghost of Daniel in the lines of Jackson's face, in his laugh, the sound of his voice. In Kerry's memory, her sorrow. She says we are, both of us, carrying our ghosts around all the time—and if she can live with mine, then I can certainly live with hers.

Jackson has been quiet a long while. Then he says, "I've heard you two talking about Daniel before."

I feel my breath catch again. "You did?"

"Yeah. I mean, it's not like you never talk about him."

Kerry looks over at me again. We didn't think we were so obvious.

"I didn't realize he was my father. My biological father, that is. But I'm glad."

"You are?" Kerry asks.

Jackson is thoughtful for a moment. "Well, he sounds like a good person. Someone who would help other people like that. I'm glad I know more about him now. But Dad is my dad. It's weird to think he might not have been, if things were different. But I'm not sorry."

"No," Kerry says. "Neither am I."

And it's true. I feel a strange lightening, as if a weight I hadn't been aware I was carrying has suddenly fallen away. Whenever I've thought of Daniel these past ten years, it's always been tinged with guilt. I took his place, this good man who did so much to help others—to help me—and I've wondered for a long time if I did the right thing, if I was worthy. Would Daniel have been a better father, a better husband? Would he have been more patient with Jackson, more fun? Would he have made Kerry happier, made her feel more loved? Has it really worried me so much that Jackson would reject me? Or would he understand that once Daniel was gone, we needed each other, Kerry and I?

No, I think—*he does understand*. Or he's beginning to. This is the family he's always known. He accepts it, the way he accepts his red hair and his freckles. It's a part of him, like I am. Like Daniel is.

From the back Jackson says, "Will you tell me more about him? What he was like?"

"Of course, honey. We'll tell you everything we know." Kerry takes the journal in both hands, turns in her seat and offers it to him. "Here," she says. "Start with this."

Jackson opens the book and says, "Was this Daniel's?"

"It was. Now it's yours," Kerry says. "It will tell you how brave he was."

"Oh." I see him in the rearview, smiling a private smile to himself. "Thanks." Then he says, "You must have been pretty brave too, Dad."

My eyes are blurry, but I don't want either of them to see me wipe my face. "Why's that, buddy?" I say.

"Helping Mom. Keeping everyone calm. If everyone had started fighting over the fire that time, you might all have died." He's quiet for a minute, thoughtful. "And then everything you did for Mom, afterward. You took care of us."

"I love your mom, and I love you. I'd have done anything for you two."

We're coming around the bend now. In a few more minutes we'll be back in the city of Whitehorse, back where everything changed. Where we lost one future and gained a new one.

"So what are you thinking, honey?" asks Kerry. "Are you glad we told you?"

He's quiet for a minute, then he says, "I guess so. I feel—lucky,

I guess. Not everyone gets to say they're the son of a hero." He grins. "Much less *three*."

I take a breath as the city comes into view around the bend. It's a bright blue October day, the sun washing the green hills gold. I take my wife's hand and say, "We made it. Look."

First Light

BILL RANCIC

————

Discussion Guide

————

BOOK
ENDS

PUTNAM

Discussion Guide

1. Prior to the accident, Kerry is a workaholic who has a hard time prioritizing her relationship with Daniel over her demanding job. But then the accident happens, and it turns her world upside down. How does Kerry change throughout the book? How does the accident affect the way she treats those around her?

2. Does your perception of Phil change as the story unfolds? If so, how and why?

3. How does Kerry's relationship with Daniel differ from her relationship with Phil? How are the two relationships similar?

4. What is the emotional turning point of the book? Do your emotional alliances change at any point? Whom do you root for, and does your answer change as you read along?

5. How does each character react to trauma and conflict? What does this book tell us about human connection in the face of tragedy?

6. What is the meaning of the book's title—and why do you think it was chosen?

7. Suppose the crash never happened. Based on your knowledge of the characters, how would each one continue to live his or her life if it had been just an ordinary plane ride after all?

8. How does Bob's character change over time, if at all? By the end of the book, is he still the intimidating, demanding boss he was first made out to be?

9. Were you surprised by Jackson's reaction to his parents' story? How else could he have reacted?

10. What is the role of time in this novel? How would the story be different if it did not include the interwoven present tense narrative? Would you feel differently about the story's outcome?

11. Were you surprised by the ending? What mechanisms and hints does the story employ to create suspense and surprise?